To Wendy for believing in me. To Carissa for helping me become an author. To my children showing them you can do anything at any stage. To all my family and friends.

Contents

Only do good with one's magic.
One's magic is not for one's self.
Respect one's magic on others.

Chapter One

"Hurry Stephen! She's getting closer and I can't stop her from coming."

Stephen tried not to show his worry on his face as he weaved in and out of traffic. "The car is going as fast as it can go."

"She's getting closer, hurry!"

Stephen glanced over to see Gloria, his wife of 5 years, sweating and tears rolling down her face. She performed her breathing exercises she learned in her Lamaze classes. She thought it was easier in class when someone was not trying to enter the world sooner than she was supposed to.

Gloria thought back to the day's events. She was standing in her kitchen by the island eating a slice of apple when her water broke; she panicked, knowing her husband was at work at a meeting.

She hurried over to the telephone hanging on the wall; she screamed at her phone when she heard a busy signal.

A knock on her front door got her attention.

"I am not up to having visitors. Please, not today," Gloria clinched the edge of the counter as a wave of pain shot through her.

Another knock came on the door.

Gloria closed her eyes with pain, walking over to the door with tears flowing down her face. When she swung the door open, an older woman stood, dressed all in black except for a white spot on the front of her dress.

"I am sorry you must leave, I am having a baby," Gloria silently panics, holding her stomach.

"Don't be alarmed. You are carrying a very special girl. I am here to give you something for her," the old lady just smiling.

"How did you find out it is a girl, I am having? Who are you?" Gloria inquired, letting out a labored breath.

"I am a friend."

The old lady pulled out a green velvet sack and opened it, and held out a necklace to Gloria.

"I don't want the necklace. Thank you anyway, "Gloria exclaimed.

"Please, look at it," the old woman persisted.

"Present this to your daughter when she turns twenty-one and not before," the old woman said.

Gloria focused on the elderly lady, then back to the necklace. A tingling feeling caresses her entire body; without realizing it, she reached out for the chain.

The sun made the necklace almost glow when Gloria held it up to the sun, putting it back into the sack.

"Please, take this back."

There was no answer. She glanced up to see that the old lady had disappeared.

"What's going...." smile framed her face as a feeling of peace came over her. The panic subsided for now, and she knew at that moment everything was going to be okay.

She noticed Stephen rolling up to the house.

"I tried to call you, but your phone was busy. How did you know I needed you?" Gloria wondered, shuffling out to the car.

"Something told me to come home," Stephen ran up and helped her.

"The hospital is up ahead, "Stephen said, trying to reassure himself that everything will be all right.

The car tires screeched to a stop in front of the emergency entrance. Stephen jumped out and ran into the hospital to grab a wheelchair.

"My wife is having a baby, and the baby is three weeks early!" He yelled at a nurse sitting behind a desk. He scurried around until he spotted a wheelchair and hurried towards the car.

"Sir, sir... What is your wife's name?!" the nurse asked, running behind him.

"Gloria, Gloria Wolff, I am Stephen, her husband," He yelled as he helped his wife out of the car.

The nurse rushed Gloria up to the maternity ward and then into a delivery room. The nurses helped her to put on a hospital gown, then laid her on the bed. A doctor with dark skin came into the room and examined her; he looked up at Stephen holding his wife's hand. "Everything will be okay."

"The doc said everything is fine," Stephen relayed to her.

"Now, push, "the doctor said.

Stephen stood by her side, trying to comfort and helped her as much as he could. They have been trying for so many years to have a baby. They had lost two children by premature deliveries; he worried this one would not make it.

The doctors had to operate on her the last time she was carrying, and they explained to them both that it was unlikely that she could get pregnant again.

The day she found out she was pregnant, it took them both by surprise, and to ensure that nothing would go wrong, they went to a specialist and followed what they said.

A loud cry of a baby filled the room and an enormous relief to everyone in the delivery room, especially Gloria and Stephen. The doctor places the little girl on Gloria's chest.

"Thank you, Doctor Abraham, "Stephen said as he read the name tag on the doctor's lanyard.

Gloria gazed at her new little girl. Her head was full of red hair and the deepest green eyes that she had ever seen.

"Hello Jazmyn, you are the most beautiful baby your momma has ever seen." Gloria brushed her baby's cheek and smiled.

"Jazmyn?, I thought we would name her after my grandmother, Allison," Stephen questioned.

"I know we were but Jazmyn seems to fit her better We can make her middle name Allison."

"Jazmyn Allison Wolff, you're right. I like it," Stephen smiled.

A nurse came in. "Would you like a picture of this moment?,"

They were agreed. Stephen stood proudly next to his wife and his new daughter, and the nurse snapped the picture.

"I will get this developed before you leave."

Doctor Abraham stopped the nurse just outside Gloria's room door. "Any sign of him?"

"No."

Doctor Abraham nodded his head as he walked into the room.

"I just came in to check on things," Doctor Abraham exclaimed, examining Jazmyn and Gloria.

"Thank you, Doctor, she's perfect," Gloria said.

"I did nothing except bring her into this world. You did the hard part, rest now."

With thanks in his eyes, Stephen shook the doctor's hand as Abraham was leaving.

A full moon was rising outside the hospital window, but a thick, foreboding fog dimmed its shine—an unsettling presence in the bushes outside the window. A pair of red glowing eyes looked in on the new parents.

Chapter Two

Jazmyn lived in a one-bedroom apartment above a small-town bar; she made her way up the stairs; each one had its creak; she could walk up blindfolded and know what step she was on. There was an elevator, but it is stuck between the first and second floors; the landlord never fixed it.

The peeling paint on the walls created a mosaic of colors as she walked to her door. She fumbled for her keys, dropping them along with a hand full of mail she had in her hand, creating an echo down the hall.

"Damn it.," she grumbled.

She didn't have to worry about disturbing anyone else. The only other person was the landlord, Mr. Wilson; he also ran the bar, so he wasn't home, anyway.

As soon as she walked across the threshold, her phone rang; she dropped everything again, trying pull it out of her back pocket.

She threw everything onto the table and plopped herself down on her garage sale couch between a pile of unfolded and folded clothes.

She looked at her phone and saw it was her mother; she rolled her eyes, knowing what the subject was.

"Hi, Mom. Just walked in from work."

"How was your day, dear?" her mom asked.

"Another day in paradise," Jazmyn smirked.

"Well, that's nice. Are you coming here for your birthday?" mom said.

"You know I made plans to be with my friend Izzie."

"But it is a special birthday, and I need to give you something."

"Yes, I know it is, but can't you just send it to me. If you send it now, it should be here before my birthday."

"I want to give it to you in person. Honey."

"But Ma," Jazmyn pleaded.

"Please."

Jazmyn flails her arms out as if she was a speaker behind a podium and sighed.

"Okay, okay! I'll see what I can do. Love you."

"Take care, and I love you too, goodbye."

"Bye," Jazmyn said, shaking her head. "Mothers!"

She stared at the pile of clothes. "I should do them someday soon."

She got up and went to her table and turning her attention to the mail.

"Junk, junk, need to pay that, and this one too," saying rifling through her mail. "Oh, look, Shoppers America magazine, let see what I can buy."

Jazmyn quickly flipped through and glanced at a few pairs of pants she liked, then closed it and threw her mail on her card table, her all-around crap collector, and desk.

She looked around her small apartment; on the far wall sat a small bookcase filled with books she never got around to read, and it doubled as a TV stand. The cluttered shelves held books on photography, nature, scenery, the animal kingdom, and crammed in between was a notebook full of poetry she would write on occasions to sort out her feelings or thoughts.

First things first, get this thing off. She stood up, reached under her shirt and undid her bra, and took it off.

"AW, better."

An angry growl from her stomach told her it was time to eat. She headed for the kitchen to grab something to eat and glanced out at the looming Oak Stone water tower standing guard.

The pictures on the refrigerator door caught her attention.

That silly Izzie, she smiled at the picture of her and friend Izzie goofing around. They were acting like a monkey hanging from one tree at the local park.

The picture she loved most was the one of her when she was born, laying in her mother's arms and her dad standing next to them. When she was seven, he disappeared one night, and her mother couldn't or wouldn't tell her what happened to him. She missed him so much.

Jazmyn glanced at her calendar on a corkboard and saw she had a self-defense class coming up. Her mom made her take them when she moved to the 'big city'.

She opened the door of the refrigerator and stood there, scanning the shelves.

What should I have? Too tired to cook anything. Leftovers, frozen dinner, or that science project in the back, I should throw that out; okay frozen dinner it is.

Jazmyn let out a little sigh and popped her dinner in the microwave. She turned around, and her foot got attacked.

"Oh, Onyx. You startled me."

She bent down and picked up Onyx, and her purr motor started. Onyx was all black except for a small patch of white hair on her chest.

The microwave alerted her, giving Onyx one last pet, then put her down.

She cleared a spot on her table and turned her laptop on and sorted through her emails, checked her Facebook as she ate. Coming across a post from a coworker's birthday party, it made her think about her plans to hit the bar with Izzie. She didn't want to drive anywhere, so both of them could have some fun. She had taken that day off from work, and she didn't work for the next two days after.

I have time in the morning to see mom, and then I can come back and get ready to go out and have fun. That reminds me, I need to talk to Izzie when she gets here.

She got up, threw her empty dinner tray away. "Shower time,"

In the bedroom she stripped off her work clothes. She felt light-headed; she felt for the edge of the bed and sat down, looked towards her dresser, and saw her cat jump up and was about to knock over her makeup mirror.

"Get down. You know you can't be in here. Now, get." Onyx meowed and got down.

She turned her head, looked through her door into the living room, and saw Onyx lying on the couch.

"How did you get over there so quickly?" Jazmyn said, scratching her head. "Weird."

Jazmyn's head cleared, and made her way into the shower. She just stood and let the warm water flow down her body. It felt so inviting she could stay in there forever, but the hot water was running out. She hurried to get the day's dirt off.

After drying herself off; caught a glance of herself in the full-length mirror; she was a reasonably pretty young woman. She thought of herself as built above average, and she worked out a few times after her defense classes.

She combed her semi-curly shoulder-length red hair when something caught her eye, a reflection of an older woman behind her. Her eyes grew wide, twisted, but no one was there. She looked around, nevertheless, there was nothing except Onyx sitting just outside her door.

"I have had a long day, I guess," she said, trying to calm her nerves.

A familiar knock came on the door; Izzie always knocks the same way. "Come in, Izzie."

"Hey, hey. What's happening?" Izzie said, strolling in the door.

"Just got out of the shower," Jazmyn said, clearing a spot off the couch.

"Ah, you smell fresh," Izzie said.

"Thanks," Jazmyn giggled. Izzie could always make her laugh.

Izzie sat down, kicked her legs out, missing the makeshift coffee table, "Damn." she sat back up and adjusted the two crates and aboard.

"You and your short legs," Jazmyn said.

"Yep, I'm fun-sized. You were in a rush to get out of work," Izzie remarked.

"Yeah, just had one of those days."

"Been there, done that a few times. Hey there, Onyx," Onyx jumped up on Izzie's lap, "How are you doing today? You've had her for a while now."

"Yeah, a few years. Ever since my mom's neighbor, Abraham, gave her to me before I moved into town."

"What movies did you bring over?" Jazmyn asked, getting up. "Do ya need anything from refrig?"

"Have any grape soda? If so, grab me one. I brought over Charmed."

Jazmyn handed Izzie her soda and sat back down on the couch. "You believe in all that magical stuff, don't you?"

"Yes, I believe magic is real."

"Yeah, real enough for the entertainment purposes. Magic is not real. I stopped believing a long time ago," Jazmyn stated.

She remembered when she believed in magic; it was a little time after her dad went missing. Many nights went by when she wished he would come back home, but it never happened. She would whirl around a stick and pretend it was her wand, trying to make her dad reappear. It lasted a few years until she thought it was just dumb to believe in such stupid things as magic.

"You believe what you want. What would you do if you were magic?"

Jazmyn thought for a bit. "I...hum. I would turn you into a toad."

"Ah, shut up," Izzie said, picking up a pillow and hit Jazmyn with it.

"Hey, not to change the subject, but I am; my mother wants me to go see her on my birthday to give me this 'special gift'. Do you mind if I go out there to see her?"

"Sure, no prob. Hey, I could tag along to see your mother figure. She's cool. Maybe she is going to tell you that you're a witch," Izzie smiled.

"Ya, right. You watch too many of these shows."

As they watched the 3rd episode, Jazmyn thought what if she was a witch and how she would help people that needed help and do good deeds with her magic.

Jazmyn shook her head and mumbled, "What am I thinking. A witch, never."

"What did you say?" Izzie turned to her.

"Nothing. would you look at the time. We need to work tomorrow."

"Oh, yeah. What time do you want me over here to go to your mother's with you," Izzie asked as she got ready to leave.

Jazmyn stretched and yawned. "Oh eight-ish, I guess."

"Oklie, doklie, Jazzy. See ya," Izzie responded as she left.

Jazmyn sat back on the couch and finished her soda, yawned again, then headed for bed. She threw back her covers to crawl into bed when she saw Onyx jump up on her dresser again and was about to knock over her makeup mirror.

"Get down..." She trailed off, and she realized she just saw this.

"Major deja vu. Whoa," she said as Onyx jumped down and ran out, but not before meowing.

Jazmyn has had deja vu a few times she had seen what was going to happen before it did. Usually, it wasn't this real.

She shrugged it off and laid down and checked to make sure her alarm is set and shut out the light and turned over and quickly fell asleep.

∞∞∞

"Shut up, would ya," Jazmyn yelled at her annoying alarm; with half of her face buried in her pillow, she struggled to find the off button.

Finally, she killed the alarm; she sat up, ran her fingers through her wild hair, trying to tame it down.

When she had enough energy, she began her morning routine. It was coffee first, always.

Her head still had morning fog, and it was a challenge trying to find the cleanest dirtiest cup. She grabbed an apple for something easy for breakfast.

Jazmyn sat at her small table, flipping through her messages on her phone. She felt Onyx graze her leg; it was her way of saying good morning; her purr engine began when Jazmyn bent over and ran her hand through Onyx's soft fur.

After her third cup of coffee, she had enough energy to get herself dressed and do her hair and makeup.

She took this time to prepare mentally for what she thought her workday would entail. She loved the customers and some of her coworkers, and some she would rather avoid.

"See you later, be a good kitty," Jazmyn said.

Onyx weaved in and out of her legs. "Do you want some attention?"

Jazmyn picked her little friend up and cuddled her; she started purring.

"Got to go," Trying to put the cat down, but Onyx wouldn't let go.

"Let go, Onyx."

Onyx meowed loudly in protest before Jazmyn managed to put her down and headed out the door.

She could drive her beater SUV, but she decided to walk to work; it was just a few blocks. She considered her vehicle a grocery getter and used it when she wanted to visit her mother.

The early spring wind took its bite when she opened the door to the street. A scattering of people littered the sidewalks this early in the morning. She glanced into the window of the thrift store as she made her way to work. That's where she got most of her furniture for her apartment and household goods. It was a place where she and her mother would spend hours.

The familiar scent of the freshly baked bread caught her nose, it was coming from the Oak Stone Cafe, and it happens to be the place she gets her coffee.

A bell rang as she opened the door to the cafe; a waitress popped her head up and smiled.

"Good morning, Helen. The usual, please,"

"You got it, Dear," Helen said, giving her a wink and a smile from behind the counter.

The locals were all at their usual tables, filling the air with stories. Sometimes Jazmyn would sit in her favorite spot with her coffee and listen to the older people talk, but not today.

"Thanks, see you later," Jazmyn said, handing Helen some money and headed out the door.

She stood just outside the door to take a sip of coffee.

"Hey, Jaz."

The coffee almost flew out of her hand as Jazmyn turned to see Izzie running up to her, "Hey."

"How's it going?. Hey, that looks good. Where's mine?" Izzie asked, eying Jazmyn's coffee.

"I'm sorry, I didn't know you wanted one," Jazmyn said.

"No worries, mate. You don't have to be so accommodating all the time."

Jazmyn bowed her head then opened the door.

They both walked back to the backroom where the break room was, then grabbed their vests they needed to wear and the name badges.

"Catch you later, Tater," Izzie said. "A cashiering, I go, hi ho, hi, ho."

"You goof-ball, you're just as funny as my first day I started here, Jazmyn said, shaking her head. Izzie helped show her the ropes and became fast friends.

"It's a gift," Izzy twittered her fingers as she walked off.

Izzie lived just two blocks on the other side of the department store. She moved there a few years ago from her father's house.

Jazmyn was about to walk out of the backroom when she

caught sight of her manager; she quickly tried to hide. He was always one of the people she wanted to avoid. The way he handles his job was just short of being in the military.

"Jazmyn!" her manager barked.

Jazmyn sauntered over to meet him, knew what her manager wanted. "Yes, Mr. Albertson,"

"I gave you only a few tasks to do yesterday, and I asked you to get them done before you left, but no, what did you do?" Mr. Albertson demanded.

"I was helping customers," Jazmyn answered.

"What the hell were you doing on the sales floor? You were to stay in the backroom to do what I asked," Mr. Albertson trolled.

"I know, but...," Jazmyn's voice cracked; she could feel her world closing in on her.

Her manager took one step closer to Jazmyn and bent down and got in her face, "But nothing, I want you to get them done today! We have a delivery tonight, and we need the room."

"Okay."

"Okay, what?"

"Okay, Sir."

"Miss Wolff, you will not amount to anything in this world. You're weak!" Mr. Albertson screamed, shaking his finger at her.

His soul-piercing stare belittled her. She tried to open her mouth to say something, but she just stood there and watched Mr. Albertson storm off, probably to yell at someone else.

"I'm not weak," she whispered to herself, then turned, lowered her head, and went on with her day.

She tried to stay on task but stocking the backroom warehouse wasn't fun. It was one of those tasks she hated doing; she would rather be out helping customers with their needs.

Jazmyn felt driven to help people; ever since her father died, she saw how helpless her mother was in dealing with the loss. She would put her needs on the back burner to help her mother instead of doing other fun activities.

It was break time; she went to the vending machine to grab a snack. She put her money in and made her choice, and again, it refused to give up the goods.

"Damn, machine!" Jazmyn spouted off and kicked it.

"You're going to hurt its feelings," Izzie said.

"It seems this machine has it out for me, and it works for everyone else but me. This is a piece of shit," Jazmyn said.

"Issues much," Izzie said.

"Give my money back!" Jazmyn yelled.

She went to shake the machine when a green spark flashed before she touched it, and then coins dropped in the tray. "What?"

"I guess it decided to like you today."

Jazmyn took her money and walked into the break room, and Izzie sat down next to her.

"What's illn'n you?" Izzie asked.

"The drill Sergeant got on my back," Jazmyn complained.

"Berty is that way to everyone. So don't sweat it, just forget it," Izzie said.

"Yeah, I know, but he called me weak," Jazmyn said.

"What an ass," Izzie said. "You should have got in his face and told him off."

"I can't."

"Yes, you can." Izzie encouraged.

Jazmyn just shook her head and sat back. "Let's change the subject, okay."

∞∞∞

"K, Did you hear that they are hiring a new stock person to work at night, Heidi in HR said his name is Luc, and he is hot." Izzie's boasted.

"Really, that's nice," Jazmyn answered.

"That's nice, are you feeling alright, I said he is hot." Izzie moved closer to Jazmyn.

Jazmyn rolled her eyes, "Why do you always have to tell me when a new hot guy is starting?"

"Because It's been a while since you had a date."

"I don't want to date anyone." Jazmyn scuffed.

Izzie put her finger to her head, "I think the last person you went out with was Trevor, right?"

Jazmyn nodded, "So?"

"As I remember, you told me it was High School."

"Yeah, that went well. Trevor was put up to it by the rest of the football team. Just to see if he could score with the shyest girl in school." Jazmyn crumpled into her chair.

"I'm sorry, that's why you need to find someone else," Izzie stated and leaned forward. "On the bright side, I saw him go through my line last week, and he was flaunting his rich wife's money like it was his until she came up behind him and gave his ass down a few notches."

Jazmyn smiled and sat up straighter glanced at the clock, "Back to the mines."

"Mines? You come up with some funny sayings." Izzie said, pushing her chair out with her feet.

"I get them from my mom. She is an old fashion gal."

∞ ∞ ∞

The rest of the day, Jazmyn avoided her manager as much as she could until quitting time. She met Izzie back at the lockers, and they headed for the front door.

"What are you going to do now?" Izzie asked.

"Just go home and...," the sound of screeching tires stopped Jazmyn.

She caught sight of a truck plowing into a car. An enormous explosion followed, throwing car and truck parts everywhere. The driver of the truck got out and stumbled a little.

"We need to help them," Izzie said, looking at Jazmyn.

"No, It's too dangerous." Jazmyn's voice wavered.

"Come on, let's go. I will see if the truck driver is fine, and you go check on the person in the car," Izzie ordered.

"Okay, I guess, you're braver than me."

Jazmyn ran up to the car, cringing at the crackling of the fire. She went around to the driver's side, but no one was there; she looked around and noticed skid marks starting from the curb, following to where the car is now. It looked like somehow took the parked car, and it pushed it sideways. Jazmyn went back to the sidewalk, where Izzie was with the driver of the truck.

"Where is the driver of the car?" Izzie asked.

"I don't know."

"Maybe someone else helped them. This is Brad. Isn't he cute?"

"Leave it up to you," Jazmyn said, looking around for the other person.

The entire police department showed up in front of the building. An overweight cop came up to Jazmyn; his untucked shirt had stains on it; he had a cigarette dangling from his lips. "I am Officer Briggs, and I like to ask you a few questions."

"Alright," Jazmyn answered.

"What do you know about what happened here?" Briggs asked, eying Jazmyn up and down.

Jazmyn told him what she knew, feeling uneasy about this officer. He would lean in too close for her comfort and kept staring at her.

"That's all I know. Can I go now?" Jazmyn asked.

"Yes, but first I have a couple more questions," Briggs stated. "Has anyone given you anything lately?"

"No. Why? What does that have to do with this?"

He leaned in even closer. "Have you been feeling different?"

Jazmyn shook her head and stepped back. "No."

Briggs took a long drag. "I see your birthday is coming up, and you'll be turning 21."

"Yes," Jazmyn answered, feeling anxious.

"That will be all. I will see you around," Briggs smirked,

throwing his cigarette butt down at her feet.

"He's eerie," Izzie commented, walking away with Jazmyn following.

"You got that right. Let's get out of here."

I wonder what his malfunction was," Izzie said.

"I don't know. I don't want to think about it anymore. I am going home to forget today."

She arrived at her apartment; Dropped onto her couch and tried to chill, but her thoughts led her to her father. She would think of him every once in a while. The memories she had of him were precious to her. It almost always made her eyes tear up.

She remembered when he took her out to the park on a windy day to fly a homemade kite; She created a tail with her hair ribbons. They played all day and into the night; she loved that day.

Her daydream ended with a flash that shot through her mind of him; she could see his face like he was standing in front of her, but he was nothing but skin and bones, and his clothes were ragged looking. The feeling of hope came over her with the thought that he was still alive. Another flash saw him bounded and enduring the punishment of being tortured.

Her back reeled with pain, with every lash from the whip as though she was there. Tears ran down her face.

"No! Stop, please stop!" she screamed.

Everything stopped, the vision faded, the pain disappeared, and she was still sitting on her couch.

"What in the hell was that?" Jazmyn jumped up and ran to her full-length mirror, grabbing a smaller mirror, and tried to see her back. Her shirt was all in one piece.

"I must have had one of those lucid dreams I read about once," she said, trying to radicalize what just happened.

"Besides, what am I thinking, he's dead. I don't need to save him," she said, walking back to the couch and slowly sat down again.

Onyx jumped up on her lap and just looked at her; it was almost like she understood what she was going through. She stroked Onyx's fur, and it always relaxed her.

"Thanks, kitty." Jazmyn hugged Onyx, then got up and went to find something to eat.

After she ate, she went back to the couch and wasted the rest of the night channel surfing.

She glanced at the time and saw it was a little after nine, and then neon light from the bar flashed red in her window.

"Shit, have to call Mom." She dug her phone out of her back pocket, then touched her mother's icon to call her.

"Hi, Mom, sorry to call you this late. I just wanted to let you know Izzie is coming with me, to see you," Jazmyn said.

"That's good. At least you won't be alone driving here," her mom answered.

"We will probably be there in the morning sometime." Jazmyn voice wavered, then trailed off.

"Is there anything going on?" her mom asked.

"No, everything is fine," Jazmyn lied.

"Remember, you can tell me anything."

"Yes, I know."

"Are you sure?" her mother pushed.

"Really, nothing is wrong. I got to go; it's getting late."

"Okay, love you."

"Love you too. Bye."

Onyx meowed at her and jumped up into her lap.

"Yes, I know I should have told her, but I think I can handle it," Jazmyn stated. "I am just having one of those days. I am not going crazy, am I?"

Onyx tilted her head and stared at her.

"Of course, I am not crazy, just because I am talking to a cat," Jazmyn said.

She got up, put her phone on the charger, headed for her bedroom and changed into her nightclothes, then went to bed.

Chapter Three

Jazmyn had an early shift today; she noticed Onyx wasn't around bugging her when she was doing her morning routine.

Before leaving for work, she called again, but she never showed. I guess she doesn't want to be bothered this morning.

When she opened the doors at her work, she saw a co-worker she had never seen before.

That must be Luc.

He spotted Jazmyn and monitored her as she passed, giving her a creepy feeling. Something about him was familiar to her, but she couldn't figure it out.

"Hey, hey,"

"Wha...What are you doing here so early? Izzie, You don't work until later," Jazmyn stammered.

"I wanted to check out the new guy," Izzie said, glancing at Luc. "And to see if you were alright."

"At least your concern for me was in there somewhere. I am doing good,"

"He is something to look at, isn't he?"

"He is something," Jazmyn replied, then glanced back as they went into the backroom; Luc was still looking at her.

A few minutes later, Luc walked by them as he went to his locker and flashed a smile at Jazmyn. He then took his vest off and punch out, and left.

"He must be hot-blooded to go out in this cold," Izzie said, watching him as he left. "Nice butt, um."

"Ya, must be," Jazmyn said.

"Girl, I think he is into you," Izzie said.

"I-I don't think so."

"You should ask him out."

Izzie always tries to hook her up. Jazmyn shook her head. "No. I got to punch in now. I will talk to you later."

"I still think you should ask him." Izzie turned and raised her hand and twiddled her fingers. "Byee."

Jazmyn went about her day stocking shelves and helping customers, avoiding her boss.

She opened a box of little cars to hang on the peg when she came across one that reminded her of the vehicle in the accident yesterday.

I still can't figure out how that car moved sideways; I glad that no one got hurt.

"Jazmyn!" the drill Sargent's voice carried across the store. *What did I not do now?*

She turned to see him barreling towards her. "Did you finish what I ask you to do on the note I left you?"

"What note?" Jazmyn had to back up onto the shelf to avoid him running into her.

"The note I left pasted to your locker." Mr. Albertson said.

"I didn't see a note." Jazmyn could feel her stomach getting tighter.

He looked her up and down, then flailed his arms out. "I suppose you saw it and just threw it away, didn't you?"

She shook her head. "No, I didn't. There wasn't…"

"Yes, there was a note, don't tell me there wasn't. I put it there myself!" He spatted.

Jazmyn cringed, and a tear let loose from her eye.

"Now get done what I wanted you to do," He said as he walked away.

She just stood there with a lost look on her face, not knowing what to do. Her mind was running wild; she felt sick to her stomach.

After a few minutes, she wiped the sweat off her face; she trudged back to her locker to see if she missed it. By the time she got there, her heart had returned to an average pace.

God, I hate feeling like that. I should have stood up to him.

She looked around her locker and up and down at the other locker; she spends a few minutes looking for it, but it wasn't anywhere.

I don't want to face him again to ask.

She felt her pulse pick up and took a deep breath, and she plodded down the hall. She glanced down in the trash can and crumbled up was a piece of paper. The paper was the same color as the paper that Mr. Albertson always uses, army green. Jazmyn picked it up out of the garbage, wiped off the leftover food, and read it. 'Ms. Jazmyn, I want you to move the palettes in the backroom to a different location'.

Who threw this away, probably him, to yell at me and make me feel like shit.

∞∞∞

She was glad her day had ended; the door was in sight when she glanced over and saw Izzie as she passed by the checkouts. She noticed Izzie was mocking the customer, yelling at her when the customer wasn't looking. Jazmyn smiled and continued out the door.

Jazmyn spotted a black fuzzy animal hanging around her door to her apartment.

"How did you get out here?, Onyx," Jazmyn said.

"Are you cold?"

Jazmyn picked her up with a meow, carried her up the stairs, and went into her apartment.

The night seemed to drag on as she sat in front of the television, trying to find something good to watch; Onyx was curled up on her lap, keeping her warm. She looked at her phone a few times to check to see if anything changed, but nothing new, so she called it a night.

She drifted off to dreamland; it was a beautiful day out,

and she was a little girl playing hide and seek with her dad.

"3-2-1- ready or not here I come," Jazmyn yelled.

She laughed as she looked for her dad everywhere, around the outside of the house, in the garage; it seemed like hours of searching.

"Dad, dad? Daddy?" little Jazmyn said. "Where are you?"

"Let me show you," an angelic woman's voice spoke as if a beautiful symphony of music was playing.

"Who are you?" Jazmyn asked.

"It is not time to know me yet." the voice replied.

Suddenly a green flash of light blinded her; she shielded her eyes, then darkness consumed her. A moment later, she tried to yell out, but no sound came out.

It was pitch black except for a very dim light, and she fumbled her way towards it. She found herself inside a cave. Fear stuck her when it seemed there was no exit. An opening just appeared, she peered in, and at the opposite end she saw her dad, and he was in some weird cage.

Tears flowed as she ran to him, she tried to tug on the bars but her hands when through them causing her to fall into the dirt. She look up then everything vanished.

She woke up with tears running down her face, turned the light on.

Sweat covered her entire body. She got out of bed, ran to the bathroom, and looked into the mirror; it revealed that her hair was a mess, and Jazmyn's face and body was coated with black mud.

What the hell is going on?

She looked down, and Onyx looked up at her, giving her some comfort.

It seemed that Onyx always had that effect on her. Whenever she felt down or depressed, the cat somehow cheered her up. And when someone was at the door, Jazmyn didn't know Onyx would be right there, ready to protect her.

She bent down and gave Onyx a few strokes. "Thanks. I'll you tell all about it, later."

Jazmyn got into the shower and cleaned up when she got out.

Thank God I don't work tomorrow, I mean today. Looking at the bathroom clock.

She felt exhausted and crawled back into bed and fell asleep again.

∞ ∞ ∞

The day was almost half gone before Jazmyn rolled over and glanced at the clock. "Oh, shit, I am going to be late!" she yelled, throwing the covers off of her.

A meow came from just across her bedroom threshold; she looked, then it hit her; it was her day off. "Damn, I was nice and comfy too."

After getting dressed, she went to make some breakfast and grabbed some eggs.

The dream she had the night before kept working its way through her mind.

"Why would I have a dream like that? It makes little sense."

She was close to her dad when he was alive. When he worked in the office at home, Jazmyn would sneak in, wanting him to play, but ended up watching him.

"Daddy, what are you doing?" Jazmyn asks, gazing at his artwork.

"Just making a design for someone." Her dad answered.

"Why?" She peered up at him.

"Because they ask me too." He glances over at her.

"Why?"

Her dad put his pencil down on his art easel and picked Jazmyn, and place her on his lap. "So the design can be printed on a shirt or anything they want."

"Why?" Jazmyn smiled.

"They-" he put her down and bopped her on her nose. "-

Never mind, now go on. I need to work."

The smell of burnt eggs stung her nose, snapping her back. "Shit!"

She grabbed the handle of the pan and tossed the whole thing into the sink, and turn the water on, the crackling of the pan cooling filled her apartment.

"I guess I'll go down to the coffee shop and grab something, Onyx," she said.

Onyx sneezed and let out a friendly meow.

She didn't want to cook, anyway; she slipped on her favorite knee-high boots on, grabbed her coat, and threw it on, took her phone off the charger, and headed for the door.

The coffee shop was sprinkled with a few customers when she entered. The aroma filling the air made her stomach growled loudly. A customer looked her way. Embarrassed, she quickly found her table and sat down.

"Hey, Jazmyn," Helen said as she approached the table

"Hey." Jazmyn flashed a smile. "I like my usual and frosted Carmel roll, please."

"You got it," Helen said, and headed for the kitchen.

Jazmyn pulled her phone out and checked her messages; there was nothing new. She put her phone down on the table, looked out the window. People went about their busy lives, some she recognized as customers from her work.

The one person she didn't want to see was Officer Briggs; he walked in with a cigarette hanging from his mouth.

"You need to put that out. There is no smoking in here," Helen yelled from behind the counter.

"I am the police. I can do what I want," Briggs scoffed.

"Are you doing any police business in here?" Helen asked, placing her hand on her hips.

"No, came in for coffee."

"Then you're not the police in here, your a customer, put that cigarette out."

Briggs crushed it out on a table with a couple sitting at it. "There you go. I want a black coffee to go."

Jazmyn just shook her head and mumbled, "Asshole."

"What did you say? Ms. Wolff," Briggs said, strolling over to her table.

"Nothing." Jazmyn dropped her head and crushed herself into the corner of the booth.

Briggs looked her over like she was less than human and sat down across from her.

A creepy feeling ran through her body as he just stared at her.

"So, has anything weird happened to you lately? Maybe about your daddy." Briggs asked.

Jazmyn's eyes widen, and her mouths dropped open, then quickly shut them again, "What did you say?"

"You heard me."

How does he know?

Her eyes were darting around, trying to think, when the bell above the door rang, catching her attention.

A sharply dressed woman walked with a confident stride, stopped, and looked directly at Officer Briggs.

Briggs's eyes met her stare; he dropped his eyes, quickly got up, and shot out the door.

Without missing a beat, the woman sat down in a booth across from Jazmyn.

She watched the woman as she took her black jacket off, revealing a maroon-colored sweater, and around her neck was a necklace with a white gem hanging from it.

Why was that pig scared of that woman?

The woman turned to Jazmyn and smiled; a flush came across Jazmyn's face when she realized she was still staring.

"Here you go, Hun," Helen said, sitting her roll down with her coffee.

Jazmyn jumped a little, "Do you know that lady over there." Nodding her head in the woman's direction.

Helen turned to find the booth was empty. "What woman?"

"There was a woman -" Jazmyn looked around. "-in that

booth a second ago."

"After that ass left, the only other person was the delivery guy sitting up at the counter."

"Never mind, I guess, thanks."

She took the last bite of her role; she paid her bill, "Thanks, Helen."

"Have a good rest of your day," Helen said.

"Yeah, thanks, going to see what other what kind of trouble I can get into." Jazmyn waved.

Jazmyn looked around when she stepped out onto the sidewalk; her day was free, and she had no plans to fill her day, so she went to the thrift store to browse.

"Hi, Jazmyn," the clerk behind the counter said as she walked in.

Jazmyn waved and went over to where the purses were hanging.

She thought of how living in a small town, and everyone knows everything and everyone. It was appealing to her, but at the same time, it was hard. A person couldn't get away with anything here without someone's aunt telling someone that you did something.

She sorted through the purses when she reached one; she saw the woman from the bakery looking at some jewelry.

The other people around her seemed to disappear as she walked towards the woman, *Just going over to thank her. Why am I so nervous?*

She looked to see that her hands were shaking.

"Your welcome," the woman said briefly, turning to Jazmyn then headed out the door.

Dumbfounded, Jazmyn just stood there for a second. "How?"

The woman left; once Jazmyn could move again, she sought the woman and spotted her across the street, heading for a building. The building had a mural painted on the side of a forest.

Jazmyn crossed the street after the woman, but the

woman walked right into the painting and disappeared.

"What the hell?" Jazmyn looked twice, but it didn't help her with what she saw.

Not believing, she looked down the alley next to the building, but no one was there. "Am I going crazy?"

"If you are, take me along. I want to have some fun, too," Izzie said, walking up to Jazmyn.

Jazmyn put her hand up to her chest and let out a little scream, "Damn, you almost gave me a heart attack."

"Sorry," Izzie said.

"What are you doing here, aren't you supposed to be at work?"

"I am on lunch, and I saw ya out here. What are you doing here?" Izzie asked.

"Um, nothing, just walking." Jazmyn lowered her head.

"Kinda chilly out here," Izzie rubbed her arms.

"Well, you're the one that came out here without a coat. I'll join you for the rest of your lunch. Come on," Jazmyn said.

"Okie, Dokie Smokie," Izzie replied.

As she walked with Izzie, she turned briefly to see nothing behind her.

Jazmyn left Izzie after her lunch; did some shopping since she gets a discount. She browsed through the clothing section, looking for whatever caught her eye; she didn't need clothes. Her closet can attest to that.

I should have told Izzie about what happened, but she would think I am crazy.

It was getting late when she got done shopping, so she went back to her apartment. The smell of burnt egg still hung in the air.

"I will clean that tomorrow." she went to the closet and grabbed a can of air freshener, and sprayed it around. "I love that lilac smell, don't you? Onyx."

Her cat meowed in agreement.

She got ready for bed and sat in front of the TV and vegged. After a few big yawns, she got up and crawled into bed;

soon, she was carried off into the land of dreams. The dream was of a forest near her mother's cabin. She was sitting in an opening, and she could feel the sun warming her; she felt happy. The birds were singing; they sounded as though they celebrate the day. Jazmyn spotted all kinds of forest creatures joining in the celebration.

The wind picked up; the clouds rolled in, all the animals stopped.

She sat by a tree when a bird dropped out of the tree. It fluttered, struggling to sit up with stressful chirping. She bent to pick it up, and it died in her hands.

She looked up and found animals were lying all around her, dead. The forest grew dark, and an orange-red glow lit up the scene. Fire raged, encircling her, and Jazmyn gasped for air, trying to get away. The flames inched closer until it was at her feet; Jazmyn screamed. She could feel the heat.

A big, booming voice came from the fire. "DIE!"

Jazmyn woke up, still screaming, and found Onyx next to her; she reached for Onyx and cuddled her; tears filled her eyes. She shook her head, trying to get the visions out of her head.

"What the hell is going on with me."

A reassuring meow came from her cat and an extra snuggle.

She got up out of bed, wiping the tears from her eyes, and grabbed a tissue for her nose.

She walked out to the kitchen and grabbed a bottle of water out of the refrigerator. She went and sat on her couch and channel surfed until she came across some country music videos. Watching and listening helped to fade the dream; soon, she fell asleep again.

Chapter Four

The night greeted Officer Briggs exiting the police station; he dug his coat pocket and found his cigarettes. He snapped his fingers; they sparked then a flame, his face glowed orange as he put it to his cigarette. He rounded the corner to the dark alley, looked around. He took a drag and held it in for a few footfalls, exhaling; he walked through the smoke when he reached the end of the ally.

The darkness concealed his morphing into a well-built, tall man. He proceeded for a few blocks out of town and came to a run-down house that had been abandon many years ago.

He waded through the waist-high grass. He kicked an ornamental bunny aside. Glancing at the boarded-up windows as he walked up the steps. The door opened with a loud creak; he took one last drag of his cigarette, the red glow matched his eyes, then toss it away. He slowly disappeared behind the closing door.

He motioned his arm as though shoeing a fly; a moment later, a creature appeared with a shimmer. He was much shorter than Diomedes; it stood on two legs, but its face and arms bore scars. The creature's head was covered with raised scales, and it wore a tattered cloak with a black vest and pants.

"What can I do for you? My master," The creature asked.

Diomedes strolled up to the creature; he raised his hands with fingers together, "Morzell, aren't you forgetting something?"

"What?" Morzell spatted back.

"Bow to me! When speaking to me." Diomedes ordered.

With a snarl of his fangs, Morzell slowly bowed.

"Better," Diomedes gloated. "I want you to send one of your soldiers, I mean one of my soldiers and to go to the place where she dwells and find that for what I seek and have them bring it to me right away."

"Of course, master," Morzell glare up at Diomedes. "Will that be all?"

"Have you found a suitable place for me to execute my plan?"

"Yes, I have found a cave that will be big enough to build an army."

"Show me," Diomedes demanded.

Morzell shimmered away and Diomedes followed.

They appeared outside of a cave. A sign posted next to the entrance 'Closed due to unstable rocks.'

Diomedes paused before going in, turned to notice camping areas sprinkled throughout the dense forest. Narrowing his eyes, "This looks promising."

Morzell made his way into the cave; Diomedes straightens up, proudly walking in like he owns the cave.

"Let me clear these stones out of your way," Morzell said and picked up the boulders with no effort at all and threw them aside.

Diomedes strolled into the caverns; the stale air filled his nose as he made his way deeper into the darkness. Lit torches would appear on the rocky walls; he finally came to a sign outside of a room called the Cathedral of the moon.

He looked up to see the almost full moon filter its light through an oculus in the ceiling.

Diomedes walked in farther, peered around with his glowing red eyes, then closed them, held his arms out to his side, and slowly raised them. The cave floor started to shake, and as it did, the ground rose in the shape of a giant throne. He fell to his knees, almost collapsing to the floor.

Morzell rushed to him to help him up. "You shouldn't be using your power like that, Master, you are weak, you need to get that necklace to regain all your strength."

"Leave me alone, I am not weak," Diomedes snapped, brushing Morzell away, then struggled to his newly made throne.

"Your not strong enough to take on that witch," Morzell pointed out cautiously, walking up next to his master. "I will take care of her and get your treasure."

"I will take care of it myself, don't forget who I am." Diomedes sat up and glared at his servant.

"As you command," Morzell lowered his head with a smirk on his face.

Diomedes relaxed a little, "Leave me and do what I asked.

∞ ∞ ∞

The air was a little crisp; a chill went down her spine when Jazmyn opened the door to the street. The sun just came up over the horizon. Spring was on its way, soon the trees would start celebrating with new leaves, and the grass would begin to turn green.

Jazmyn loved nature and all it can gives to you. Any season was her favorite; she could find fun things to do at any time, from enjoying time on a lake in summer or a walk in the woods in the spring or the fall in the winter; she liked to play in the snow. She felt somehow connected to nature more than most people.

"Hey, Iz!," Jazmyn yelled, trotting up to her friend.

"Hey, girl," Izzie said. "What's up?"

"Nothing much."

"So, I think Luc likes you," Izzie said with a smile on her face. "He was totally eyeing you yesterday."

"No, he wasn't."

"Oh, yes. He was too."

"Hi, Bernie," Izzie and Jazmyn said as they opened the door to go to their work.

"Hi, Ladies," Bernie said as he collected pop cans out of the garbages. Bernie was a homeless man that visits the department store every morning, almost like clockwork.

"I think you should at least go talk to him," Izzie said, pushing the doors open to the back room.

"Get your mind off of that guy. I will pick you up around eight in the morning on Friday to head to my Mom's," Jazmyn said.

"Okay, time to punch in now, talk to you on break."

"K."

The day was stretching on too long for Jazmyn's liking. She was down the pet aisle stocking shelves, occasionally helping a customer or two out. A few who knew her or her mother asked how things were, making some small talk, trying to make the day go by faster.

A young woman walked up behind Jazmyn and tapped her on the shoulder to get her attention, it sent a shock through her, and she quickly turned around.

"Wow, you were so quiet, I didn't even hear you," Jazmyn turned to a woman with black hair and wearing a black leather jacket with a white t-shirt hiding under it.

"Sorry, my name is ah.. Holly," She said.

"Is there something I can help you with?" Jazmyn asked.

"I can help you," Holly said.

"What? Help me? With what? I don't even know you." Jazmyn said, trying to back away, but she hit the shelf behind her.

"You do know me, at least not like this. I come to warn you." Holly said as she approached closer to Jazmyn; the woman spotted a furry toy mouse on a peg and batted at it.

"Warn me?" Jazmyn asked nervously, "About?"

"About..." Holly paused as a customer passed. "About an evil that is coming for you."

"Evil is coming for me? What are you talking about?"

"I am not even supposed to be here telling you this."

Jazmyn turned and saw Luc, who was coming out of the

back room, and when she turned back to the woman, she was gone.

"Did you see her?" Jazmyn said, looking at Luc

"See who?"

"That woman," Jazmyn said, looking around. "Oh, never mind."

"Are you alright? You seem shaken," Luc said.

Jazmyn took a deep breath to clear her head and to stop her nerves from tingling. She wasn't going to say anything to someone she does not know; she quickly change the subject.

"So, you are the new guy. I saw you the other day," Jazmyn said.

"My name is Luc and you are Jazmyn Wolff, right?"

"Ah, yeah. How did you know?"

"I have magical powers and read your mind," Luc smirked.

"You can't read minds," Jazmyn stated.

He is good-looking. His face and his beautiful tanned body were well chiseled. He had short blond hair; Jazmyn had to look up at him.

"You are right, I saw your picture on the employee of the month board."

"Oh, sorry, been having one of those days," Jazmyn said.

"That was kind of strange what happened the other day?" Luc inquired.

"You the mean accident that happened outside the store? Yeah, kinda strange."

"Especially how that car slid sideways," Luc almost whispered, leaning in closer.

She cocked her one eyebrow up, "How did you know that it did that?" She backed away.

Luc's eye gleamed a little, "It's a small town."

"That's true," she nodded.

"I got a lot to do before my shift ends so I'll see you around," Jazmyn said as she quickly took her stock cart and left.

It was finally time to call it a day; Jazmyn and Izzie left the store together and headed towards Jazmyn's apartment.

The stairs seemed to snap and crack louder than usual as they climbed. Izzie stopped at the top step.

"Jazmyn...," she pointed to her door. "Your door is opened."

"What?!" She turned her head, they both slowly crept towards the door.

The door wasn't forced opened; Jazmyn cautiously opens the door but stopped when they heard something hit the floor. She reached just in the door and grabbed a baseball bat that she always kept next to the door. Jazmyn put her hand out behind her to signal Izzie to stay back.

"Yep, I'm not going anywhere," Izzie whispered.

Jazmyn went in quietly; the living room was a mess; the furniture was either turned upside down or out of place. She carefully walked towards her bedroom, where she heard another noise.

The hair on the back of her neck stood up when she approached the bedroom door opening. She readied herself as much as she could; her fear was trying to tell her to run back out and call the police, but she fought it off.

"Whoever is in there get ready for a world of hurt!" Jazmyn yelled and ran in, ready to swing at anyone in there.

When she got in, the only thing she saw was a veil of misty smoke and Onyx sitting on top of one of her dresser drawer which was flipped upside down on the floor.

Onyx meowed; she jumped onto the bed. The top mattress was hanging over the box spring and covering it were all of her clothes.

"You can come in, Izzie, there is no one in here!" Jazmyn shouted as she went back out to the living room.

"I am calling the police," Izzie said, stepping in with her cell phone in her hand.

"I am going to look around to see if anything is missing," Jazmyn said, starting to straighten up cushions on her couch and pick up her belongings on the floor.

"Don't touch anything; maybe there are fingerprints on something," Izzie said, dialing her phone.

"Okay, P.I. Izzie." Jazmyn said.

Jazmyn looked around; some pictures were ripped off the wall, scattered all over the floor, frames broken and the refrigerator left opened.

She went back into the bedroom and saw her jewelry box scattered on her dresser, but nothing seems to be missing. The emergency cash was all there also. The bathroom had been gone through.

She sat down on the couch and put her head in her hands, and started to cry. Everything that has happened lately was getting to her. The deja vu, the dream, and the woman at her work now.

What is happening to me.

Up until now, her life was good, and she liked it that way. She had a decent job that paid her bills and a few bucks saved and have a little fun. She had this tiny, now messed up apartment that was hers, and she had some pride in that.

She talks to her mother at least once a week, if not twice; Izzie is a good friend she could talk to and have fun times with. Onyx is there talk to when no one was around. Her life is what she made it, and now things are going crazy.

Izzie hung up the phone, sat next to her best friend, put an arm around her, and tried to comfort her.

"Thanks, it's almost getting too much to handle," Jazmyn said between the tears.

"You're strong enough to handle this."

Onyx jumped up onto Jazmyn's lap and started to purr, with the look of empathy in her eyes.

A while later, a knock came on the partially opened door, and a couple of police came in.

"It is sure nice that we live in a small town, it doesn't take the cops long to get anywhere," Izzie said.

"Hello, my name is Dan McQuaid, and this is my partner Phillip Morris. Who is the renter here?" one of the police asked.

"The one over there crying," Izzie stated.

Jazmyn told Officer Dan what happened before and after

they came into the apartment. The other police officer took fin-gerprints and photos of the scene when he picked up a picture off the floor.

"Was there a fire in here?" the policeman asked and held up the photo to Jazmyn.

She took the picture and saw that it was her family pic-ture, but her father was the only one burnt off.

"No, there was no fire," Jazmyn said, holding the picture against her chest.

That was the only picture she owned that had her dad in it; it was like he was gone again.

"I believe that will be all for now. Is there anything we can do for you?" Officer McQuaid asked.

"Yes, Do you know an Officer Briggs?" Jazmyn inquired.

"No, No, I don't. Why?"

"He was asking me too many weird questions the other day; he was kinda creepy."

"Sorry, I am new to this department, so I don't know everyone."

"Oh, okay, thanks."

After the police left, Izzie helped Jazmyn clean up the apartment, trying to put it back like it was. All the drawers in the kitchen were pulled out and dumped; everything was pushed aside in the cupboards.

"It looked like whoever was looking for something," Izzie said, putting her books back in the bookcase. "Whoever it was wasn't after money, because all it looks like all the money you had hidden in these books is still here."

"Yeah, I got that habit from my mother. I used to find her money in her cookbooks." Jazmyn said, still trying to settle her nerves.

"Do you want me to order a pizza? I don't think any of the food you had is probably any good." Izzie said.

"Sure, go ahead. Could you stay here tonight?" Jazmyn said.

"Yeah, no problem. We can have a slumber party."

"Are you ten years old or what?" Jazmyn barked.

"Just trying to liven up the mood, Jaz." Izzie snaps back at her.

"Sorry, just my nerves are little on edge. That officer didn't know that creepy cop. It's a small town, wouldn't you think he would at least know him."

"So," Izzie said as she sat on the couch. "Don't worry about it."

"Yeah, I guess," Jazmyn replied.

Izzie called the local pizza place, and after it came, they ate and watched TV.

Chapter Five

Izzie volunteered to help Jazmyn clean up her trashed apartment the following day since they both had it off.

"Whoever did this was a pro at messing up places," Izzie said. "It reminds me of my brother's room."

Jazmyn smiled, shoving her books back in the bookcase, then stopped to look around, "It's missing."

"What's missing?" Izzie turned around from throwing away the pizza box they shared the night before.

"My journal, it always laid on this shelf and now it's not here," Jazmyn started scratching her head.

"That's it, that's why someone broke in here to steal your journal," Izzie tried to hold back a smile. "We need to inform the police."

"Shut up."

Izzie went over to the sink to fill it with soapy water, "It's probably hiding behind the bookcase."

"Yeah, maybe," Jazmyn said, trying to move the bookcase, but the TV was too heavy. "I'll look for it later, I guess."

The sun was high in the sky when they both sat down on the couch. Izzie was wiping her hands with a dish towel to dry them off from doing the dishes.

"Thanks, Izzie."

"No, prob, I was in the neighborhood," Izzie said with a wink.

"At least it's cleaner than it was."

"Yeah, whoever done this sure did a number," Jazmyn said,

looking around.

"I meant from before someone broke in," Izzie smirked.

"Funny, ha-ha," Jazmyn wrinkled her lip. "I am too tired to fix anything. Want to go to the cafe? I'm buying."

"Yeppers," Izzie said, springing up from the couch.

"Guard the house, Onyx." Jazmyn said, grabbing her wallet.

Onyx sat up and let out a meow.

She shut her door making sure both locks were locked this time.

The tables in the cafe were dabbled with a few people, primarily regulars, when they got there. They sat down in a booth by the window, and a waitress came over, "What would you like to start with?"

"I'll have a hot chocolate, please. I got a shiver in my timbers," Izzie said.

Jazmyn smiled, "I'll have the same, thanks."

Izzie put the menu down after a few seconds, "I think I am going to have the double cheeseburger with fries."

Jazmyn just stared at the front of her menu at the picture of an oak tree, which she had seen a thousand times before.

"Are you going to stare at that all day?"

"Sorry, it just reminded me of a dream I had the other night," Jazmyn said as she became aware of her surroundings again.

"Really, fill me in."

The waitress came over with their hot chocolates and took their order. After she left, Jazmyn told her about her dream.

"That's a weird dream," Izzie stated.

"Even weirder, I had another dream that the forest around my mom's place was on fire and at the end, a voice said to me 'Die.' That freaked me out," Jazmyn's hands trembled.

"What do you think your dreams are telling you?"

Jazmyn sipped her hot chocolate, trying to settle down, "I wish I knew."

"Humm, let me see," Izzie said, setting back against the

booth, picking up her sunglasses, and acted wisely. "Dreams are a way for a person to deal with events happening in their lives."

"I don't think these dreams are helping me deal with any-thing.-" she shuffled her cup back and forth "-On top of all of that I had this woman come up to me to warn me about some kind of evil coming for me."

"What kind of evil?" Izzie leaned forward a little.

"She didn't tell me, she disappeared just before Luc came out of the back room."

"That's crazy. Speaking of Luc, did you talk to him?" Izzie asked.

"A little."

"Did you think he was cute?" Izzie said.

"Um, yeah, I guess."

A big Cheshire cat grin came across Izzie's face, "Told you."

"Still not interested."

"Ok, fine then, I'm just telling you you should go for it." Izzie said, sitting back to let the waitress put the food on the table.

"Yeah, you can tell my girl here she needs to get hooked up."

"Izzie!" Jazmyn face flushed. "If I don't want to date some-one, I won't."

As the waitress just smiled and walked away, Jazmyn put her head down and took a bite of her cheeseburger.

Izzie knew not to push her friend, "Tell me more about this woman that warned you."

"Not much else, but she kinda looked familiar."

"Do you believe her?" Izzie asked.

"Really, Izzie, I don't know." Jazmyn shrugged her shoulder a little.

They both finished, Jazmyn laid some money on the table, and they left and walked back to her apartment.

Jazmyn looked around, "Are you still willing to help? There is the bathroom and my bedroom left."

"I will stay and I will rub-a-dub the bathroom." Izzie threw her coat on the back of the couch and headed towards the bathroom.

Jazmyn smiled and followed her, and stopped at her bedroom door, "What the hell was someone looking for?"

When the daylight gave in to the dark, Jazmyn's apartment was almost back to the way it was.

"Thanks, Izzie." Jazmyn said as Izzie was putting on her coat to leave.

"No prob girl. Catch ya tomorrow." Izzie gave her a big smile and a wink and stepped out the door.

Jazmyn walked back into her bedroom, let out a yawn when she saw her bed, crawled in without changing first, and fell asleep.

∞∞∞

The next day at work, Jazmyn tried to avoid answering questions about what happened to her apartment. Big news travels fast in a small town. After a while, she just stayed in the back room.

She was putting products away when Luc came around the corner.

"How are you doing?" Luc asked.

"I am fine, I guess," Jazmyn said. "I suppose you want to know everything too?"

"No, It doesn't interest me at all except that you are OK."

Jazmyn leaned against a wall and put her head back, "I'm fine, thanks. I couldn't answer another question about it."

"I do have one question." Luc smiled.

She looked at him, shook her head, turned and started to walk away, "I knew it. You are just like the rest of them."

"No, no, I was going to ask if you would like me to take you somewhere after work to get away from all this," Luc said, walking towards her.

"What?"

She stopped and turned around, meeting Luc, face to face. Her cheeks flushed and backed away, and she bowed her head then looked up.

"Sorry, I didn't mean to be so forward. Excuse me, I will leave you alone," Luc exclaimed, turning to leave.

"Where would you take me?"

"I know this place across the county line, we could grab a bite to eat," Luc said as he turned halfway around with a smile on his face.

Jazmyn's stomach fluttered, "That sounds alright. I would like to go home and change first."

"OK, great, um, I'll pick you up around six then," Luc said, then went out the door and back out to the sales floor.

Jazmyn kind of smiled. *He doesn't know where I lived*

She shot out of the back door to run after him, but he was gone.

She flashed a look around but he just disappeared. *That's strange he couldn't of gotten to the exit that quick.*

She slowly walk back to where she started and caught sight of Izzie when she was walking back to the time clock.

"Have you seen Luc?" Jazmyn asked.

"No, it is his day off. See, right here on the schedule board." Izzie pointed at his name.

"That's weird, he came in and asked me out tonight," Jazmyn said as they grab their coats before heading out.

"Ooh, I knew he liked you. I'm so excited for you." Izzie said, clapping her hands a little.

"It's not like that. Luc just wanted to take me away from of all this mess for a bit."

"Where is he taking you to?"

"He said someplace across the county line."

"Must be that restaurant that entertains you while you eat. I think it's called 'The Show' or something like that." Izzie said as she pushed the door to go outside. "Have a fun time, call me. Bye."

∞ ∞ ∞

Jazmyn stopped and cautiously looked towards her door and let out a sigh of relief to find it wasn't open.

She went in and got ready for her company to come and pick her up. She didn't want to call it a date that would imply that they were dating, and they are not.

She stepped out of the shower and dried herself off, and went to find something to wear, but her cat seemed to be right under her feet, meowing at her.

"Get out of here. I fed you, which you haven't touch again, and you have water now go." Jazmyn waved her hand, but the cat wouldn't move.

She went to the closet and threw a shirt on the bed, and Onyx balled it up and laid on it. The cat did the same with her pants.

Jazmyn picked Onyx up and tossed her out of the bedroom, and shut the door.

"What's with that cat," Jazmyn stated as she finished getting dressed.

As she was putting on her earrings, a knock came on the door.

"Shit." She said, then glanced at her alarm clock. It read 5:45. "I will be right out."

She quickly put her shoes on, swung the bedroom door open, and almost tripped over her cat.

"Onyx?!" Jazmyn yelled.

She opened the door. "Hi, your a little early," Jazmyn said.

"Sorry, I guess I wanted to get an early start," Luc said.

"Let me grab my coat, stay right there."

Onyx jumped onto the back of the couch, faced the man standing in the doorway, and hissed and growled.

"Nice kitty," Luc said, then smiled at Onyx and winked.

The cat jumped down and darted at Luc, but Jazmyn

caught her.

"That's a naughty kitty. No! I'm sorry about this; she has been acting weird all night." Jazmyn said as she put the cat down and shut the door, and then locked it.

"Cats can act that way sometimes," Luc said, putting his hand on the small of her back and gently pushed her towards the door.

The night was warm; there was a southern wind blowing when they stepped out of the door to the sidewalk. She followed him towards his new shiny-looking all-black Camaro.

"Nice car. Where did you get this?" Jazmyn asked as he opened the car door and guided her in.

"I got it from someone who wasn't going to use it anymore," Luc said, then closed the door and slid across the hood to get to the driver's side.

Jazmyn looked up towards her apartment window, feeling it would be the last time she would see it; she could feel her body shake and held herself tight.

"Watch out," the angelic voice said.

"What?" Jazmyn blurted out.

Luc turns and looks at her, "Did you say something?'

Jazmyn just shook her head and looked around.

The engine roared like some creature in pain. Jazmyn stared out into the night, watching mailboxes flew by. She answered a few questions he'd asked but could not shake the feeling that this was wrong.

The car screeched to a stop in front of the restaurant, snapping her back to reality. She climbed out of the car to a giant flashing marquee sign reading 'The Show.' The sign on the door read, 'Now Playing the magical talents of Abe B. Ham.'

Luc opened the door, and she went inside. The place had a theater feel to it; there was a small stage off the far wall with tables lining in front of it, the set of half-moon booths facing the stage. There was a bar over to one side with a few patrons sitting, drinking. Behind the bar was the entrance to the kitchen.

"How many?" a hostess asked.

"Just us-" Luc said; he flashed a fifty in her face. "-We want one of the booths, darling."

"Right this way." the hostess tucked the money in her bra and led them to the booth.

"Thank you," Jazmyn said as she sat and caught a glimpse of the hostess, and she felt like she knew her, but before she could ask, the hostess winked at her and shot off towards the kitchen.

"Nice place," Jazmyn said, taking one of the menus from the stand in the middle of the table.

"Yep," Luc answered.

"What's good to eat here?" Jazmyn asked.

"I don't know, don't care." Luc barked at her.

"What?" Jazmyn said, looking at him, confused.

"I said I don't know, never been here."

"Oh."

A waitress came over, took their order, and a few minutes later, came back with a glass of water for Jazmyn and beer for Luc.

"This kind of reminds me of the place my parents used to take me when I was younger," Jazmyn said.

"Oh, really," Luc said with a condescending tone.

They both sat silently at the table than an announcement over the intercom system.

"Ladies and gentlemen! Put your hands together for a really talented magician, Abe B. Ham."

Jazmyn clapped along with someone else, the curtain was drawn back, but no one was on stage. Jazmyn looked puzzled, but Luc just sat there, not even paying attention except staring at Jazmyn.

She avoided his stare as she waited for the entertainment to start. A young man stepped out onto the stage; he was a tall, dark-skinned man with glasses. He wore a suit with tails and a white ruffled shirt set off by a black bow tie.

He carried out a stand with a top hat on it, but he dropped it when he got to the middle of the stage.

"Loser!" Someone yelled from the back.

"Sorry, I am kind of nervous." the man said, then took a deep breath. "Welcome, My name is Abe. I, along with my assistant, will bring you to the land of magic and marvel you with amazing tricks."

Jazmyn was the only one that clapped.

"Thank you. Help me welcome my lovely assistant, Teressa."

The hostess that helped them when they came in the door walked out on stage, and they both bowed when they returned to the upright position. They both glanced at Jazmyn.

The food arrived at their table; it looked good to Jazmyn. She began to eat her salad; she ordered and noticed that Luc didn't even look at his almost raw steak, which turned her stomach. She liked her steak well done, not just out of the pasture.

"So, what do you have planned for your birthday tomorrow?" Luc asked, then took a swig of his beer.

"'How did..." Jazmyn said but was interrupted by a flash made by Abe on stage; a few doves flew over to Teressa.

"You didn't answer me," Luc said as he got closer to her.

"Hang out with my friend and go see my mother. How did you know it was my birthday?" Jazmyn questioned, sliding away.

"I know things about you, a lot of things. There is one thing I don't know.

Luc turned, touched his forefinger to his lips. "Where is the necklace?

"What are you talking about? What necklace?" Jazmyn's mind reeled as vision of the last few days permeated her thoughts.

"The one that was given to you!" Luc's eyes turned fire red.

"You..." Jazmyn held her hand over her mouth. "You were the one that trashed my apartment."

Jazmyn got up but was stopped by Luc, grabbing her arm. "Let go of me!"

The magician and his assistant jumped down from the stage but were forced backward by the wave of Luc's arm; he pushed the table across the room like it was nothing.

Everyone in the place looked then went on like nothing was happening. Luc dragged Jazmyn towards the back of the stage, his grip was like steel prevented her from getting away. She started to scream, but her voice went silent after Luc waved his hand.

"If you tell me, I have no used for you. You will not see your twenty-first birthday," Luc said, laughing

Jazmyn tried to say something but still no sound; she latched her arms around a pole to try to anchor herself from being pulled out of the back door, but her body felt like it was being torn apart, she released her hold, and he took her outside.

Luc picked her up by her arms and threw her down on the cold, hard dirt. The wind rushed from her lungs, and she desperately tried to regain the air she had lost, then her head met the ground.

"Now die!"

She tried to scream, but still nothing.

Steam from the warm blood seeping out of a gash on her head caused Luc to smile.

He stood over her, and he began to change; he grew much taller, his hair turned jet black, and a beard appeared on his face, and he held his hand out, and a ball of red light appeared. Jazmyn tried to focus and saw two people coming up behind Luc.

"You first." a woman's voice said.

Luc turned around and dodged a white ball of energy. He launched the one he had back at them; it missed them. He turned to grab her, but his hand was held at bay, he fought to push his hand down, but it won't move.

Jazmyn heard him growl like a beast.

The two people approached, and Jazmyn thought she recognized both of them. One was the hostess/assistant, and the other looked like her old neighbor Abraham, but her vision was blurred. She couldn't believe why they would be here, she reached out for them, but everything faded to black.

"I will get her yet," Luc said, and then there was a flash of light, then he was gone.

Jazmyn laid back, She tried to stay awake, but she kept fading in and out. She heard voices, they sounded familiar, but she couldn't focus.

"She isn't ready to know this, it would jeopardize everything." a woman's voice said.

"Yes, I agree. Come here," a man's voice said as he motioned with his hand.

Jazmyn felt a tingling feeling about her head, in her daze, and she saw a new face of a young man appeared above her, and he had his hands on her head, then everything went black.

Chapter Six

With a pounding on the door, Jazmyn's eyes popped open; she quickly sat up and looked around, found herself in her bed and her nightshirt. She reached up and felt the back of her head; there was nothing but hair.

Why did I do that?

Her head was sore, and she had a killer headache, but she knew something had happened, but the memories of the night before were like a fast-fading dream.

"Wake up, sleepyhead. It's me, Izzie. It's going on 8:30. Wake up and let me in!" Izzie yelled through the door.

"Yeah, I'm getting there. Don't pound so hard," Jazmyn said, getting up and headed to the door, and they're sitting so pretty; on top of the couch was Onyx.

"Morning, pretty kitty."

"Happy Birthday," Izzie said when the door open. "It's about time I've been pounding on the door for 15 minutes. Must of had a wonderful night."

"Thanks, I don't remember it too well," Jazmyn said as her friend went by her into the living room.

"Oh, had too much fun, uh," Izzie said as she held her hand out with a gift in it.

"Ah, thank you," Jazmyn said as she hugged her friend.

Jazmyn sat down and opened her gift; it was a bracelet with the word 'BEST' on it.

"I have one too, mine has the word 'FRIENDS,' see." Izzie held her bracelet out to her.

"I love it. Thanks again. I will put it on after I take a shower, it seems somehow my arms have dirt on them."

"Okay, I'll make you some coffee, and maybe you'll remember more about last night," Izzie said as she opened the cupboard and took down the coffee.

Jazmyn tried to recall what happened the night before, but nothing was there except she knew Luc picked her up, and they headed out of town and got to the restaurant, but after that, it was blank.

The hot water soothed her sore head and arms, but she couldn't remember what she did to make them so painful. She thought maybe it was from work, but nothing came in off the truck to stock that wasn't too heavy. It didn't explain why her head hurt.

She stepped out of the shower and dried herself, then put on a t-shirt and jeans. She debated on putting on that sweater her mother made for her. It was a multitude of colors, and one arm was a little shorter than the other.

Her mom has been trying new things lately, and knitting was her latest endeavor. She loved her mother, but some of the things she's tried don't turn out.

Jazmyn put it on and fixed her hair, put on the bracelet she just received, and went out to the kitchen.

"I have been dying to hear what you did last night," Izzie said, pouring a cup of coffee for both of them.

"I can't for the life of me remember. I must have had a good time, but curiously I have a headache this morning, and my arms are sore." Jazmyn said, taking a sip of her coffee. "Thanks for making coffee."

"Yea. I guess if you don't want to tell me, you don't have to tell your best friend of all times."

"It's not like I am holding back on you. It's just I don't know." Jazmyn shook her head, "Sorry."

"Okay. I know the last few days have been a little rough on you."

"Yes, they certainly have. Are you ready to hit the road?"

Jazmyn asked, checking through her purse to make sure every-thing was there, and pulled out her keys.

The day turned out to be very warm. The heat from the sun was beating off the snow from the ground, the green grass was stretching its blades to touch the light.

They headed east out of town; her mother lived about a half-hour away. The girls were chatting and jamming to country music from Jazmyn's cell phone since the car radio didn't work.

"Now that you are twenty one like I am, we can go out and have fun together," Izzie said between songs.

"Got that right, Izzie," Jazmyn said, nodding her head.

"I wish we had money so we could go on a trip to the Baha-mas or Jamaica. We could sit on the beach with drinks, getting a tan, and watching cute guys surfing." Izzie said.

"That would be a lot of fun, but the best we could do would be to sit in front of a heater and drinking sex on the beach, watching surfers on TV."

They both glanced at each other and broke out laughing.

Jazmyn pulled onto her mother's very long driveway; her mother liked her privacy. A little shed stood on the corner of the driveway. Jazmyn remembered using it when she would wait for her bus, rain or shine. She also pretended it was her tiny little house.

Her Mother's house was more like a big cabin; the old rope swing was still hanging from an oak tree in the yard. She re-membered her dad, mom, and her, used to have picnics under that tree, and her dad would push her high up into the sky. She believed she was flying. There was a small lake just beyond the back door.

Her mother was sitting out on a swinging couch on the wrap-around porch. Jazmyn spent hours swinging there think-ing of her dad after he had gone away.

By the time Jazmyn put the car in park her mom was half-way down the steps and stopped and waved.

"Hi, Honey. Happy Birthday." Her mother went the rest of the way down and spread her arms.

"Hi, Mom. Thanks. Glad to see you." Jazmyn said, giving her a hug and a kiss on the cheek.

"Hi, Izzie. How are you doing?" Her mom hugged her.

"Fine, Mrs. W," Izzie said.

"Come in, come in. It's nice out here, but the wind still has a bite to it." her mom said.

They walked into the house, and it had the same smells that it always had, of pine and oak; most of the furniture, was made from wood.

Her mom likes the rustic look. There was also the smell of freshly baked cinnamon rolls drifting through the air.

Jazmyn and Izzie took their coats off and hung them on a sturdy oak coat tree.

"I see you wore that sweater I made for you. It doesn't look bad on you at all. You said it looked ugly on you." Her mother commented.

"I agree you look pretty sweet in it," Izzie added.

"I know, I said that, but it's actually comfortable," Jazmyn said, wrapping her arms about herself and rubbing her arms.

"I knew you would like it." Her mom said. "There is a surprise in the living room for you."

"Ah, you finally got that pony I always wanted," Jazmyn said with a small laugh.

"Maybe." Her mother said, leading them to the living room.

"Surprise!" a multitude of voices rang out as Jazmyn entered the living room.

The first person she saw was Abraham, with a big smile. His same old smile that was on his face as on her eighth birthday. He had given her a thick storybook, and it had a lot of little stories in it, some she had never heard.

Then she saw her childhood friends Abraham had

adopted.

There were the twins, a boy, and a girl; Tony and Tina Neevision. Both were short with blond hair and their eyes were strange. Tony left eye was blue and the right eye had no color. Tina's eye were just the opposite.

Abraham then took in another girl named Miryssia Black. She was a tall thin Asian,

dressed all in black.

Jazmyn used to play with them, but they usually had to study. Abraham home-schooled his children.

A young man standing off to the side, with a face she thought she recognized, was keeping to himself, drinking a can of soda.

"Nice to see you guys, how have you all been?" Jazmyn said.

"Just grand," Miryssia said, giving Jazmyn a wink. "Happy birthday."

"We're fine, we seen you coming. Happy Birthday." Tony and Tina said together.

Abraham reached his hand out and moved the new young man over to the group. "Hello, Jazmyn, nice to see you again. This is Arion, Arion; this is Jazmyn."

"Nice to meet you," Jazmyn said, offering her hand to Arion.

"He isn't much into touching," Miryssia said.

"Oh." Jazmyn pulled her hand away and waved instead at him.

"Hey," Arion said, nodding his head.

Jazmyn looked into his eyes. Something deep inside her stirred, her heart skipped a beat, she felt her cheeks warming up, then quickly turned away.

"Are you alright?" Abraham asked, sitting next to her.

"Ah, yeah, I guess," Jazmyn said.

Abraham just smiled, glanced over to Arion then back to her.

As Jazmyn was growing up, Abraham would be something of a dad to her. She felt comfortable around him, and he would give encouragement when needed and help her when her mother wasn't home.

Her mother opened the door, and an old lady was there.

"Hello, Theia, glad you could join us. come in." Her mother said.

Miryssia and the others went over to the older woman; they must have known her. They all welcome her in.

Theia walked into the living room and looked around, and spotted Jazmyn. A big smile came to her face, and she walked over to Jazmyn.

"Happy Birthday, Jazmyn. This is a special birthday for you." Theia said. "My name is Theia."

"Thank you. You look familiar, do I know you?" Jazmyn inquired.

"We have met, but you know me better in a different form," Theia said, turning attention to Izzie. "Hello, Izzie"

"Hello," Izzie replied, glancing over at Jazmyn.

Theia turned to her mother. "It's time."

Jazmyn stood up and met her mother before she left the room.

"Mom, who is she?"

"She is a very old friend I met on the day you were born. She gave me something to give to you." Her mom said.

"I don't remember her at all."

"Probably not, Dear, she has only been here a few times when you were a little girl."

"How could she be a friend if you only knew her through a few visits? I have a bad feeling about all of this." Jazmyn said nervously.

"I trust her; nothing bad is going to happen." Her mom said and put her hand on her shoulder, and then went to her bedroom.

Jazmyn went back to sit down, and Izzie came over and sat down next to her.

"What's going on here? I thought we were going to have a party with presents, cake, and balloons at this time. Instead, we are just hanging out doing nothing." Izzie said.

"I know."

Her mother came back, holding a green velvet sack with drawstrings. She handed it to Theia.

"This has been given to me by your ancestor, and it was given to her by the ones who are all-powerful," Theia said, looking at Jazmyn, then handed her the sack.

"What do you mean?" Jazmyn asked.

"Just open it take and what is rightfully yours."

Jazmyn opened the sack and pulled out a necklace, and it was beautiful. Hanging from a leather strap was a pendant. It had an emerald seated in a gold backing, with a golden tree cut into the emerald, and it glowed brightly. Jazmyn could feel the energy coming from it; the necklace was beckoning to her, wanting her to put it on.

"Now, put it on," Theia said.

Jazmyn looked towards her mother, and she had a big smile on her face and tears in her eyes. Everyone in the room except Izzie, who was sitting there; the others gathered closer.

"What is going on, Mama?" Jazmyn widens her eyes.

"As it was explained to me is that you must take the necklace so you can become one of the most powerful witch that has ever been born," Her mother said as she came closer to her.

"What do you mean a witch. There are no such things, the only ones I have seen have been on TV." Jazmyn said.

"Yea, She is not a witch, I mean she can be a bitch at times but not a witch," Izzie commented.

Jazmyn looked at Izzie and then at Theia. "Take this. I don't want it."

"You must take it if you want to save your father," Theia said.

"Save my father?" Jazmyn creased her eyebrows together. "What the hell are you talking about? He is dead."

"No, he is not," Theia replied.

"Mom, is this true? Jazmyn turned to her.

Her mother nodded her head with tears in her eyes.

"The dream that you had about father is true too. Your father is trapped, and you are the only one who can save him." Theia explained.

"How did you know about my dream? The only person I told was Izzie and my cat."

"Yes, I know, it is time that you know something about me," Theia said.

Theia stood up and faced Jazmyn, whips of smoke came out of nowhere, Theia started to shrink, she bent over, put her hands on the floor, and they became paws, her face grew fur and whiskers popped out next to her nose, suddenly Onyx her cat was in front of her.

"Whoa, this is crazy," Izzie said as Theia turned back into a human.

"You are my cat? You've been with me all this time listening to me when I thought no one was there. Abraham, you gave her I mean Onyx to me." Jazmyn said, turning to Abraham.

"Yes, I gave Theia to you to watch over you," Abraham answered. "Until this day, when you received your necklace."

She turned back to Theia and studied her, and finally said. "Are you the one that came to the store to warn me?"

"That was I."

"You saw me naked," Jazmyn exclaimed and held her arm as to cover her breasts.

"Yes, that I have," Theia said. "That's part of watching over you. Sorry."

Jazmyn looked at everyone in the room in a different light. She grew up and played with Miryssia and the twins and never knew who they were.

"So, are you all witches too?" Jazmyn said, looking back at the crowd.

"Yes, except for Arion, he is a healer, he has the ability to heal people, and he also can fix things," Abraham answered.

Jazmyn locked eyes with Arion, and he shook his head. He emptied the can of soda and crushed it, then he held it in the palm of his hand, he placed his other hand over it, and it began to fix itself. The can seal itself, and Arion popped the top and wink at her, and took a gulp.

"He hasn't bought a new can of soda for months," Miryssia said as she waved, and the can jumped from Arion's hand to hers.

"That's cool," Izzie said.

"Do you remember when we used to play hide go seek, and whenever one of us was with you, we would have our eyes closed," Tina said.

"Yes, I always wondered why," Jazmyn said.

"We share each other sight," Tony said. "We can see what the other is looking at, so when we played that game to stay hidden, we closed our eyes."

Suddenly the whole house shook, and Izzie let out a scream. Everyone jumped up and ran to the window. There standing outside, was Luc with his hands in the air.

"Knock, knock," He said as he threw his arms down, and the house shook again. "Can I come in?"

Theia stepped out of the house and stood on the porch. Abraham stood next to her.

"Leave this place. You can not approach this house. Now leave!" Theia shouted.

"You can't tell me what to do," Luc stated and walked towards the house, but he was flung backward and landed on his back.

"You can't protect this house forever, you wretched witch. I am growing stronger every day, and soon, I will kill you both." Luc said, standing up again.

"Jazmyn! Did you enjoyed our date?. Let me introduce myself properly. I am Diomedes," Diomedes shouted.

Jazmyn stood by the window with disbelief and horror. The memory filled her head of that night when he attacked her. Her emotions were on a wild roller coaster with all these new feelings.

"All these years, my mother had been lying to me about my father being dead when he wasn't. I am a freak of nature, a witch, and my destiny is to save my father. I didn't ask for this."

The thought made her stomach twist in a ball.

"I can make this easy for you. I can feel that you don't want to be a freak, and you didn't want this. I can give your daddy back to you if you give me that necklace," Diomedes said.

"Don't listen to him; if he gets that necklace, there will be no stopping him. He will use that to control the whole world," Theia said, "You need to help us defeat him and become who you really are."

Jazmyn looked back, terror-filled the eyes of her mother and Izzie.

Abraham, Miryssia, Arion, and even the twins stood ready to fight.

"Why aren't they scared?"

"Oh, Jazzy, give me that necklace now! If you don't, I will kill your father," Diomedes said, making the house shake again; this time, pictures fell off the walls and shattered.

Jazmyn wanted to run, but a vision flashed in her mind of her dad. He was yelling, "Save me!"

She went outside with the necklace in her hand.

"What should I do?" She asked.

"Follow what's deep inside you. He will not kill your father as long as you have the necklace," Abraham said.

The necklace slowly began to slip from her hands. She looked and saw Diomedes holding his hands out, beckoning for it. Jazmyn used everything she had and managed to pull it back using both hands, then forced it around her neck. The emerald lit up so bright it blinded her, she felt the energy flow through her again, and it shot out in all directions. One of the rays of light struck Diomedes throwing him off his feet. The last thing she saw before the power overwhelmed her was Diomedes vanishing, then darkness.

∞∞∞

Jazmyn woke up, and she was in her bed at her mother's

house. It was just like it was on the day she left to move out.

She looked at the end of the bed where her vanity dresser was, and it's where she used to do her hair and put her makeup on; there were pictures of her mother and other people she knew, crammed in under the edges the wooden framed mirror. Her pink jewelry box, holding all of her childhood jewelry, was sitting right where she left it. She had her old clock radio on her nightstand, and the time read 9:06 am. She sat up quickly, and her head started to pound and felt the necklace move and rest between her breasts. She was hoping it was some bad dream and could go back to her life, but she knew that things would not be the same from now on.

She tried to get out of bed but found her legs were a little weak and sat back down; she cradled her head, she saw the nursery book that Abraham gave her, sitting on the chair next to her desk. Her emerald around her neck began to glow; the book came to her and laid itself on her lap.

"Whoa." She said.

The picture on the front morphed into a symbol that looked like her necklace. A leather cover appeared, the edges of the pages turn brown and weathered.

The book opened, the pages began to flip. Jazmyn saw symbols, pictures of creatures and people, and a lot of writing. It stopped on a page with a sketch of her, but she was dressed in colonial-style clothing. She read the name, and it was her own 'Jazmyn Allison Wolff. Then she heard her voice speaking from the pages.

"Welcome. If you are hearing me, then that means you have received your necklace. The book you are holding is yours."

"What?" Jazmyn said.

"This book is yours to use and to learn from."

"Oh my god, you heard that?" She asked.

"Yes I did, We are the same person but I lived long ago."

"This is confusing; it's like talking to myself."

"In a way, it is true. I can answer your questions, teach you from this book, your Book of Shadows. The contents of these pages is

what I had learned, spells, potions, and other things I wanted to pass them onto you when you reached your twenty-first birthday."

"How did you know I was going to be born?" Jazmyn said, getting up and moving to her desk with the book.

"300 years ago, a demon named Diomedes, also goes by Luc Stalin, came up from hell to claim the necklace that you wear. He wanted to use the forces of nature to help him with his army of crea-tures to wipe out the human race so he can ruled the world. I was the wearer of that necklace then, and I needed to learn my craft to end him, but I failed. I severely wounded him and he vowed he would be back and find the necklace to use it for evil."

"How can I? I am not a witch. Besides Luc, I mean Dio-medes, seems too powerful to defeat." Jazmyn thought for a bit. "Just tell me how you did it and that will be the end of it."

"I can not tell you, and yes, you are a witch."

"Why can't you? You said you'd teach me."

"With the help of your necklace, I will teach you the things that will help you defeat him, but you will need to learn more that I."

A light knock came on her door and she heard her mother's voice say. "Is everything alright in there?"

"Not sure, I am just talking to my book," Jazmyn said.

"What did you say?" Her mom opened the door and walk-in.

"I found what I thought was my nursery book but it turns out to be my Book of Shadows? Its talking to me." Jazmyn said.

"Yes, I put it there," Her mom said.

"You knew? You knew of all of this?" Jazmyn stated.

"Yes, I did. Theia told me this would happen."

"Why didn't you tell me about all of this?" Jazmyn asked.

"I was told not too. It will be explained to you later, but for now, come downstairs and have some breakfast, it will make you feel better," her mother said and walked out.

"I am going crazy," Jazmyn said

"No, you are not," Allison said.

"I am going to join the land of the real now," Jazmyn said.

"Magic is real, Goodbye for now."

Jazmyn closed the book and laid it on her desk, thought everything in her life has been routine, and regular, now her life is and will be different. Knowing magic does exist, and she had some part. Being in it was almost too much for her to wrap her mind around. She wanted nothing more than to forget all this.

She grabbed clothes out of a suitcase and changed and went downstairs.

When Jazmyn got to the last step, she found Izzie sitting in the dining room talking to her mother and Theia.

"Morning, Jaz, glad to see you are alright. I have been talking to Theia; she is a really cool woman." Izzie said

"Good morning, Jazmyn," Theia said.

"Hi. I talked with my book this morning." Jazmyn said as she headed towards the kitchen to get some eggs and bacon that was left.

"Jaz, did you say you talked with a book?" Izzie questioned.

"Yes, but it seems that only freaks like me are the only one who can do that sort of thing," Jazmyn said, sitting down across from Izzie.

"You are not a freak, Jazmyn." Her mother said. "You are my daughter and you have a special gift."

"Gloria is right. You have a special gift. Learn to use your magic and you will," Theia smiled. "After we teach you with the help of your book, you will see that it is a gift."

"Who's we?" Jazmyn inquired as she took a bite of her bacon.

"Abraham and I and his children. You must start learning your craft today." Theia said.

"Today? Oh no, after I am done here, Izzie and I are going back home, where I have my life, my job and my cat, forget the cat who wasn't even a cat, who was a person all this time," Jazmyn got up and paced, waving her hands "This is just crazy."

"We are going back?" Izzie asked.

"Yes, we are," Jazmyn said, turning to face Izzie.

"I think all of this so cool," Izzie said. "I'd like to have magical powers."

"Well, here you can have this stupid necklace, and you can have the book too," Jazmyn said.

"The necklace is meant for you," Theia said.

"Oh, honey. This is a good thing that happened to you. So, try to look on the bright side." Her mother pleaded.

"Bright side?! What is the bright side, now I can learn to turn people into a toad, if I wanted or is it to have the chance to be killed by some strange demon, monster or whatever the hell he is." Jazmyn said as she pushed her plate away, grabbed her coat, and stormed out of the house.

The lake was calm, encircled with a ring of ice. Jazmyn stopped at the end of the dock, and she looked across the lake, and she could see Abraham's place. Her mother's house and his were the only two houses on this lake. The lake wasn't huge; it only took five minutes to walk between the two houses.

When she would play games with the kids next door, they seemed normal at the time, but they weren't; hell, she wasn't even normal anymore. Thinking back, she could tell something was different about them. Little things like when Miryssia and her were playing, and Miryssia fell into a deep hole, and when she got back with help, Miryssia was out of the pit; she must use her gift to help her out. She used to play guess the next card with Tina, and she would always guess the right card, and so would her brother.

Jazmyn was snap back to reality when she heard a sound behind her; it was Abraham.

"How are you doing?" Abraham asked

"This is too much for me. I am not a witch. I can't stop him."

"You are a witch, and yes, you can," Abraham said, walking with her back to the house.

"I don't want to be a witch."

When she got into the house, she walked by everyone and went up to her room, and slammed the door; she sat down in front of her makeup mirror, "Happy birthday, Jazmyn, surprise you're a witch."

Her necklace felt very heavy on her, like the weight of the world was around her neck. She took it off and put it next to her; it began to glow; it seems to beckon for her to put it back on.

Jazmyn just stared at it, "Why me?"

A light knock came from her door, "Can I come in?"

When she heard it was her mother's voice, tears began to flow, "Why didn't you tell me about all of this earlier?"

"I was keeping you safe." Gloria said peeking in the door.

"I am not strong enough to do this," Jazmyn confessed.

"Yes, you are," Her mother answered.

The thought of her trying to do what was set in motion a long time ago and now fell on her made her panic.

"I am not going to do it," Jazmyn said.

"You have too. To save the world," her mom pleaded. "More importantly, your father."

"I was just getting over the fact that he wasn't going to be in my life anymore, but now you are telling me that I can save him," Jazmyn pushed past her mother. "To top it all off, I am a witch. Forget it. I am leaving."

When Jazmyn got downstairs, she grabbed her coat and headed for the door; she looked at Izzie, "Are you coming?"

"Aren't you staying?" Izzie wondered.

"No."

Chapter Seven

After dropping Izzie at her place, Jazmyn arrived at her apartment; it seemed like years went by instead of a day. She knew the life she lived before wasn't going to be the same now, knowing that magic is real and she is part of it.

She dropped her coat on the back of the couch and went to the bedroom, sat down on the edge of her bed, and put her head in her hands, trying to put everything into perspective.

She knew that she would never be brave enough to face down Diomedes, even with the help of magic that she had no clue. It best to leave everything like it was.

She was never any good with confrontation; she would always find a way to avoid it. Jazmyn remembers a time in school a bully that kept teasing her about her daddy just left them because he didn't want Jazmyn as his daughter. She would agree with her insults than to stand up to her. There were times it would hurt her so much that Jazmyn wanted to pound the bully but never did.

It would scare her, and she would avoid seeing her aggressor. She thought if she didn't hear the hurtful words, it wouldn't bother her.

This became her philosophy for all of her life.

The day was moving on even though Jazmyn didn't. She decided to change into her comfy clothes and do a whole lot of nothing.

The couch looked inviting and plopped down and grabbed the remote, and began to flip through the channels. She came across the same show that she and Izzie watched the other night. She quickly changes the channel then came upon a documentary about the history of magic.

"Good grief, can't even getaway here. I just want to forget about this." Jazmyn said, then shut the TV off.

A sound caught her ear, and she turned to see her necklace appear next to her, "What the hell?"

She looked at it and then slowly reached for it but grabbed her phone instead and dial her mother.

"Hi, Mom," Jazmyn said, staring at the necklace.

"Is everything alright?" her mom stressed.

"I'm fine. Who sent me my necklace?"

"I don't know, hold on."

Her mom muffled the phone, Jazmyn waited, and it seemed a long time when she heard her mother's voice, "Nobody did."

"No one, so it sent itself here?" Jazmyn huffed, rolling her eyes. "Well, I don't want it here, have someone take it back. Ask your friend Theia to take it back."

"Well, honey, it is yours to keep. Besides Theia said she can't, once it's given it is yours. Are you coming back here?"

"No, I am not coming back. I will talk to you later. Bye."

Jazmyn threw her phone down and got up off the couch, trying to forget about everything. She could call up Izzie and maybe do something, but Izzie would want to talk about all this magic stuff. She decided to go down to the Cafe to get her mind off of things.

She grabbed her coat and was about to walk out the door when she almost forgot her phone. She reached for it from the couch and picked it up, glancing over to the necklace.

She felt a chill run down her spine, and the room got dark, suddenly she saw a terrible vision of children and adults. Tens of thousands of them dressed in black were working hard; they were crying and screaming in pain. There were hideous creatures yelling orders and using whips on them. Some people were dead or dying, and we're left right where they dropped to rot.

Jazmyn felt tears stream down her face, and she saw herself leaning over a person on the ground. When she looked closer, it was her friend Izzie, and she was dead.

The vision of herself, turned, look at her, and with the pain of the loss in her face and pleaded. "Don't let this happen, please, don't let this happen." then she trailed off with her voice and looked back down.

Jazmyn then saw a giant hand with claws, and the knuckles had bony growths on them. When she turned around, she saw Diomedes, and he was five times the size he was before. He had horns coming out of his head; he had armor lie skin covering his body.

He grabbed her and picked her up, and brought her to his face.

"Thanks for the necklace," Diomedes said and held it in front of her. "It gave me the power to become my full self and to control all."

The necklace had changed, it had a black stone in the middle, and it had grown to fit the owner.

"No!" Jazmyn yelled. "How did you get that?"

He began to laugh with a baritone laugh; it ran chills down her spine. "Well, from you, when you didn't want to be a witch. It made everything so much easier," Diomedes said as he started to crush her.

The next thing she knew was that she was lying on the floor gasping for air, the room around her came into focus again. She slowly got up off the floor; her head was pounding; it felt like someone hit her with a steel beam.

She barely made her way to her kitchen chair before she fell onto it. She was finding it difficult to breathe, and her throat felt as dry as the desert. She grabbed an almost empty bottle of water and drank it all, "What the hell was that? Is this what I am going have to look forward too? I want my life back."

A flush of heat rose from somewhere deep inside; she felt as though the room was closing in on her. She shot out of that chair and ran out her door, slamming it. The staircase was a blur as she almost flew down them, the cold of the outside hit her; she stopped and took a deep breath to calm herself down.

She leaned up against the building, and she looked around to see a few people looking at her. One of them came up to her and asked if she was alright. Jazmyn just nodded and began to walk towards the Cafe.

An empty booth was what she was seeking when she pushed the door open; she spied one over in the corner and quickly sat down, then picked up the menu.

"Is there anything I start you off with?" A voice said.

"A coke," Jazmyn blurted out.

"K, I'll be right back with that," the waitress answered and darted behind the counter.

Jazmyn's mind was full of visions of evil creatures and people in torment. She shook her head, trying to clear it.

A dreadful feeling came over her; it felt as though some-one was watching her. She looked around and caught a glimpse of Diomedes sitting across the room, but the waitress blocked her view when she brought her coke over.

Jazmyn tried to look around her, but the waitress kept moving.

"Did you want to order something?" The waitress asked.

"No," Jazmyn snapped.

As the waitress made a face, she moved off.

The table was empty where she saw Diomedes. Jazmyn cautiously looked to see if he was there but no sight of him.

"Maybe, I was just seeing things," she said to herself.

She couldn't shake the feeling that Diomedes was some-where watching her. She threw a five-dollar bill on the table.

Leary of watching her back on the way out of the door, she ran into Izzie walking in.

"Oh, sorry Izzie, I didn't see you," Jazmyn said.

"That's ok, no harm," Izzie replied.

"Could you walk with me?" Jazmyn pleaded.

"Is there something wrong?"

Jazmyn just nodded her head and grab Izzie by her arm,

headed back to her place.

When they arrived back at her place, Jazmyn locked her door.

"What's going on?" Izzie asked with a hint of panic.

"I thought I saw Diomedes in the Cafe," Jazmyn said, pacing the floor.

"What? He's here?"

"Yes, I'm pretty sure," Jazmyn said.

"I think we should call Theia or Abraham or someone to tell them."

"I don't have their number."

"Can you use the force or something to talk to them, then," Izzie asked.

Jazmyn paced her floor, "I don't know how, I think we should just stay calm and hope I was wrong."

"You sure didn't look like you were wrong,"

"I am feeling overwhelmed with all that has happened; maybe I just need time to process it or something," Jazmyn said but not knowing who she was trying to convince more, Izzie or herself.

Izzie walked over to her couch and sat down. She saw the necklace lying there and picked it up. "How did this get here, I thought you left it at your mom's."

Jazmyn seized the necklace from Izzie, "It just appeared here."

"Maybe it's trying to tell you something," Izzie said.

"No, I don't think so," Jazmyn argued, putting the necklace down on her table.

Jazmyn walked over to her kitchen counter and pulled herself up, "I really don't know anything anymore, Izzie."

Izzie walked over and sat next to her friend, "Everything will be alright."

Jazmyn felt that the world was closing in on her; a panic feeling came over her again. The visions that she had earlier haunted her. Tears rain down her face, "I don't think everything is going to be alright anymore."

"What do you mean?" Izzie wondered as she hoisted herself up next to Jazmyn.

"I had a vision of people dying and that asshole was ruling the world because I gave him the necklace," Jazmyn sobbed.

Izzie thought for a moment, "Maybe, you could change that. Being a science freak, I believe nothing is set in stone until it actually happens, So, we will make sure it doesn't happen."

"But how?" Jazmyn asked.

The necklace began to glow brightly; within moments, a pounding came at Jazmyn's door. "It's him."

Both of the girls jumped off the counter and hugged, trying to comfort each other.

"Let me in!" A haunting voice came through the door.

"What are we going to do?" Izzie panicked.

"The fire escape," Jazmyn screamed, and they both ran towards her bedroom.

The door blew apart; Diomedes stepped in and spotted the glow from the necklace, "This is too easy."

Diomedes approached the necklace, and in a bold move, Jazmyn ran and grabbed it first but was blocked by him.

"What are you going to do, little girl," Diomedes teased.

Without thinking, Izzie picked up a heavy vase next to her and threw it, striking Diomedes's back of his head; Diomedes fell to the ground.

"Hurry, Jaz," Izzie screamed, waving her hands in a hurry motion.

"I never opened this window before, it's stuck," Jazmyn told, trying to pull up on the window.

The crashing of furniture echoed loudly from the other room. They both worked franticly on the window. Finally, the window gave in and opened; they both hurried out and went down to the street and ran. Diomedes screamed at them as they disappeared around the block.

It seemed forever before they stopped. They finally ended up in the preschool playground.

"Are you alright?" Jazmyn asked, caught her breath.

Izzie placed her hand over her heart, "Yeah, that was close. Do you think we lost him."

"I hope so."

"I guess your necklace glows when something bad is going to happen," Izzie said. "Like a spider-sense for Spider-man."

Jazmyn cracked a smile while trying to catch her breath, "You would see it that way. Yeah, maybe it does."

The night was cold and clear, the stars twinkled to life in the sky, and the parking lot lights pop on.

"I think we should go to my apartment," Izzie said.

"Yeah."

Izzie unlock the door to her tiny little house; it had only two rooms, living space, and the bathroom.

Jazmyn went to the window facing the street and peek out to see if he was out there. "I don't see him."

"That's good," Izzie replied.

"Izzie," Jazmyn said.

"Yep?"

"I am sorry for all of this. You shouldn't have to go through this shit. I got you drugged into this." Jazmyn lowered her head.

"No worries, mate. I would help you through anything; you're my bestie. Besides, living in this town is really boring, and a little change is good." Izzie said, then came over and draped her arm over Jazmyn's shoulders.

"I think this would be more like a big change and thanks for being here for me. I need it."

Izzie hugged Jazmyn, "I think it's time that you have your first 'legal' beer."

"I guess we never did celebrate my birthday," Jazmyn said, sitting down on Izzie's hide-a-bed couch.

Izzie went to her refrigerator and grabbed a couple of beers.

"Happy Birthday, Jaz," Izzie said, raising her beer.

"Yeah, what a birthday," Jazmyn said to herself.

∞ ∞ ∞

Monday morning greeted Jazmyn too early, all night she wrestled with her thoughts and blankets, sharing a small hide-a-bed with Izzie.

Jazmyn stretched to work out the kink in her neck and got up, took a few steps to Izzie's kitchen to make coffee.

She looked around to where Izzie kept the coffee. Izzie likes to move things constantly, so it is always a guessing game where things are.

Trying to keep her mind off of what's been happening, she quietly walked around Izzie's house; she is pretty organized with her things.

Jazmyn bent down to pick up her jacket she worn last night, and her necklace fell out.

She stared at the necklace; It beckons to her to pick it up. She reaches for it and placed the emerald in her hand; she could feel a stimulating pulse traveled through her hand up her arm to her soul. It felt like it was a part of her, and it needed to reunite with her. She placed it over her head; it felt right. The emerald burst into a very bright light, and she could feel the energy flow through her body, waking all of her senses.

"Dad, turn out the light, I don't want to go to school today," Izzie mumbled, still more asleep than awake.

Jazmyn tucked the necklace down her shirt and walked back into the kitchen. Its light disappeared, and she pulled it back out.

What the hell am I going to do?

"What time is it?" Izzie said, sitting up.

"Jazmyn glanced at the clock hanging over the stove, "7:38."

"Aw, shit, we both need to work at nine, remember?" Izzie hurried out of bed and headed for the coffee. "Thanks for making coffee."

"Your right, I totally forgot."

"It's not like you have anything else on your mind," Izzie smirked.

A realization came over Jazmyn, her heart began to beat harder, and her mind went wild, "I can't go back to work," Jazmyn panicked.

"Why?" Izzie said, raising her eyebrow.

"I am," Jazmyn hesitated. "Different."

"Just chill," Izzie spouted. "How are you different?. Just because you found out you are a witch. It's not like a switch was turned on and suddenly you became one, you were always one."

"What will happen if I do something," Jazmyn paused to find the right word. "Weird."

"Don't worry about it, just act like you don't know what happened and just walk away," Izzie said before finishing her cup of coffee.

"I have nothing to wear. I don't feel safe going back to my apartment."

"You can wear some of my clothes. It not like we haven't borrowed each others clothes before."

"Thanks, Izzie," Jazmyn felt a little better.

"By the way, you rock that necklace, it matches your eyes," Izzie said, heading toward the bathroom. "Just grab what you need from my dresser."

"Okay," Jazmyn said, walking over to Izzie's dresser with also had her TV and her gaming computer on it.

∞∞∞

On the way to their work, Jazmyn kept looking at everything that moved.

"Would you just chill, Jazmyn."

"I can't help it, what happens if he attacks us there?"

Izzie turned to look at Jazmyn, "In all the shows I have watched about this stuff, no one on either good or evil side of magic, wants to be exposed. He will not attack when we are in public."

"You are basing all this on something you watch!" Jazmyn exclaimed.

"Yes, I also have books." Izzie smiled.

"I am going back to your place. I am not doing this." Jazmyn turned to head back.

"Deciding you're not going to work, Ms. Wolff," A voice came from behind her.

Jazmyn slowly turned back around, afraid of who she would see. Her heart was in her throat.

"It's the drill Sargent," Izzie said.

"No, I was...um...I was going back because I thought I forgot something," Jazmyn lied.

"Good, I got things for you to do today." Mr. Albertson said as he opened the door to usher them in.

After Jazmyn punch in, Mr. Albertson was true to his word; he had made a list that seemed not to end.

A few hours went by, and she couldn't keep her mind on her job, never mind the list.

She just stood there and stared at nothing while her thoughts kept playing through her mind.

What am I capable of? Am I going to be able to have an everyday life? What if I get found out that I am different than everyone.

Her heart skipped a beat when she heard the scuffing of feet behind her.

"What are you staring at? Get back to work," Her manager yelled from the back room.

She jumped, then caught her breath and just shook her head and went back to the backroom, walking past him.

"We don't pay you to stand around," Her manager got in her face.

A timid voice came out of her, "I am going on break."

She turned to walk away but was stopped by a hand on her shoulder.

"Get back here, I am not done talking to you," he huffed.

"Okay, what?" Jazmyn stopped.

"I don't like that attitude you have. I am your manager, and you are small for me. I will not..."

It felt like her mind was shutting down; she hated how he made her feel; he made her feel small.

Jazmyn turned her head, "I am not small, you are."

Her necklace began to glow, and suddenly, Mr. Albertson shrunk until he was not more than a few inches tall.

"Holy shit, oh no," Jazmyn cried. "What am I going to do? I can't just walk away from this."

Mr. Albertson began to run down the hallway, Jazmyn chased after him. It didn't take her long to catch up to him. "Please, stop Mr. Albertson, I can fix this. I don't know how but I will"

"What happened to me?" He asked in a meek voice.

Jazmyn was about to answer heard footsteps behind her. She froze in place; she panicked and reached down and pick her manager up and hid him behind her back as she turned around.

"What's happening, girl," Izzie said, oblivious to what was going on.

"I am in some serious trouble," Jazmyn pleaded.

"Why did drill Sargent bitch at you again, he's a loser," Izzie said.

"No, but it is about Mr. Albertson," Jazmyn stated, showing Izzie what was in her hands.

"No way, that's rad," Izzie smiled and began to laugh.

"This is not funny," Jazmyn fumed.

Jazmyn put her manager back on the floor and began to pace, then grabbed her phone and called her mom.

"Hey, mom, is Theia there?"

"Yes," her mom answered.

"Could you put on the phone," Jazmyn paced around?

"What's going on?"

"Nothing," Jazmyn lied. "Everything is almost fine, mom. I'll tell you later, just put her on the phone."

"Here, she is."

"Theia, um, I need your help."

"What the matter, Jazmyn?" Theia said, appearing next to her.

"Whoa! "Jazmyn screamed, stepping back a few steps.

"Cool," Izzie stated.

Jazmyn caught her breath and just pointed at Mr. Albertson.

"Oh, I can fix this. I do believe you should come back with me and let us teach you," Theia relayed to her.

"Could we talk about this later after you fix this, please."

"Yes, Dear,"

Theia waved her hand, and her manager returned to his normal size. She shook her hand again, and he froze in place.

"What did you?" Jazmyn exclaimed.

"She froze him in time," Izzie excitedly said.

"Izzie, your acting like a nerd at a comic-con convention," Jazmyn said.

"So what, this is the coolest thing ever," Izzie jumped around a little.

"Sorry, just going through a mental breakdown here.", Jazmyn began to pace the floor again.

"No, you are not, Jazmyn. It's natural to feel this way," Theia calmly said.

"Is he going to remember this?" Jazmyn asked, pointing at her manager.

"No," Theia assured her; she lifted her head like she sensed something. "I must be going. Think about what I said; you need guidance."

Theia waved her hand and disappeared; then, her manager began to move.

"Done with your break yet. How did you get here, Ms. Osgood?" Mr. Albertson wondered. "Never mind."

"No, not yet. Still heading there," Jazmyn said.

"Go, then get back to work," He said, checked his watch, and walked away.

For the rest of the day, Jazmyn watched what she said and

tried to stay away from anybody. When it was quitting time, she almost ran out of the store.

"Hey, wait for me!" Izzie shouted from behind her.

"Sorry, Iz, I just needed to get out of there," Jazmyn said.

"That's okay. I am having one of those days too." Izzie said as they walked towards her place.

"Not like this. I have been thinking of quitting my job. I can't be around people." Jazmyn admitted. "I am not safe to be with."

"Well, why don't you go back and let Theia teach you."

"I am not sure yet...." Jazmyn stopped when she noticed Officer Briggs approaching them, and her necklace began to glow.

"I have a few more questions for you ladies about the incident last week," Briggs said; he looked down at Jazmyn's necklace. "Nice necklace; why does it glow?"

Jazmyn felt uneasy, her instincts told her to run, but she just stood there, unsure why her necklace was glowing.

"What do you need from us, we told you everything we knew," Izzie stated, stepping between him and Jazmyn.

"I don't need anything from you." Briggs pushed Izzie out of the way, causing her to fall into the street; a car just missed her.

"Who do you think you are?" Jazmyn spouted, helping Izzie back up.

"I think you know who I am," Briggs said.

"What do you mean?" Jazmyn inquired.

Briggs threw his hand out in front of him, began to raise it, and Jazmyn lifted off the ground. "How are you doing this?"

"Let's not waste my time with any more questions," Briggs said.

The officer masquerade disappeared, revealing Diomedes standing there; he wore a black trench coat.

Jazmyn struggled to break free; his iron grip stopped. She noticed Izzie trying to help her, but something stopped her, an invisible force, "Let me down!"

"Give me the necklace, and I will," Diomedes sneered.

"Aren't you afraid of letting the world know about magic," Jazmyn said.

"To the world, it looks as though your friend is crazy. This is my world, and no one can see us."

"Let me down and do what you ask," Jazmyn bagged.

Diomedes brought her down, "Give it here."

Jazmyn knew she couldn't let him have it, but she froze with fear, all of her muscles locked up, her mind was in overdrive trying to think of something, she glanced at the necklace, and words popped into her head, "Take this evil far away. With this command, you will not stay."

The necklace burst out with a brilliant of a thousand lights, and Diomedes disappeared.

Jazmyn fell to the ground; she almost passed out; she propped herself up on one elbow. She felt weak and could hardly breathe. It felt like she hadn't slept for days.

Izzie fell forward when the wall vanished but caught herself. She ran to Jazmyn's side, "Are you alright?"

"I am fine, I guess."

"That's awesome. You did your first witchy thing." Izzie said ecstatically, helping Jazmyn to her feet.

"Yeah, I guess I did," Jazmyn stood there bewildered, a car honked, snapped her back, "Let get out of here. I don't want to be here when he gets back."

The setting sun lit the way into Izzie's house. She looked around before shutting the door and locking it.

"What am I going to do? Iz," Jazmyn worried.

"I think you should take Theia's advice and let them teach you. I know I would."

Jazmyn knew Izzie was right, but her mind was telling her that this was somehow all make-believe, and she would wake up soon, and all of this would be gone.

"This is so unreal," Jazmyn said.

"Believe it, girl, it's real."

Jazmyn tried to push it to the back of her mind, like she

always does, "Got anything to eat?"

"What? How could you think of eating?" Izzie flashed her an odd look.

"I don't want to think about this anymore. Besides, I have been nervous all day and didn't eat much. Okay?"

"Alright, but we will talk about this later. I think I have a pizza."

Yes, Mom," Jazmyn tried to make a joke.

They shared the pizza in silence. Jazmyn mind was numb. She wrestled with the thought of her having powers, and it scared her, but at the same time, she knew it felt natural to her when she made Diomedes disappear, for the first time in her life, since she was born, things strangely made sense.

"Earth to Jazmyn, come in, Jazmyn," Izzie called.

"What?... I'm sorry, did you say something?" Jazmyn said, wandering back from her thoughts.

"Are you going to have the last piece?"

"Aw... no, you can have it," Jazmyn offered.

"Thanks."

"You have tomorrow off, right?" Jazmyn inquired.

"Yes, Why? Izzie said, chewing on her pizza.

"I think I am going to give this witch thing a chance," Jazmyn said, which brought her relief in some way.

"Hurray!" Izzie shouted, raising her arms over her head, causing the topping from the pizza to land on her lap.

"Oh, Izzie," Jazmyn smiled, then they both burst out in laughter.

Chapter Eight

"Are you almost ready to go?" Izzie yelled.

Jazmyn stood in the bathroom, staring at herself in the mirror.

She didn't look any different than she did before realization of her new destiny besides the necklace she wore now but the one thing the mirror doesn't show the turmoil inside.

"I need to embrace the fact that I am a witch, but how," Jazmyn said to her reflection.

"Jaz?"

"Yeah," Jazmyn yelled out.

She picked a brush and ran it through her hair, but her brush argued with her hair. Frustrated, she gave up and threw the brush down.

Damn hair.

She looked in the mirror for one last time, straighten her shirt then left the bathroom.

Izzie stood there, waiting like a puppy that wants out. "Ready?"

"As much as I can be. When we pick up my car, I need to get some clothes."

"Hopefully, weirdo isn't there," Izzie said, zipping her coat up slowly.

"Yeah, you got that right. I need to call mom to let her know we're on our way."

"Ok," Izzie said.

"Hi, mom. Just letting you know were on are way...yes, we

will be careful...Love you. Bye"

Jazmyn hit the end button on her phone, "Mom is excited the were coming back."

"I kinda figured."

Both women walked carefully over to Jazmyn's place; she kept looking down at her necklace so she wouldn't miss the first hint of trouble.

When they got to her apartment door, Izzie stood guard out the door, nervously pacing, stopping at every noise, "Hurry up. If creepy comes, I will probably scream, besides it's kinda creepy out here."

Jazmyn came out with a small travel bag, almost dropping it, trying to lock her door.

They headed down the stairs then stopped when they saw the door at the bottom slowly open. Jazmyn's heart skipped. She dropped everything, trying to get to her necklace, buried under her coat and shirt.

She got it out at the same time the door burst opened, and standing there was Bernie.

"Sorry, ladies, if I scared you. It's kinda cold out there, needed to warm up." Bernie said.

They both let out a big sigh. Izzie helped Jazmyn pick up her stuff. "That's ok, Bernie," Jazmyn said, feeling her heart resuming its regular beat.

The car rode down the road like it wanted to get away and never want to come back.

"What's it like?" Izzie asked.

"It's kind of weird, I guess, it's overwhelming to think that I could do what I want but can't," Jazmyn answered.

"What does the magic feel like?"

"When I said that spell," Jazmyn paused, searching for the words. "You know when you hit your funny bone; it kind of like that. It comes from somewhere by my heart. Magic is very draining."

"Yeah, I noticed."

Arriving at her mom's cabin, Jazmyn was afraid to own up

to his mistake for leaving as she did.

Put the car in park, slowly open the door. A cold blast of air hit her face when she stepped out. She hurried to get into the cabin as the wind bit into her skin.

"Welcome back, you two," Gloria said, coming up to Jazmyn and hugging her, then Izzie.

"Hi, Mom."

"Hey, Mrs. W," Izzie said, taking off her coat and headed for the living room.

"How are you? Dear."

At that moment, it seemed that the world was coming down on her knowing that becoming a witch and defeating Diomedes was now her fate in life, "Fine. I'm sorry about the other day."

"That's alright, honey. You must be hungry," her mom said, trying to hide the fact that she knew a little what her daughter was feeling.

"Not really," Jazmyn said.

"I made one of your favorite cakes, German chocolate. I'll get you a piece," Gloria said and headed for the kitchen. "Go sit in the living room."

Jazmyn found Theia talking to Izzie. Theia got up and hugged Jazmyn, and escorted her to the couch.

"How are you? Never mind I can see you are overwhelmed. Everything will be fine." Theia assured her.

"Izzie told me that Diomedes tried to get the necklace, and you fought him off," Theia said.

"It wasn't anything. It was more an accident than intentional that I fought him off. The necklace did it, not me," Jazmyn said unconvincingly.

"The necklace can help you out at times, but the will of it comes from you. Somewhere deep inside of you, there is a connection with your necklace," Theia informed.

"Here is your cake, I brought one for Izzie," Her mom said, entering the room.

"Thanks, Mrs. W.," Izzie blurted. "I love your cakes."

"Thank you."

Jazmyn reached for her plate, "Thanks, Mom."

"I have planned a big supper; afterward, I guess Theia has a surprise for you."

"I'm not really ready for any more surprises, had enough in the last few days," Jazmyn stated.

"This one you will cherish," Theia said with a gleam in her voice.

Jazmyn finished her cake, "I'm going to go up to my room and take a nap."

"Yes, you must be tired, magic can take a toll on a new witch," Theia said.

"Plus, she had to spend a few nights at my house. That would take a lot out of anyone," Izzie said in her sarcastic way.

"Yeah, that too," Jazmyn said. She pauses at the bottom of the stairs.

A new witch, I kind of like that.

Jazmyn nodded and walked up the steps.

She opened the door to her room; she felt safe here. She fell on her bed, letting out a sigh; she rolled over and curled up, hugging her pillow. "My life is going to change," she mumbled, with a single tear that fell and stained her pillow.

∞ ∞ ∞

A light knock on came to her bedroom door. "Time to wake up," Her mom's muffled voice said.

"Alright, getting up," Jazmyn answered, but her body didn't agree.

She laid there for a while, then finally convinced herself to get up. She made her way downstairs and found everyone there in the living room. The twins were sitting next to the couch on the floor, next to Abraham and Theia.

Izzie was talking to Theia; Miryssia was relaxing across the recliner.

Jazmyn heart skipped a beat or two when her eyes meant Arion's.

"Hi," Arion said.

"Hello," Jazmyn answered timidly.

"Supper is about ready. How was your nap?" Her mom asked, wiping her hands on a towel when she entered.

"It was good."

"Let's eat," Izzie said.

After the supper mess was cleaned up, her mother and Izzie stayed at the house while the rest went into the woods. The afternoon stretched on to become dusk, and the woods were growing darker as they gathered around the same giant old oak tree that she took a picture of.

When Jazmyn was a young girl, she marveled at the house size base and how the grass around its roots would stay green even when there was deep snow on the ground. Jazmyn used to spend hours under the arms of this tree, and she would imagine fairies were hiding around the tree. Jazmyn now wonders if those fairies were real.

"What are we doing here?" Jazmyn asked.

"You will see. Now all of you form a half-circle, Jazmyn, you stand here." Theia said, handing Jazmyn's book of shadows to her.

"All of you except for Jazmyn, hold your hands out in front of you, with one under the other," Abraham said.

"Are we going to catch a cold with our hands? It's cold out here," Miryssia said.

"No, Just wait," Abraham said, waving his hands, a lighted candle appearing in their hands.

"Thanks, getting warmer now," Miryssia said.

"Quiet, please," Abraham said, eyeing Miryssia.

"Welcome, Jazmyn, you can do this." the angelic voice spoke, causing a strange feeling to come over her; it felt as tho she needed to be here to do this.

She took a deep breath and noticed that everyone around her was wearing necklaces. For some reason, she never saw them before today except for Theia's gem, which was white with a hint of a rose color. Abraham's gem was amber, Miryssia had an amethyst gem, the twins had sapphire, and Arion wore a citron-colored gem.

"Jazmyn, open your book, it will know what you need and present it to you." Theia moved her eyes from the book to Jazmyn. "Please, read out loud the spell on the page, " Theia said.

"I am not a witch, but, OK," Jazmyn rolled her eyes.

She turned her attention to the book and opened it; the pages came alive and flipped wildly, causing her hair to flutter until it stopped. Almost like on cue, little sparkles of light raised off the pages and hovered to help her read.

Jazmyn cleared her throat and began:
> **"With these candles of light. Show me**
> **the entrance to honor my right,"**

Jazmyn could feel a tingling sensation start from her heart and spread all over her body.

Beams of light shot out from each of the candles, striking the tree trunk. The ground shook, and a ribbon of light framed a door on the side of the tree.
> **"With the power given to me, open**
> **the door, for I am the key."**

She felt as though all of her nerves were firing at once.

Her emerald lit up the night; with a green glow. It began to hum; as it did, it shot a beam of light at the door, causing it to open, and a staircase just inside leads downward.

What is this place?" Jazmyn inquired.

"This is your place, your sanctuary and a place to learn and study," Theia said.

"It will keep you hidden from evil. The door will open only to the ones you invite," Abraham told.

"Totally, cool," Miryssia said as the candles disappeared.

Jazmyn looked above the door and seen the same emblem carved into the bark as her necklace, she entered the doorway, and a path of candles lit the way down the spiral staircase. The others followed her as she went down.

When they got to the bottom, a large circular room beyond a grand archway illuminated. Jazmyn stepped in; the space could hold her apartment, with a podium opposite the door made of marble, and along the walls were a few shelves and cupboards with bottles inside.

She placed her book on the podium. The book opened itself to the page with the portrait of her ancestor on it.

"Hello again, Jazmyn," Allison said.

"Hi," Jazmyn answered.

"Hello Theia, it is nice to hear your voice again, it has been a while," Allison said.

"Yes, yes it has. So many years, it hadn't seemed that long, Allison," Theia said, going to Jazmyn side.

"You know her?" Jazmyn asked.

Theia nodded her head. "We met when we were around your age. She was my best friend, or as you kids say she's my BFF."

Tony and Tina giggled.

Jazmyn looked at the book and noticed writing below Allison's picture that wasn't there before. "Where did this come from?"

"Speak it out loud and you will find out," Allison said.

Jazmyn recited:

"I call to my ancestor from the past. Come back to us, appear here with this spell I cast."

Suddenly her necklace lit up, from the pages in front of her, sprouted a ball of light, and floated to the ground, then Allison appeared and became real.

"That's better," Allison said as she strolled around the room. "It's nice to be whole again."

Jazmyn felt strange seeing someone that looked like her, and it was like seeing your reflection coming to life.

"How can you be alive again after 300 years?" Jazmyn asked.

"Jazmyn, we really don't die, our life force is always alive, but I only can hold my body within this ancient tree," Allison said.

Allison turned and pointed to the center of the room, and a huge round table materialized. "We'll need a place to work," With a wave of her hand, chairs seemed to come out of the floor.

"All of you, come sit," Theia said.

Jazmyn sat down with Allison on her right and Theia on her left, and the rest followed.

In the center of the table was a carving of an oak tree. Encircling the tree were four triangles pointing to the north, south, east, and west.

"I announce the first gathering of the oak tree coven. We are all here to teach Jazmyn her craft and to prepare her to defeat Diomedes," Theia said as they all glanced at each other.

"I still don't understand why it is up to me to destroy Diomedes," Jazmyn asked.

"When I was living, I met this gentleman, we courted; I fell in love with him. He was the one for me until I found out that he was a demon from hell and he was here to take that necklace from me," Allison said, pointing at Jazmyn's necklace.

"Sounds familiar," Jazmyn stated.

"When he couldn't get it from me, he sent a wolf after my family," Allison lowered her head, and tears fell. "I found my mother and father were all torn up. It devastated me, I lost my whole world when he killed them. So, I vowed I would destroy him. I could not, one of my descendants would. That is why it falls to you to rid the earth of that beast."

Everyone was silent.

"I will teach you about what is in the book," Allison said, wiping the tear away.

"I got your back on levitating things," Miryssia said.

"We will guide you on using premonition," Tina said, with Tony nodding along.

"So, who's going to show me how to fly on a broomstick?" Jazmyn said with a smirk on her face.

All of them looked at her then Jazmyn smiled a little "Don't you guys fly?"

"That's not how we travel, we teleport places. I will show you how to do that too. Besides, it's much faster. If you want to fly, you can turn yourself into a bird," Miryssia said.

"Oh. Can you teach me to heal?" Jazmyn said, turning to Arion.

"I can't, sorry," he shrugged his shoulders and shook his head. "Only people born as healers can heal."

"I guess we can't do everything," Jazmyn said.

Arion just smirked.

"We will start tomorrow morning," Theia said.

"Good, I am getting hungry," Arion said.

"You are always hungry," Miryssia said.

"Yeah, I am sure my mom is worried about me. This is still a lot for me to take in," Jazmyn said.

"Yes, I guess it is," Allison said.

They all got up and proceeded out the door. Allison turned back into a bright ball of light and went back into the book. Jazmyn was the last to leave; she turned to look and thought all of this is real and she was a part of it.

As she walked up the stairs, the candle went out one by one. The cold breeze hit her when she stepped out of the tree. The door shut, and it disappeared.

Arion was waiting for her.

"I can walk you back to the house if you wish," Arion said.

"Thanks," Jazmyn said as they walked without saying another word.

Chapter Nine

"So, what have you been doing? Witchy stuff?" Izzie said as Jazmyn walked into the house.

"I guess you can say that," Jazmyn said.

She sat down on the couch and told them about what happened in the woods.

"You must be hungry." Her mother asked.

"Not really, got a lot on my mind," Jazmyn answered.

"I suppose you do. That doesn't mean you can't eat." Her mother said, getting up and heading towards the kitchen. "I will make you a sandwich."

"No, you don't have too, mom," Jazmyn said, but it was too late. Her mother was gone.

"I guess you have to give up your job." Her mother said, walking back into the living room with a sandwich with chips on a plate and a glass of milk.

"Thanks." Jazmyn said, taking the plate." I can't quit my job. I have bills to pay and an apartment to deal with and not to mention my car."

"Honey, you know all these crafts and other things I have been doing." Her mom said.

"Yeah."

"Well, I been selling them, and I have saved up for this moment for you so you won't have to worry about your bills. You can give up your apartment and move back here, so you can become what you are meant to be." Her mother said.

"I can't let you do that, mom."

"I have known about this since your father disappeared." Her mom stopped for a moment, then grab a tissue to dry the tears from her eyes." If there is a chance for you to save your father, I would do almost anything for you."

"You won't need your car; you can fly on your broom where ever you want to go. I can take over the payments for you." Izzie added.

"I was told that we witches teleport places, and we don't use brooms," Jazmyn said. "I can't let you do that, Izzie, You barely have enough money as it is. You won't be able to afford the payments."

"It sounds like you are meant to do this, I will manage," Izzie said.

"Let me think on it, I have had a long day," Jazmyn said. "I am going up to my room."

Jazmyn looked down at her plate and realized that her sandwich was gone; she must have been hungry. She got up, went to the kitchen and rinsed her plate off and put it in the dish-washer, then headed up to her room.

When she got to her room, she left the light off and went to the window, and her thoughts seemed endless as the darkness outside.

What if she couldn't stop him?, what if he comes after her mother or her friends?, what if she couldn't save her father?.

A river of tears broke free from her eye as her brain worked overtime.

"What ifs never did anyone much good." her dad's words ran true, stopping her mind from spinning.

She remembered when he said that to her. It was when she had to give a short speech in front of her class. She was scared of the kids and the what-ifs. What if they laugh at me? What if they don't like her anymore? Her father told her those words, and it helped her get over her fear.

She was turning from the window not before noticing there was a glow in the direction of her oak tree.

"This light is only for you, you will always see the glow, so you will always know where your tree is." Alison voice traveled through her mind.

Jazmyn smiled a little, then went to the lamp on her dresser when a ghostly image of Diomedes appeared and illuminated the room.

Jazmyn let out a little scream.

"Be scared of me; you will never beat me. You're just a little girl that is playing a witch in the hope of getting her daddy back." Diomedes taunted.

Cringing, Jazmyn hands started to tremble. She could see the evil in his eyes. Her throat felt like it was closing. She took a deep breath and forced her fear back; she stood up tall.

"I will defeat you," Jazmyn blurted. The necklace began to glow.

"No, you won't. You are weak."

"Get out, Get out of this house," Jazmyn said, then her necklace shot a green light out, which scattered Diomedes's image, and then he was gone.

The door of her room flew open, and her mother and Izzie ran in. Izzie was holding her hairbrush like a weapon.

"Are you alright?" Her mom asked, going to Jazmyn's side.

"Yeah, I think I am. Diomedes visited me. He was trying to scare me."

"How did he get in here? this house is protected." Her mother asked.

"It wasn't him exactly, it was a ghost of him," Jazmyn stated.

"Were you scared?" Izzie said.

"Yes, a lot, but I stood my ground." Jazmyn still felt her heart beating hard.

"Good." Her mother said.

"Do you want me to stay in here with you?" Izzie asked.

"No, I will be fine. Now put down that hairbrush it could be loaded." Jazmyn said, smiling at Izzie and her mom.

"Goodnight." Her mother said.

"Goodnight, to the both of you," Jazmyn said. "Izzie, you

can have my car. I am staying."

∞ ∞ ∞

The light of the morning sun pried Jazmyn's eyes opened. She looked at the clock; it was 7:35 am. It was funny how well she did sleep despite everything that had happened lastnight.

After she got dressed, she walked downstairs to find no one up yet. She went to the kitchen and started a pot of coffee. It was like she never left; she knew that her mother never changed where things were in her kitchen. She could never forget her mother bringing that to her attention every time Jazmyn would put something in the wrong place.

She poured the water into the coffeemaker, turned it on, turned, and leaned on the counter. Grabbed her phone, checked for messages, emails, nothing new there.

She sat at the table and scrolled Facebook, she came across a picture of her and Onyx, and it was now strange to know that a person was there with her through her life since she moved away. She told her Onyx/Theia everything that she didn't want anyone to know, on her good and bad days. She even confided to her cat her dreams and also her fears.

The aroma of the coffee brought her back from her thoughts. She got up but saw her mother getting a couple of cups out of the cupboard.

"Morning, Mom," Jazmyn said.

"Good morning, Dear." Her mom said, bringing two full cups of coffee over to the table. "How are you this morning?"

"I feel good. I slept through the whole night."

"That's good. You needed it."

"Mom, when you found out about what I was. What did you do?" Jazmyn asked.

"Of course, I didn't believe it at first, but Theia explained that on my side of the family tree, there are witches." Her mother explained. "I was unaware of that fact because your grandmother took that to her grave. Both of my grandparents died before I was born."

"How does Theia fit into all of this?"

"After she explained things to me, she told me she was in the same coven as our ancestor."

"Yeah, I've met her," Jazmyn said.

"What?" Her mom looked over the top of the coffee cup.

"Remember when I said I was talking to my book, well, I was talking to her. She shares the same name as me, but I call her Allison."

"Oh."

"Last night, when I was down in the oak tree, I seen her in person or something close to that, she said she would help me understand my book."

"The smelled coffee drew me here. I hope I am not interrupting anything." Izzie said, walking into the kitchen.

"No, we're just talking," Jazmyn said. "Help yourself to some coffee."

"Thanks, I will," Izzie said.

Izzie poured herself some coffee, then the doorbell rang.

"I will get it," Izzie said, darting out of the kitchen. A minute later, Izzie came back, followed by Theia and Abraham.

"Good morning, you two. I think I am going to start some breakfast. Is everyone hungry?" Gloria asked.

"I am," Jazmyn said.

"So am I," Izzie said.

"Sit down Gloria, I got this," Theia said.

With a wave of her arm, food appeared on the table, eggs, bacon, sausages, and pancakes.

"Boy, a person could save a lot of money, getting food this way," Izzie said. "How are you about putting gas in a car?"

"Sit and enjoy," Theia said, just smiling at Izzie.

Jazmyn told Theia and Abraham what had happened the night before; after everyone had their fill, Theia waved her arm again, and everything disappeared.

"Jazmyn, when you are ready, Abraham, and I will meet

you at the tree. it is time for your first lesson." Theia said.

"Okay, Give me a few," Jazmyn said as Theia and Abraham left.

"Can I come with you to the tree," Izzie asked.

"Sure," Jazmyn said. "See you later, mom. Love you."

"Okay, love you too." Her mother said.

The morning air had a bite to it as they stepped out of the house. Jazmyn and Izzie put their coats on and headed out to the tree.

"Just think a week ago you were Jazmyn, the stock girl, and now you are Jazmyn, the witch," Izzie said.

"Yeah, it is kind of weird."

"Everything is going to change now, isn't it."

"I guess so, but I am not going to change who I am," Jazmyn said.

"Kind of wish I was one of you," Izzie said. "I could get anything I wanted."

"Getting everything you wanted, would make you not appreciate what you have," Jazmyn said, stopping close to the oak tree.

"I guess you are right. Look at you, getting wise now that you are a witch," Izzie said with a giggle, then turned and looked at the tree. "That is one big ass tree."

"The privilege of having magic is the one of respect," Theia said, approaching them.

"I take it that Mr. tall, dark, and gross doesn't have any respect," Izzie commented.

"You are right," Theia said. "Excuse us, Izzie, it is time for the teaching to begin."

"Okay, you have fun at school now, love you, bye, bye," Izzie said, twiddling her fingers at Jazmyn and turned and walked back to the house.

"Goofball." Jazmyn laughed.

Jazmyn approached the tree, and the door opened, and out of nowhere, Abraham joined them.

"Sorry, had some things to check on," Abraham said as

they went into the tree.

When Jazmyn walked into the room, she headed for the book and opened it, and Allison appeared.

"Good morning, everyone," Allison said.

"Morning.' Jazmyn said. "So, what is the first lesson?"

"So glad to see you are eager to learn your craft," Allison said.

"Yeah, I was visited by Diomedes last night that kind of wanted to make me kick his ass," Jazmyn said.

"I understand, He used to try to scare me also," Allison said.

"Remember, He will try anything to get you to give up that necklace. Do not believe anything he says or does. As he grows stronger, he will be able to project images and false memories into your head." Theia said.

"How can I tell the difference?" Jazmyn asked.

"We will teach you. He is not strong enough yet," Allison said.

"You will begin by reading out of your book," Abraham said, and motion with his hand, the book floated down in front of where Jazmyn sat.

"Abraham and I will leave you for now. If you have questions, Allison will answer you." Theia said.

"Well, okay," Jazmyn said.

Theia and Abraham got up and walked up the stairs, and went out

"There is something I need you to read first," Allison said, coming up next to Jazmyn.

"Sure, What is it?"

"This will give you an understanding of where the stone came from that is in your necklace."

The book opened, and it turned itself to one of the first pages. Text appeared on the page; it describes how the necklace is connected to the earth. The green gemstone comes from the heart of the earth. The passage said it sparked the began of the creation of the earth. The gemstone power comes from the earth.

A thousand years ago, a witch discovered the gemstone embedded inside of this oak tree. For generations, the necklace had been passed down. The gemstone was called the Eye of Nature and the center of the Oak stone Coven ever since. A powerful spell was cast to protect the tree from evil. No evil can see the oak tree or enter it without being invited.

The person who found it was the first incarnation of you; after that, it has been passed to each succeeding embodiment.

"Where is the rest of the text? it just ends," Jazmyn asked.

"The rest has been lost," Allison said. "What I told you when you first opened the book is my part of the history of the gemstone. Demons of all kinds throughout the eons have tried to get the gemstone to use its power to evil. Diomedes is the one that has come the closes, and he is very hard to stop."

Jazmyn looked at her necklace, "So this struggle over this gemstone has been going on for a long time?"

"Yes, many sister witches have died protecting it," Allison answered with a tear rolling down her face. "Time to read your book now."

"I have questions," Jazmyn said.

"Later."

Jazmyn began to reread her book. The following page was the Witches Rede, the law of their coven.

It read:

> **"Only do good with one's magic.**
> **One's magic is not for one's self.**
> **Respect one's magic on others."**

"That sounds reasonable," She said to herself.

Then she read the instruction on how to move objects and make them appear and disappear. She learned about all types of different demons and what they can do. She read about casting spells; some were long and some very short.

"Allison?" Jazmyn said.

"Yes?"

"When you say a spell do you need to be read it out loud to

work," Jazmyn asked.

"Some do, some don't. It just depends on how much power you want behind them and what they do." Allison said.

"Can spells be made on the fly?"

"On the fly? What does a fly have to do with spells?" Allison inquired with a puzzled look on her face.

"Oh, I mean, can you make one up if need be," Jazmyn said.

"Yes, but you have to make sure that you think it through first because every word could mean something. Your spell could do what you want, or it could be dangerous. When you write a spell or say one 'on the fly', as you say, you must also make sure it is a spell that does good, not evil or not for oneself."

"So, I can't do a spell to, let's say bring me wealth."

"No, you can not. Once you start, evil will enter your soul and corrupt you." Allison said in a stern voice.

"I will do my best not to say a bad spell then," Jazmyn said.

She spent the rest of the morning reading her book until her eyes and head hurt.

"I am going to go get something to eat, okay," Jazmyn said.

"Alright," Allison said.

'Do you want anything?" Jazmyn asked. "Oops, sorry, I forgot."

"That is okay. I haven't eaten for so long I forgot what food is like to eat." Allison said.

"I will see you in a bit."

Allison disappeared into the book as Jazmyn walked out.

Chapter Ten

On the way back to her mother's house, Jazmyn took it slowly; she sorted through what she had read from the book. It was almost like a fantasy, she still couldn't believe all these demons and spells, and the whole subject of magic was real.

All the people worldwide live their lives oblivious to the whole other world working behind the scene. Ordinary people who believe in magic are shunned and laughed at, and not taken seriously. Jazmyn was one of those people who didn't believe in magic, and now she felt guilty of that fact.

Now with the wave of her hand, she could do almost anything to an object or a person.

After what she had done to her boss, she knew she had to be careful with every thought that goes through her mind because she could make someone disappear if so wanted or worse. She was kind of nervous about all of this now.

"Earth to Jazmyn, come in Jazmyn."

Jazmyn jumped a little, then realizing it was Arion. "Oh, sorry, hi."

"Deep in thought, I see," Arion said.

"Yeah. Can I ask you a question?"

"Go for it."

"When did you know you were...different?"

"That's easy; I knew since I was really young. My parents were both witches and my mother told me when I was old enough to understand," Arion said.

"But you only can heal and fix things. Can you do other

stuff?"

"No. As it was explained to me every so often, a witch is born with the gift of healing only," he spread his arms out. "And here I am."

"Is it possible for someone," she paused. "I mean a witch, is it possible for me to heal?"

"Yes," he smirked, "By a potion only."

Arion and Jazmyn walked a few paces, Arion stopped.

"I have heard somewhere-" He put his finger on his chin and tapped it a few times. "-Not sure if I read it or someone told me that there are witches that heal by touch, but there hasn't been one in five or six hundred years. In other words, very rare.

"Oh,"

Jazmyn turned to Arion; she opened her mouth but closed it again.

"What?"

She stopped and looked at him, "What? what?"

I can see you have another question."

"Are your parents still alive?" Jazmyn asked. "No, wait, I don't need to know. It's too personal."

"It's OK, Yes they are," Arion answered with a smirk.

A strange feeling crawled through Jazmyn's body, her gemstone glowed. She looked around and felt the wind pick up; within a few seconds, the trees began to sway.

"There is some..." Jazmyn was interrupted when the ground shook under their feet.

A small tree was ripped out of the ground and fell, pinning Jazmyn, knocking the wind out of her.

"Jazmyn!" Arion yelled over the wind.

He tried to get to her, but some force pushed him back against a big tree.

"Hello, Jazmyn." a deep voice pounded through the air.

Jazmyn looked around through the dust and debris; a figure came towards her. She tried to take a deep breath; she couldn't.

She saw a hand reach for her necklace, Jazmyn tried to

squirm out from the weight of the tree, but it trapped her there.

"No, get away from me!" Jazmyn screamed.

"Give me what is mine and I will leave you alone," Diomedes said, standing over her.

The tree on her was suddenly lifted and knocked him away from Jazmyn. Her breath rushed back into her lungs, struggling. She got up and ran towards the house. Miryssia was standing with her arms out; her necklace was glowing. She was controlling the tree like a bat and struck Diomedes again and again. He fell to the ground; Miryssia kept at him. He struggled but managed to get up. Diomedes destroyed the tree with a burst of energy then disappeared.

Miryssia ran up to Jazmyn and was joined by Arion. The door of the house opened; Izzie and her mother came out.

"Are you alright?" her mother asked.

"Yeah, I think so. Just a few cuts." Jazmyn said, looking at her arms.

"Here, give me your hands," Arion said.

Jazmyn gave Miryssia an edgy look; Miryssia just nodded.

She hesitated but held them out. Arion grabbed her hands and closed his eyes.

A warm surge of energy flow through her arms and through her whole body. She felt peaceful, like feeling the sun on your face sitting in an open field.

The feeling faded away when Arion let go. She looked at her arms, and all of the cuts disappeared, and there was no pain.

"Who needs health insurance when you're around," Izzie said.

"Thank you," Jazmyn face flushed, looking into Arion's eyes.

"You are welcome," Arion said, pretending not to notice.

He helped her up and followed her into the house, and she sat down on the couch.

"Thanks, Miryssia, for saving me," Jazmyn said.

"No problem," Miryssia said, giving her a wink.

Theia and Abraham appeared and went to Jazmyn.

"Are you alright?" Theia asked.

"Yeah," Jazmyn said, trying to fix her hair.

"That is good," Abraham said.

"Thank you for being there for her, Miryssia and Arion," Theia said.

A silence settled over all of them, then Theia and Abraham moved off into a corner of the living room and began to talk.

"I am going to go get a sandwich or something, that's what I was going to do before he attacked me," Jazmyn said when she got up from the couch.

"Just sit, Dear. I will make you a sandwich, you need to rest," Her mom said.

"I could get it, but thanks," Jazmyn answered.

"So, what have you been doing since you moved away?" Miryssia asked as if nothing happened.

"Oh, um. Just making a living working at a department store just west of here." Jazmyn replied.

"What's it like to work?" Miryssia wondered.

"What?" Jazmyn puzzled. "You never had a job?"

"Nope never had one. We all have been getting ready, ready to help you,"

"Getting ready for me?"

"Yeah, ever since we have known each other, we have been learning our unique gifts. Miryssia said.

"So, Tony, Tina and you have known about this encounter since we were kids? What do you mean, own special gifts?"

"No, we didn't know about Diomedes, we were told a month ago," Miryssia said. "Each one of us specialized in our type of magic. Tony and Tina have specialized insight. They can see through each other's eyes as they told you before. Each can see what is going to happen hours or days ahead, by themselves, but together they can see months ahead."

"So that's what they meant the other day when they saw me coming," Jazmyn said.

"Yep, I have been honing my ability to move and control things with my mind. Arion joined us a few months after you moved away." Miryssia said, looking at Arion.

"Abraham and Theia came to my parent's house." Arion began. "They help me to learn to heal, which was a relief on my parents because they couldn't teach me. My parents didn't know the proper way to develop my healing skills."

"Oh, I see," Jazmyn said.

"I also learned, I could fix objects too, like refrigerators, cars or whatever needs fixing."

"I'd hire you as a handyman," Izzie added.

Jazmyn shot a look over to her.

"What? I would." Izzie said.

Gloria walked back into the room with a sandwich and a glass of milk. She sat down next to Jazmyn.

"Did you know all of this, mom?" Jazmyn asked, grabbing the sandwich and taking a bite.

"Yes, I did, after you moved out, Abraham explain it to that his children and their abilities," Gloria said.

Jazmyn noticed that Theia and Abraham were done talking. Theia came up to her, "We have decided from now on someone will be with you until you have mastered your craft."

"I guess that would be a good idea," Jazmyn said.

"It's getting late and I have to go back home," Izzie said.

"That's right. I need to go to pick up a few things." Jazmyn said.

"You need to stay for your lessons," Theia said.

"But I need some stuff other than what I packed. I didn't think I was going to stay here that long." Jazmyn said.

"You need to stay here and learn your craft as fast as you can," Abraham said.

"Look, I will be back in a few hours, then we can continue." Jazmyn snapped back.

"Wait, Wait. I can get you there and back in less time. Besides, I haven't been out of here in months." Miryssia said.

Theia stood there for a bit, glancing over to Abraham.

It looked as though, to Jazmyn, they were talking to each other without moving their lips.

"They are talking it over, they do that when they don't want anyone to hear," Miryssia said.

"That will be fine," Theia said.

"Just hurry back," Abraham said.

"Can I go with you guys?" Izzie asked.

"Izzie, you have to drive my, I mean your car back," Jazmyn said.

"Oh, that's right." Izzie sighed.

"I promise when I learn to teleport, I will take you anywhere you want," Jazmyn said as she walked up to her and hugged her. "I will keep in touch with you."

"OK, bye. I will go pack now." Izzie said. "Thanks for everything, Mrs. W. and it was nice to meet you all."

"It was a pleasure meeting you, Izzie," Abraham said.

Izzie went upstairs, Jazmyn watched her go, and she knew that the next time she would see her friend, her life would be dramatically different.

∞∞∞

"Ready?" Miryssia said.

"Yeah, I guess," Jazmyn said.

"Everything will be fine. All you have to do is hold my hand, and I will do the rest. Miryssia said.

"Hey, Wait," Jazmyn exclaimed.

"What?" Miryssia asked.

"How do you know where to go? Do you need directions, or do you have a GPS built-in?"

"No," Miryssia snickered, giving Jazmyn a sideways glance. "You need to picture it in your head and I will use that to get us there."

"Okay," Jazmyn said.

Jazmyn pictured her living room then held her hands out; Miryssia took hold of them; she closed her eyes then opened them again. "You need to concentrate, clear your mind of everything, close your eyes and then picture where you are going."

"I have never done this before," Jazmyn cracked a nervous smile.

She closed her eyes, pictured her living room again, a feeling of millions of tiny bubbles of air tingling her body, lifting her into the air. The next thing she knew, she was in her apartment, and the tingling in her body went away, but it left a massive headache.

"Breathe, your headache will go away in a few minutes. Besides that's minor compared to non-witch folks when teleporting, they have a headache and throw up several times." Miryssia said, noticing that Jazmyn was holding her head.

"Feels like a freight train hit me. That's nice to know." Jazmyn said.

"Once you get used to it, the headaches will go away."

Jazmyn stood there breathing while Miryssia took a tour of her apartment.

"Nice place you have here," Miryssia said.

"Thanks," Jazmyn said, slowly walking to her bedroom. "Onyx, here kitty-Aw shit, never mind. I guess I can get rid of her litter box. Now I know why she never used it."

"Yeah, Theia was never litter box trained," Miryssia said, cracking a smile, and then they both chuckled.

"I'll be right back out, make yourself at home. There is a soda in the fridge."

"Okay"

Jazmyn eased her way to her bedroom, her head still pounding but not as much. She stood in front of her dresser, trying to figure out what to bring.

She decided to pack a few more shirts and pants and a few more essential things. She went into the bathroom and grabbed her shampoo and conditioner.

When she stepped back out of her bedroom, she found Miryssia lounging on her couch watching Charmed.

"I love this show," Miryssia said.

"Izzie likes that show too. I guess I should pay more attention to it," Jazmyn said as she packed up her laptop.

"Somethings are close too real, but others are way off base. All the powers they have you will learn," Miryssia stated.

"Wow, really," Jazmyn said.

"Yes, Ready to go?"

"I have to stop at my landlord's, Mr. Wilson. He just lives down the hall, and tell him I am moving out. I also have to stop at my job and tell them I am quitting." Jazmyn said.

"Okay, I guess you just don't want to leave them high and dry, but make it fast we need to go," Miryssia said, shutting the TV off without the remote.

"I also need to find time to pack the rest of my stuff. I have to cancel my cable. When am I going to find the time?" Jazmyn said, letting out a sigh.

"I am sure that Abe or Theia can get that done for you."

"How?"

"Oh, magically."

"Okay, I guess we will leave this here until we get back so we can take it with us," Jazmyn said, stacking her bags of stuff next to her couch.

"Let's do this the easy way. I will teach you how," Miryssia said.

"Am I ready to do that?" Jazmyn nervously questioned.

"I say yes, but Theia won't. Now clear your mind of everything." Miryssia instructed.

Jazmyn nodded and stood there, trying to clear her mind.

"Got that?"

Jazmyn nodded again.

"Now picture the bedroom at your mother's with your stuff there, then send it there by waving your hand."

She concentrated, and suddenly, she could see her bedroom like she was there, then waved her hand with a flash of light; her things just vanished.

"Did I do it?" Jazmyn asked.

Miryssia closed her eyes for a moment. "Yes, kinda, I didn't see your suitcase. On the bright side, I think all of your clothes are there, and let's say you need to clean a little."

"Really? Damn it."

"No sweat, the first time I did it, Abe was teaching me; he wanted me to send a chair to another room; instead, it ended up on the roof. It was his favorite chair."

"That's funny." Jazmyn laughed. "That's why that chair was up there. I remember seeing it when I came over one day. I could never figure that out."

"Could you teach me something else?." Jazmyn said.

"Maybe later," Miryssia said. "Don't you have a few things more to do?"

"Oh, yeah, that's right. Stay here while I go talk to my landlord." Jazmyn said as she darted for the door.

"No, I will go with you. You are not supposed to be left alone, remember?"

"Okay"

They went down the hall, and Jazmyn talked to Mr. Wilson about her moving out. Then they went outside to head to her job so she can talk to her boss.

"Cute little town you have here," Miryssia said. "Anything exciting happen here?"

"Well, we have 4th of July parades and usually I sit on the roof of my apartment and watch it and the fireworks," Jazmyn said.

"When I was younger, I used to go to the parades in my old hometown before my family died," Miryssia said.

"What happened to them? I never asked you when we were growing up."

"Demons killed them," Miryssia growled.

"Oh, I am sorry to hear that."

"That's alright."

"You don't need to tell me if you don't want to," Jazmyn said.

They walked a few more paces in silence.

"We were having a family picnic at the park where we lived. My dad and mom and my sister and I were having a great time. Then my mother went with my younger sister to use the biffy and they didn't come back for a long time. Dad was pushing me on the swing when he suddenly stopped and ran over to the bathrooms, which was behind the building. I couldn't see what was happening." Miryssia stopped and took a deep breath.

"Oh, my God," Jazmyn exclaimed. "You can stop if you want."

"No, it's fine. I saw a flash of light, when I got over there and my family was all dead lying on the ground. When I looked up, I saw this strange beast with a bear face. It started at me, but I put my hands out and he flew backward."

"Have you done that before that?"

"No, I didn't know I could," Miryssia said.

"Then what happened?"

"I threw it around like a rag doll. Abe and Theia came from out of nowhere, and the beast just disappeared. Abe adopted me," Miryssia wiped a tear away. "I became his student. He helped me develop my powers."

"So, you didn't know you had those powers?"

"No, Theia told me that sometimes in traumatic times, the magic is released from somewhere deep in a person. Theia said I must've had a witch as an ancestor."

"Wow, I didn't know," Jazmyn said, realizing they have been standing at the entrance to where she works, talking. "Well, this is it."

"I haven't been to a store for a long time," Miryssia said, opening the door.

"I will come to find you when I am done," Jazmyn said.

They walked in, and Miryssia nodded her head and aimed for the clothing department.

Jazmyn went and told her boss that she needed to leave; he said to her that she was a good worker. She will be missed, and if she needed a job, he would hire her back.

She felt sad about leaving; this job was her first real job. When she came to work, she thought she could make a differ-ence in at least one customer's life, which would make it worth coming to work. If she defeated Luc/Diomedes, she would make a difference to everyone on the planet.

Jazmyn wandered through the women's clothing, searching for Miryssia, and found her coming out of the fitting room with a black tank top and a pair of jean shorts.

"How do I look?" Miryssia asked.

"That outfit looks good on you," Jazmyn said.

Miryssia spun around.

"Too bad, I can't get it," Miryssia said, heading back to the fitting room.

"Why?"

"No dough to make the bread."

"I can get it for you. It's the least I can do for saving my life. Besides, I still get my discount."

"Okay, Thanks"

Miryssia changed back into her clothes, and they went to the checkout then left.

"We should be getting back. I am sure Abe and Theia are wondering where the hell we are," Miryssia said.

"Yeah, I guess."

"Let's go over there out of sight. We can leave from there," Miryssia said, pointing towards the alley next to the store.

"Okay."

They walked down the alley; out of sight of everyone, Miryssia held her hand out for Jazmyn to grab.

"Ready?" Miryssia asked.

Jazmyn nodded and waited for it to begin, but a lightning bolt struck the dumpster next to them. Miryssia dove behind it, and Jazmyn was flung and hit the wall hard with her shoulder. She saw a creature a heading down the alley.

It looked like a cross between a warthog and a human, with a goat mixed in. It had tusks coming from its mouth and a set of massive curled horns dawning its head, and its covered with thick hairy fur.

Jazmyn scurried behind a car and crouched behind it. She recognized the car as Mr. Albertson's.

"God, can they get any uglier and smellier?" Miryssia said.

"What is it?" Jazmyn said, trying to see the creature.

"I think it's one of the bad boy's henchmen."

"Give me that necklace." the creature demanded.

"Yep, it's one of his," Miryssia said and stood up. "Hey, ugly!"

"What are you doing? Get down." Jazmyn insisted.

"I got this," Miryssia said, waving her hands, then a broken pallet floated into the air and flew and knocked the beast in the head. A loud squeal came from the creature, and it raised its hand to shoot a bolt of lightning at Miryssia, hitting the dumpster again.

"Not a very good shot, Ugly!"

The creature roared, picked up an old tire, threw it, and knocked Miryssia into the wall.

"Maybe not," Miryssia grunted.

The beast turned his attention to Jazmyn; a bolt of lightning hit the car, and it burst into flames; Jazmyn picked up one of the lids and held it like a shield, trying to protect both of them.

"Enchant the lid," Miryssia said, sitting up.

"What?" Jazmyn asked.

"Say a spell to enchant the lid!"

"What?" Jazmyn shots a confused look, "What spell?"

"Make one up."

Her mind started to reel; it was like her thoughts were on the downhill side of a long steep roller coaster; words, phrases came rushing by her, then suddenly it came to her.

"Make this object become my shield,
make it strong and will not yield."

The pendant on the necklace began to shine; her hair turned a brilliant red; she could feel little pinpricks traveling all over her skin as the magic focused on enchanting the lid. The lid became a little more substantial in weight.

Jazmyn arm shook as she forced it up. The beast shot a lightning bolt at her; when it hit the shield, the force knocked Jazmyn on her ass, hard. Miryssia flung shards of the broken pallet; it pierced the creature, killing it instantly, then it vanished.

"Are you good?" Miryssia asked.

Jazmyn picked herself up off the ground.

"What in the hell just happened."

She looked at Miryssia and just nodded her head.

"Aw, shit," Miryssia said.

"What? Are you hurt?"

"No, but my brand new outfit didn't make it. Do you think I could go back in and exchange it?" Miryssia said with a smirk on her face."

"Probably not, the receipt is burnt. Never mind the store will return it anything in any condition."

They both laughed.

"Let's go before anything else happens," Miryssia said.

"Sounds good."

Miryssia took Jazmyn's hand, and then they were back in her mother's living room, and everyone was still there.

"What took you guys so long," Theia asked.

"Well I had to do a few things before we came back we also were attacked," Jazmyn said.

"Attack? Was it Diomedes?" Theia snapped.

"No, it was some warthog faced creature," Miryssia said.

"That means he must have been weakened in the last encounter. He must be using other means to try to get that necklace now." Abraham paused. "There is also another way to look at this. He could be saving his energy for something big and he is sending his minions to keep up the fight to wear us down."

"Jazmyn, you must return to your studies," Theia said.

"Okay. I have a favor to ask." Jazmyn said.

"What is it?" Theia asked.

"I left most of my stuff back at my apartment, Miryssia said you could take care of moving it for me," Jazmyn stated.

"Yes, I can help with that," Theia said.

Theia stared up at the ceiling, closed her eyes, and raised her arms; she stood there for a bit, then lowered her head to look at Jazmyn.

"It is done, It's like you never live there and all of your stuff is safely in the spare shed at Abraham's place," Theia said.

"Thank you," Jazmyn said.

"Your welcome," Theia said.

She gave Arion a long look. "Want to escort me?"

"Ah-Sure," Arion replied.

Jazmyn and Arion walked back to the oak tree, this time a little more watchful than before.

Arion walked just a little ahead of her, acting as her body-guard. Jazmyn watched him as he walked, his body with almost a majestic air about him, confident of what he was doing.

He must be hot-blooded because there was a chill in the air, but it seemed not to bother him. He wore just a tight white t-shirt with jeans. She noticed how muscular his body was; it sent tingles through her.

"Hey, Arion," Jazmyn said.

"Yes?" He said, turning his head back to look at her.

She almost forgot what she would say as her body shudders with how he looked at her.

"Umm-Do, you like to jog?" Jazmyn asked.

"Yeah. I jog every morning, sometimes at night. I also workout, Abraham set up an exercise room at his place. We use it for learning to defend ourselves and to fight."

"You guys fight too? I thought you just use magic." Jazmyn said, stopping.

"You can't use magic all the time. Especially for me, I only can heal, so defending myself is my only option." Arion said, turning around to face her.

"I guess you are right. My mom made me learn some self-defense before I moved and I continued after too."

"It's not a bad thing to know. If you want, I could teach you what I know."

"Sounds good, thanks," Jazmyn answered and continued their journey to the tree.

Chapter Eleven

Diomedes walked down a dimly lit passage that opened up into a large cavern. With a wave of his hand, a cage appeared. He clasped his hands behind his back, strolled over, looked into the cell at a man crouched in the corner.

Dirt-filled wrinkles covered the man's face except where his long tangled gray beard and mustache were.

"Hello Steve, it has been a while since I have seen you. I had to find a good place with a view," Diomedes said.

"I didn't miss you, Diomedes, and it's Stephen," Stephen said.

"Oh, sorry, my bad, as kids say these days," Diomedes said. "We should really give you a bath one of these years and those clothes or what's left to them should be burnt."

"You must have gotten bored with the last place," Stephen said.

"No, just wanted to be close to where your daughter is."

"Leave her alone!" Stephen said, using all of his energy to stand up.

"Just to catch up, your little angel is attempting to become a witch with the help of the necklace she now has," Diomedes said, strumming his finger across the bars as he walked around it.

"You don't need to-" cough, cough "-bring her into this, leave her be, "Stephen could taste blood in his mouth.

"I would, if she would just give up that necklace of hers, so I must do what it is I need to do."

"She will destroy you."

"She can try. That reminds me I must take care of something." Diomedes said as he walked back the way he came.

Stephen sat back down; it was too much for him to stand any longer; he began a coughing fit.

He knew he didn't have much time to live. He hoped that he would see his family again before he dies.

The larva and mold-covered scraps that he receives are almost enough to keep him alive. He often ended up throwing it back up.

His mind drifted back to the day when he was ripped from his family. The day started, as usual; they all were sitting around the table, eating breakfast. Stephen and Gloria were deciding what to do that day since he had the day off from being a graphic artist. They asked Jazmyn if she wanted to go to the zoo; she loved the idea.

Jazmyn spent an hour just watching the chimpanzee playing and climbing in their enclosure when they got there. She would let out a loud laugh when they would do something funny. He laughed at her when she pretended to be an elephant, putting her arm by her nose, and sauntered about. They ate at the food court and day's end; she was tired.

Jazmyn was in her bed, sleeping, probably dreaming of all the animals she had seen. He went out to put the car into the garage; when he got out, a weird creature attacked him.

He was thrown into a cage and was kept in the dark for days with nothing. Diomedes tortured Stephen for hours a day to find out where that necklace was, but Stephen would not tell. After a few months of this, Diomedes visited now and then, after a few years, Diomedes stopped.

When Diomedes arrived back to his throne, he let a groan out. Most of his wounds from the recent encounter were healing fast, but some scars were deeper. He knew he had to start conserving his energy. He wasn't strong enough to wage a full-on confrontation with Jazmyn and her ragtag band of witches.

He motioned his hand, and instantly, Morzell appeared.

"What?" Morzell asked, remembering to bow. "I mean, what can I do for you, my master?"

"Send my soldiers out to lay waste to the lands around this cave. Kill every animal insight and tell them to bring me any humans they find to me." Diomedes said.

Your army, Morzell thought.

"Yes, Master," Morzell hissed. "When are we going to make our move? I am tired of waiting."

"When I say, no sooner," Diomedes snapped back.

"She is still a weak human, and we should do it now," Morzell leered at him.

Diomedes flicked his wrist, and instantly, Morzell's neck was in his hand, crushing it.

"The only reason I keep you alive is that you helped me after my first attempt at getting that damn necklace," Diomedes said.

"You should have more respect-" Morzell chokes out "-since I helped you defeat many other demons to become who are today."

Diomedes let go, Morzell dropped to the floor, "I am letting you live, aren't I. But if you don't do as I say you will not be living much longer."

Morzell regained his footing then began to walk out, rubbing his throat.

Diomedes yelled, "Tell one of them to come to see me!"

Morzell turned and bowed when he left the throne room.

When he got to be out of earshot, he let out a loud growl.

"Damn him. I should be the one sitting on that throne."

Morzell reached where his army was training, motioning over his lead soldier.

Morzell pulled his lead closer, "Kor, you've been with me since way back. I want to know if you are loyal to me."

"You know I am," Kor said.

"Good to know, "Morzell paused to look around. "I am going after that witch, and then I will rule everything."

Kor smiled, "Just tell me when and I will be right next to

you."

Morzell nodded and glanced at the vast army, "Find me others that will join us. Now go send one of his minions to him."

∞∞∞

Inside the oak tree, an aroma filled the air of a forest after a spring rain drifted in the air and tickled Jazmyn's nose as she sat at the large wooden table down in her tree.

Jazmyn leaned forward on her elbows, trying to wrap her brain around what she was reading out of her book, how to make potions. Chemistry was a subject she was never good at, especially when using ingredients she never heard of before.

A little while later, Tony and Tina came down the staircase. They looked the through books that lined all the shelves that covered the walls of the tree.

"Don't mind us, we are here to read," they both said.

Jazmyn just nodded.

When she was growing up, the twins always seemed different to her. She knew some twins shared a particular bond, but Tony and Tina's bond was on a whole another level itself.

She was watching them as they looked through the books they picked, one would read, and the other would sit there with their eyes closed. When the one finished with a few pages, they would switch.

"How are you guys doing over there?" Jazmyn asked.

"Good." answering at the same time.

"Learning anything?"

"Yes, we are." Tina said.

"I notice that only one reads at a time."

"Our minds are connected so both of us can share what we learn," Tony said.

"Cool. Do you two ever have separate thoughts?"

"Yes, if one of us is too far from the other. "Tony said.

"But, usually, we are never apart." Tina said.

"Oh, I see." Jazmyn said.

The twins both smiled and nodded their heads, and went back to reading.

Fascinating. Jazmyn returned to her book skipping over the potion part and began reading about the earth, air, fire, and water

It was getting late, and Jazmyn was tired of reading. She got up and walked around to stretch.

"I am done, for now, too much info. My brain is about to explode," Jazmyn thought.

Tony and Tina got up and went to the bottom of the stairs and stood there.

"What are you guys waiting for?" Jazmyn asked.

"For you, We are going to escort you." They both said.

"How did you know I was going to leave?"

"We just did."

"Oh..Yeah." Jazmyn said, smiling.

They arrived at the house without anything happening, the twins went back home, and Jazmyn went into the house. Her mother was sitting in her chair, busy, crocheting.

"Hey, mom."

"Shh, I am trying to count." Her mom raised an eyebrow and gave her a glassy stare.

"Sorry," Jazmyn said, headed up to her room.

She opened the door and saw her clothes all over the place.

"So, that's what Miryssia meant."

She began to pick them up to put them away, then stopped, "I can do this the easier way,"

Jazmyn hesitated for a moment, raised her arms like she was conducting an orchestra, "Now the book said to say what needed to be done."

She cleared her throat and then spoke,

"Put everything way."

Her room came alive all her clothes began to fold themselves, the drawers opened when the clothes were near them.

"This is fun," Jazmyn said.

Her clothes were mostly done, putting themselves away. Suddenly the blankets and sheet flew off of her bed and were placed in the closet. Her jewelry went back into the box, even the clothes she had on, force their way off of her, "Shit, shit. Stop… give me my shirt back!"

The clasps on her bra came undone; she let go of her shirt to hold her bra on, "No, no, no!"

"What's going on up here?!" Gloria said.

Jazmyn turned, panic filled her eyes, "OH, I need some help."

The room, filled with clothes, and shoes were flying everywhere. Her mother had to duck a few times, "I am calling Theia."

Within seconds Theia showed up and waved her arms, the room settled back down, "What went on here?"

"I just said a spell to help me out," Jazmyn looked down and moved to her bed. "Thank you."

"You need to be careful about how you use your magic," Theia said.

"Yeah, I can see that now. I will try-" Jazmyn stopped when she realized that Arion had come along. '-Get out of here I'm half-naked."

Jazmyn grabbed something to cover herself. Arion's face flushes bright red and bolted out of the door.

"Sorry!" he yells back.

"Are you alright?" Gloria asked.

"Yeah, I guess, just need to clean up a bigger mess now."

"We will leave you to it," Theia smiled with her eyes. "Just be mindful of how you say a spell."

Jazmyn just nodded her head as Theia and her mother left. Her phone buzzed, incoming text from Izzie.

Hey girl, what's up?

Jazmyn floated her fingers over the keyboard for a moment.

Just screwing up at being a witch.

OMG, what happened?

I tried to cast a spell to clean up my room, and it backfired.

There was a pause for a moment, then Izzie answered.

So tell me more.

The whole room was just crazy. Izzie, It kind of scared me.

Y? It's just one spell that you roasted.

I have all these magical powers, and it freaks me out that I could hurt or kill someone.

Jazzy, I know u, and u wouldn't or couldn't do that.

Jazmyn thought of what Izzie stated.

I guess so.

Damn straight.

Maybe I just needed to hear it from a friend.

Glad I could help, TTFN.

K Bye.

Jazmyn threw her phone on her nightstand then proceeded to clean her room in the old fashion way.

After making her bed again, she felt her shoulder aching from what happened earlier, so she gathered her nightshirt and slippers and headed down the hall to take a hot shower. She undressed and inspected her bruised shoulder, and then she climbed in the shower letting the hot water soothe the pain away. She was guessing she would receive more battle wounds before this was over with.

Chapter Twelve

A stream of sunlight pierced through the curtains in Jazmyn's bedroom and tapped on her eyelid to wake her. She rolled over; a sudden panic ran over her. She shot straight out of bed. Her mind was on getting to work but soon realized where she was, so she stopped herself.

"Duh, I don't need to go to work." She said. "Damn, I was sleeping good too."

She went over to the curtains and pulled them all the way open to let in the full sunshine in. She could smell coffee roaming up from the kitchen, so she got dressed and went downstairs and found her mother sitting reading the newspaper at the table.

"Morning," Jazmyn said.

"Morning, Dear. Did you get your bedroom all straightened up?"

Jazmyn lazily nodded her head and went straight for the coffee, and poured a cup, and joined her mother at the table.

"How are you doing this morning?" Her mother asked.

"Good, slept through the whole night."

"Good to hear." Her mother said, putting aside her paper. "Are you hungry?"

"A little, I will just make some toast in a bit."

"How is your learning going?"

"I guess I need to learn a lot more after that dumb thing I did last night," Jazmyn said, she blew across her coffee and took a sip.

"Don't be hard on yourself. It's going to take some time."

"I hope I can do it." Jazmyn wrinkled her nose.

"You will. I believe you can." Her mom smiled.

They sat in silence for a while; Jazmyn got up and poured another cup of coffee. She turned, leaned against the cupboard when her eyes popped open wide and her face flushed.

"What's wrong?" her mother sat up straight.

"I just remembered Arion was going to teach me some martial arts." She said, putting her cup down.

"What's wrong with that? He seems like a nice boy." Her mother said.

"Yes, he is, but he saw me half-naked. I'm too embarrassed." She lowered her head and turned away.

"I am sure he didn't see anything, don't worry about it."

"Still," Jazmyn replied, noticing a smile on her mother's face.

"Then why are you smiling?-" Jazmyn thought, and her face turned another shade of red "-Mother, no."

"What? I just said he was a nice boy."

"I am not going to go there," Jazmyn said but disagreed with herself. She knew that there was something there, but she had to concentrate on the more essential things.

Jazmyn jumped up, went to the cupboard, got the peanut butter down, opened the fridge, and got the bread.

"Where's the jelly?" She asked, turning her head toward her mother.

'On the door where it always been. Changing the subject, are we." Her mother said, letting out a little chuckle.

"Yes," Jazmyn said with a quick smile, then grabbed the jelly and went to the toaster.

When the toaster popped up, Jazmyn put peanut butter and jelly on it, took her coffee, went outside onto the porch, sat, enjoyed the crisp morning air, and ate her toast.

She was enjoying the bird songs that fill the air. She saw her first robin of the year; it scurried across the ground, then stops, bob its head down, then up, then moved and repeated it all over again. She watched a gray squirrel stirring up the leaves, trying to find the nut it probably stored away last fall.

A feeling that she needed to find something came over her; it was a weird feeling. She didn't think she lost anything that needed to be found. Jazmyn tried to shake the feeling, but she couldn't.

"Nature watching, I see," Theia said.

"Hold on, I need to find something," Jazmyn stated.

"What?"

"I have no idea," The feeling was disappeared when the squirrel runoff.

"There is magic all around in nature," Theia informed, realizing what was happening. "You are connected to it."

"I am?"

"The feeling that you just had, you felt what the squirrel's need to find it's buried acorn."

Jazmyn scanned the trees and saw the squirrel again eating an acorn. "Really?!"

"The forces of nature can help you in times of need."

"What do you mean?" Jazmyn asked.

"The amulet you are wearing has a symbol of an oak tree."

"Yeah," Jazmyn said, then looked at it closer and it began to glow a little.

"You are connected to nature through it," Theia said.

Jazmyn looked down to see a rabbit climbing up on the porch and stopped by Jazmyn foot. She picked it up and cuddled it.

"I can sense what she's feeling and she is scared," Jazmyn said as her mother came out to join them.

"Of what?" Theia inquired.

Jazmyn bent over and gathered up the rabbit, held it close, petting it.

"What's the matter, little one," Jazmyn said, looking into its eyes.

Her eyes connected with the rabbit, Jazmyn felt as if someone was forcing there way in, her heart began to pound faster.

Through the connection she saw a place where darkness was shadowing an area of land not far from them.

She sat back in her chair, sifted through what she had seen.

"What is it? Dear," Her mother said.

"You know the abandoned caves north of here?" Jazmyn asked.

"Yes." Her mother said.

"There is a very dark presence in those caves," Jazmyn said.

"Yes, Abraham and I have sensed that something was happening," Theia said. "Just yesterday, Abraham check them out and we believe that Diomedes is using those caves as his lair."

"According to this rabbit, I think you are right," Jazmyn said.

"I conveyed to the rabbit we were going to get rid of the evil," Jazmyn said. "I feel like Snow White or Dr. Dolittle."

Jazmyn could feel that the rabbit needed to warn someone else, so she put the rabbit down, it scurried off into the woods.

"Who is Wen?" Jazmyn asked Theia.

Before Theia could answer, they heard shuffling of gravel coming from the driveway. Theia stood up and ready herself to act when Arion came jogging up.

"I will tell you later, for now, it is time for you to do some more studying," Theia said, letting her defense down.

"I guess." Jazmyn turned away from Arion.

"I was hoping we could jog a mile or two before you had to do that," Arion said.

Jazmyn's face flush a bit, *Just get over it, he didn't see anything. I need to run anyway.*

"Sure, let me change and I will be back down," Jazmyn said with a smile on her face.

"You need to study," Theia said.

"I need to run too. I haven't done it for a couple of days. I promised to study afterward."

"I will make sure she does," Arion said.

"That will be fine then," Theia said.

Jazmyn went in and changed into her sports bra and jogging shorts, came back out and gave her mother a quick kiss, and she smiled at Theia then joined Arion.

"Whoa, you're beautiful," Arion said, seeing Jazmyn in her outfit.

"What did you say?" She asked.

"Ah... it's a beautiful morning, isn't it." Arion stumbled to say.

"Yes, it is. Let's go."

The morning sun was warm; a few high clouds drifted their way across the sky as they headed down the road that leads around the lake.

They stopped for a bit of rest, about halfway around the lake.

"Um, sorry about last night, things got out of hand, and I didn't mean..."

"Don't be sorry. Magic is a tricky thing to learn," Arion said.

"I mean seeing me." Jazmyn face flushed.

"I didn't see anything-" He smiled with tight lips. "-anything at all."

Sweat drenched the shirt that Arion was wearing, and it clung to his body, letting Jazmyn sneaked a peek of what he was hiding underneath of it. He must keep himself in shape, and his muscles showed it; Jazmyn liked that.

"Ready to go again," Arion said.

"Ah.. yep." She said, snapping herself back from the vision she was enjoying.

"Then let' s-Shh." Arion stopped and pointed towards the woods next to them.

Jazmyn looked; she couldn't see anything, then she heard something in the brush, her heart skipped a beat. Arion slowly moved closer to Jazmyn and moved between her and the noise.

Jazmyn thought how noble he was being but moved to the side of him.

"Stay here," Arion said.

"Thanks, but no," Jazmyn said.

They moved closer to the edge of the woods; Jazmyn caught a glimpse of brown fur and then a face. She instantly could feel the pain coming from the creature.

"It's a deer, and it's hurt." She said.

Arion ran into the woods, followed by Jazmyn.

He stopped; the deer's hind leg had a giant claw mark on it. It seemed broken.

Jazmyn held its head, trying to comfort it; she looked into its eyes, suddenly, a vision pushed into her mind.

"It was attacked and chased by a hideous creature like the one that attacked us. I see other animals slaughters all around," Jazmyn yelled, sobbing. "Oh, my God! I...I see trees down and other terrible creatures, everywhere, ripping trees out of the ground. People are being put into crude cages."

Jazmyn slowly petted the deer's neck, "Everything will be fine."

"It came from that direction," Arion said as he pointed north.

"Earlier, another animal told me that Diomedes took over the caves up there," Jazmyn said.

"Wait, What? You talked with animals, Now."

Jazmyn shook her head, "I will explain later. Can you heal her?"

Arion laid his hands on the doe. He concentrated for a bit, then took his hands off and sat on the ground. Jazmyn could feel the life leaving the deer; tears fell from her eyes.

"Sorry, I couldn't, she was too far gone," Arion said.

"That is alright. You tried, she's better off now."

"Those caves are at least 20 miles from here," Arion said. "I guess this deer felt it needed to get as far as it could away from there."

"There are campgrounds around those caves."

"We should get back and tell the others."

They ran back around the lake to get back to her mother's house. They found Theia and her mother still sitting out on the porch; they ran up to them.

"Diomedes army of creatures are enslaving people. Animals are being slaughtered," Jazmyn said between breaths.

"What?!" Theia said.

"We found a deer injured. It must have come from around the caves and it showed me what it had seen before it died," Jazmyn hung her head.

"Oh, my, that's terrible. I heard there were a few early season campers up round there," Gloria added.

"We must get the others and tell them. Meet me by the oak tree in a few minutes." Theia said, then vanished.

"Are you OK? Dear," Her mother asked. "You look hurt."

"I could feel the deer's pain; it was horrible, Mama," Jazmyn said, hugging her mother.

"It will be alright." Her mother said, returning the hug.

"We should go," Arion said.

"OK," Jazmyn said, following Arion as they went to the tree.

∞∞∞

When they arrived at the tree, everyone was there, and they followed Jazmyn into the tree. Theia went over to the book and opened it, and Allison materialized.

"What is going on?" Allison asked, noticing solemn looks on Theia's and Jazmyn's faces.

"It's Diomedes, he has set up a lair in some caves north of here," Theia said.

"He is having his creatures capturing people and killing animals," Jazmyn added.

"This is something new for him," Allison said.

"What do you mean?" Jazmyn inquired.

"When I battled him, he worked alone. This means you are going to have a harder time defeating him now that he has help. What did these creatures look like?" Allison wondered.

"That's great to hear that I now have double the threat. The beast had claws and a warthog face and horns like a ram. They are like the one that attacked Miryssia and me," Jazmyn replied.

"Oh. I know those creatures, they are called Warhogs. They are used by, -I can not recall right now," Allison said, walking around with a bewildering look on her face.

"What are we going to do," The twins said.

"We must find out what is going on, Abraham and I will go to the caves to investigate," Theia said.

"I want to go with," Jazmyn said.

"You are not ready; you must stay here and resume your learning," Theia said.

"I can help," Jazmyn said, then Miryssia poked her with her elbow.

"Give it up, Jazmyn, once Theia speaks the law, its the law," Miryssia whispered.

"Morzell, Morzell is the demon's name," Allison said. "His army are the ones fighting and killing for Diomedes."

"Tony and Tina, would you teach Jazmyn sight of the mind and Miryssia, teach her to levitate things," Theia said. "Arion come with us, we might need your healing powers."

"Ok," Arion said as he walked over next to Abraham and Theia

"Be careful," Jazmyn said, looking at Arion.

Arion nodded, and in a blink of an eye, they vanished.

The long silence was broken when Allison cleared her throat, "Well, let's get to it. Tony and Tina begin your lesson. I will retire back into the book to think about what is happening."

With that, Allison disappeared into the book, and the twins faced Jazmyn.

"Alright, Jazmyn, We will teach you how to see through other's eyes," Tony said.

"Ok," Jazmyn said.

"It is quite simple to do so as long as you know the person that you want to channel," Tony explained.

"How well do you need to know them?" Jazmyn asked.

"Not long, You must have made eye contact with them," Tina said.

"What do you mean?' Jazmyn said.

"Anyone from your mother to a person that you randomly met on the street," Tony said.

"You need to focus on that person," Tina said.

"Alright," Jazmyn said as she pictured her mother.

"Now recite these words either out loud or to yourself," Tony began. "Share your vision with me to see what you see."

Jazmyn nodded her head, then repeated the words. She suddenly lost her vision of what was in front of her; all she could see was black.

"What is going on?!" Jazmyn panicked, then her sight came back.

"You were connecting; your vision has to change to the person you are trying to channel," Tina said.

"Oh, sorry. I kind of freaked out there," Jazmyn said, feeling her heartbeat returning to normal.

"Try again," Tony said.

"Ok," Jazmyn said.

She took a deep breath then saw her mother in her mind then said the words to herself. Her vision went black again, and Jazmyn just took another breath; she slowly saw her mother's hands. She was washing dishes. It reminded her of one of those 3D movies she went to see at the theater, but this was so much more real.

Jazmyn saw as her mother rinsed a glass off of soap then placed it in the drain rack. Her vision was so real it seemed like she was the one washing dishes. She heard a phone ring and knew it was her mother's house phone; she saw her mother turn and walk to it.

She felt like someone was poking her, then she heard a very faint voice calling her back to her sight. "Come back, Jazmyn, come back."

Her sight returned to see Tony in front of her face, and he

was poking her.

"Are you back?" Tina said.

"Yes, I am. That was intense," Jazmyn said. "I could see and hear what was going on."

"What do you mean, hear?" Tony asked, with a weird look on his face.

"I heard the phone ring at my mother's house. Why?"

"It usually takes years to begin to hear anything from your connection," Tina said.

"I wonder why it happened," Jazmyn said.

"Maybe it was because it was your mother and her house isn't too far away," Miryssia added.

"That could be," Tony and Tina said together.

"Should I try again with someone else, like Izzie?" Jazmyn asked.

"Yes, you could," Tony said.

"I have a question, first,"

"What's that," Tina said.

"If a person can see and hear what another person is doing, can you control them?"   "That is not allowed, we never mess with a person's free will, but yes, you can," Tony and Tina answered.

"Oh, I won't go there then," Jazmyn said.

Jazmyn focused on her friend Izzie. When her vision cleared up, she saw Izzy's hand grabbing an item off the cash register belt and swiping it across the scanner. Izzie was at work, and she was ringing up an older lady that Jazmyn seen many times at the store.

Jazmyn was ending her channeling when she heard the beeping of the register and all the sounds around Izzie. She listened to the old lady tell Izzie that an item she rang up was the wrong price. This old lady always argued about the cost of everything.

"Jazmyn, Jazmyn come back," Tina said.

"I am back; I heard everything again," Jazmyn said, shaking her head a little.

"I guess you must be one powerful witch to be able to do that so soon," Tony said.

"Maybe, My head hurts now," Jazmyn said.

"That will go away in time," Tina said.

"I'm going to go outside to get some air,"

"Ok, I will come out with you," Miryssia said, jumping up from her chair. "Be back in a bit."

"That will be fine," the twins said.

Miryssia and Jazmyn went up the stairs and went out and sat on one of the giant roots of the oak tree.

"There is a lot to learn," Jazmyn said.

"You can handle it," Miryssia said.

"I guess."

"What's the matter?" Miryssia asked.

"Just thinking about Arion and the others and if they are alright,"

"This isn't their first time at the rodeo, Abraham and Theia are well capable witches and should be able to handle it," Miryssia said.

"How about Arion?" Jazmyn questioned.

"You like him, don't you?"

"Ah, me-no," Jazmyn stumbled and pointed at herself and turned her hand and waved it. "Just worried."

"He can handle himself too. I can tell you like him," Miryssia said as she nudged Jazmyn's shoulder with hers. "Come on; you know you can tell me. Remember?"

Jazmyn thought back to when she used to tell Miryssia some of her secrets. As kids, they used to sit under this oak tree and talk for hours.

"Remember when you broke one of your mother's vases and you buried it out here somewhere so she wouldn't find it and you told me not to tell her,"

"Yes, I remember that. I did confess to breaking it about a month later," Jazmyn said.

"So, I been keeping that secret all this time for nothing," Miryssia said, then laughed.

"Yes, I think I do like him a little," Jazmyn said, smiling back at Miryssia.

"I knew it."

"Don't tell him," Jazmyn said.

"What, so a month later, you can tell him yourself," Miryssia said, smiling.

"No, I need to concentrate on this Diomedes thing first."

"Ok."

"Miryssia?"

"Yep."

"You're like a sister I never had." Jazmyn hugged her.

"Thanks," Miryssia said, giving her a wink back. "Hey, want to have some fun?"

"Sure, but we should go back in," Jazmyn said.

"Consider this a prison break so, follow me," Miryssia said as she got up.

They walked through the woods, they talked, catching up on events that happened in their lives. Occasionally they would knock over rotten trees that were ready to fall. Miryssia used her powers to help her with the bigger trees.

"Teach me that," Jazmyn asked, turning to Miryssia.

"Ok. Let's...um," Miryssia said, looking for an excellent tree to use. "See that tree over there."

"Yeah," Jazmyn said, following Miryssia's arm to a tree on the edge of the woods.

"Now, picture the tree falling in your mind."

"Got it," Jazmyn said, trying to do what she asked.

The tree tilted to one side then popped back upright.

"Try it again,"

Jazmyn concentrated on the tree. It tilted a little more this time but didn't fall.

"I can't do it,"

"Maybe you need to use your hands to focus your thoughts. Hold your hand out towards the tree," Miryssia instructed.

Jazmyn held out her hands and tried again, and this time,

the tree leaned farther but went back to a standing position.

"Damn it!" Jazmyn screamed.

She cocked her arms back then thrust her arms out in anger; the tree shattered into pieces.

"OMG!" Miryssia said.

"I didn't mean too," Jazmyn said, shaking a little.

"All of our powers are connected to our feelings. So if you are angry, your powers are forced to act, but when you are calm, your powers will flow smoothly," Miryssia explained.

"I remember reading that in my book. I felt frustrated that I couldn't knock the tree down, so I push myself to do that and then got angry."

"What you did is called molecular manipulation, there are two types, acceleration, which you did and mobilization, which you can slow time. You can slow time down as slow as one second could stretch to be two or three minutes."

"How do you slow time?" Jazmyn asked.

"Well, that really is not my area," Miryssia said. "I will let some else show you. I read about it as you did but never mastered it."

"Alright. I will try moving something," Jazmyn said. "I will try on those rocks over there."

Jazmyn took a deep breath to calm herself down, pictured the pile of rocks moving upwards in her mind. The rocks quivered a little; Jazmyn reached her hand out and motioned it upwards. They separated from each other and slowly floated up. She waved her hand back and forth, and the rocks follow her.

"I am doing it," Jazmyn said excitely; the rocks fell back to the ground.

"You did good. Glad you didn't blow them up," Miryssia said.

"Yes, that's a good thing," Jazmyn said. "What is the heaviest thing you ever moved?"

"I have moved cars, but that takes a lot out of me."

"I guess it would take..." Jazmyn stopped.

"What's the matter?" Miryssia asked.

Jazmyn just stood there; she was trying to hear a distant sound.

"Do you hear that?" Jazmyn questioned.

"Hear what?" Miryssia said, trying to hear what she was.

"Jazmyn, can you hear me?" a voice said. It sounded like hers.

"Yes, I can."

"Come back to the tree, hurry!"

"I think Allison is calling me. We have to get back to the tree, something is wrong," Jazmyn said, and they both turned and ran back to the tree.

Chapter Thirteen

The sun was getting low in the sky when they arrived at the tree. They ran down the stairs and found Abraham holding a part of a shirt on his arm like a bandage, and he was bleeding badly; next to him was Arion holding Abraham's hands with his eyes closed. He was trying to heal the wound.

"What happened?!" Jazmyn said, running to the other side of Abraham.

"We ran into some Diomedes's warhogs and we had to defend ourselves," Theia said.

Abraham pulled the blood-soaked shirt away from his arm; the wound healed. Arion sat back in the chair and took a deep breath, slowly opened his eyes.

"Thank you, Arion," Abraham said.

"No problem," Arion answered.

"Diomedes has definitely made his lair there," Theia said.

"We tried to enter into the area but he has a spell that blocked us," Abraham said. "His minions cleared an area about half a mile around the caves and he is building a fence around the whole thing using people to do it."

"We could not see to the cave mouth," Theia added.

"We need to rescue them!" Jazmyn demanded.

"I know we do, but we are not strong enough to mount a rescue, yet," Theia said.

"We will need your help, Jazmyn," Allison stated. "You need to learn at an accelerated pace."

"I've learned enough to help," Jazmyn said.

"No, you have not," Theia said. "You have learned nothing yet."

Jazmyn heard the words Theia had said but didn't want to listen to her.

"I have read the book; I've done spells," Jazmyn began to pace, gesturing with her hands. "I've teleported I have done so much. I don't see why I can't help."

"I am sorry, no," Theia said.

Jazmyn opened her mouth to speak, but she heard words coming from her past He once told her that the way to do something is to do it right the first time. Her dad said it was like taking a test that you have not studied or even knew what the test was about.

"I guess you are right." Jazmyn conceded.

"What about those people?" Miryssia asked.

"When he is done with them, he will kill them," Allison said.

"That's a relief," Miryssia said sarcastically.

"That's the way he does things," Allison remarked.

"It's getting late, everyone we should call it a night," Abraham said. "Personally I need the rest, I am not as young as I once was."

"You guys go without me, I want to study my book some more," Jazmyn said.

"Ok," Theia said.

"I'll stay behind to walk you home," Arion said.

"I'd like that," Jazmyn said with a smile.

After an hour or two studying her book, Jazmyn's eyes were getting heavy, and yawning was breaking her concentration too many times.

Arion walked Jazmyn back to her mother's house and parted ways.

Her mother was already in bed when she walked into the house, so she went up to her bedroom to get a good night's sleep.

She crawled into her bed and tried to go to sleep, but her mind would not shut off.

133

Diomedes had captured all those people with the intent of using them as slaves made her frustrated.

She rolled over, and a picture of her dad flashed in her mind.

I wish I could see him. He has suffered so much live in those horrible conditions. I want to see him.

Her pillow caught her tears as they traveled down her face. Wait, I can.

She remembered the lesson she had learned. She pictured her father and spoke the words."

"Release your vision to me to see what you see."

Her vision went blank; then she saw a pair of bony knees and a hand holding onto the cage bar. She began to hear the squeaking of rats; then, her dad's voice came in clear.

A tear left Jazmyn's eye when she heard his voice again.

"Guard, I need some water." Her dad said.

"Die of thirst, human." a warhog snorted back.

"I don't think Diomedes would like that."

Jazmyn saw the warhog straighten up, then disappear for a while, it return with a bowl of water. She saw her dad look at it, and it was dirty water, it turned her stomach.

"Thanks." Her dad said.

She saw the reflection of his face in the water; he looked ragged and weak. She smiled, happy to be able to see his face again.

Her dad looked around; Jazmyn saw he was in a cavern with torches on the wall. Screams echoed throughout the cave; it sent chills down her spine. Jazmyn broke the connection and began to cry.

"What's the matter? Dear." Her mother said, peeking her head in the door.

"I can hear people screaming," Jazmyn said, sobbing.

"Where? I can't." Her mother said, coming to the side of the bed.

"I learned to see and hear through other's eyes and ears. I connected with dad, and the screams that I heard were terrifying."

"Oh my." Her mother gasped. "How is he? Were they doing something to him?"

"He is skin and bones, but he is holding his own. No, it wasn't him, it was the people Diomedes has enslaved."

"It is good to hear about your father." Her mother said, wiping a tear from her eye.

"I want to go and rescue dad and the other people, but I am not ready."

"I wish you could. I would love to have your father home too. When you are, you will do great things." Her mother said. "Now, get some sleep."

"Ok, I will try," Jazmyn said, wiping her tears from her face.

$$\infty \infty \infty$$

The morning came too early for Jazmyn; she rolled out of bed and went to her bathroom to wash her face. At that moment, she realized that she was back in her old apartment.

"What am I doing here?" Jazmyn questioned.

She heard a knock on the door, and she went to answer it, walked towards the door, looked around, it was like it was before, her laptop was on her table, and all of her bills were there, she picked them up and headed towards the door. She reached for the knob then notice Onyx wasn't there. When she opened it, it was Izzie standing there.

"Are you going to work today," Izzie said.

"What?"

"Work, you know, where you bust your ass and get paid nothing," Izzie said, smiling.

"I thought I quit my job," Jazmyn said.

"For what? You didn't tell me. That date with Luc must have been a real hoot."

"You were there at my mom's when I decided to quit my

job and gave you my car."

"You gave me your car? If you did, I wouldn't have to walk over here. Is something wrong with you?" Izzie questioned.

"No, I don't think so. Don't you remember I am becoming a witch? We went to my mother's house on my twenty-first birthday and that's where I found out I am a witch."

"A witch, you can be a bitch sometimes, but a witch is carrying it a bit too far. Besides, we went out on your birthday."

"What is going on here?" Jazmyn half said to herself.

"All I know you were on your third date with Luc last night and we have to go to work," Izzie stated.

"Third date?. Luc is evil. He is trying to take over the world and I am supposed to stop that from happening."

"You couldn't stop anything. You are weak," Izzie said with an evil smirk on her face. "Oh yeah, I remember now you sucked on becoming a witch. You couldn't handle it. You are a pathetic being."

"What? What is the matter with you? You are starting to sound like...."

"Luc?" Izzie said, but her face distorted and turn into the face of Diomedes.

"Get away from me!" Jazmyn said.

"I am trying to make it easy on you. You are never going to be strong enough to beat me, I am just giving you a chance to give up before I have to kill you," Diomedes said, moving close to her.

"I am strong enough to beat you," Jazmyn insisted.

"Come and get me yourself, instead of sending the old folks to spy on me," Diomedes said.

"I will!, I will come for you, you bastard," Jazmyn asserted herself.

"You better hurry, I am almost ready to dispose of those humans I am using. I guess that wouldn't be a bad thing; I can always get more."

"Leave those people alone!" Jazmyn stated.

She clinched her fist as the rage building inside her more

and more with every word he said. She felt flames enveloped her hands, and she reached out towards Diomedes; the fire shot out at him. With a sinister laugh, he disappeared.

She heard words coming from what seemed far away. "Wake up. Wake up! We have to get out of here."

Jazmyn awoke and found her bedroom on fire and her mother pulling her out of her bed.

"Wha?" Jazmyn mumbled. "What happened?"

"I don't know, but we have to go, your room is on fire!" Her mother said.

Jazmyn stopped, looked at her bed engulfed in flames except where she was lying. Jazmyn's desk was ablaze; all of her clothes were burning. It looked like someone had used a blowtorch in here.

"I can stop this," Jazmyn stated.

Jazmyn held her arms out, "Stop, flames, stop!"

The fire continued its feeding; She began to wave her hands, "I command you to stop!"

"Let's get out of here," Gloria exclaimed.

The smoke engulfed Jazmyn, choking her, "I can do this."

"Come on. Now!" Gloria panicked, pulling at Jazmyn's arm.

Suddenly the flames froze as though they were looking at a picture.

Jazmyn and her mother turned and found Theia standing there and spoke:

"I call on the power of fire, to cease and retire."

The fire went out.

"Are you both alright?" Theia asked.

"Yes," Jazmyn lower her eyes.

"How did this happen?" Her mom said.

"I think I did it," Jazmyn shamelessly said.

"How?" Her mother said with a stunned look on her face.

"I had a nightmare and Diomedes was messing with me telling me that I was no good and never will be, and he made me very angry and my hands caught on fire. I am sorry."

"As long as you are alright. Look at your room; it is ruined."

Theia walked into the chard shell of the bedroom, with a wave the bedroom suddenly came to life, her bed went back to the way it was, the burn marks disappeared, all of her pictures, her clothes, and her desk looked like nothing happened.

"I could have lost the whole house before the fire trucks would have ever got here. Thank you," Her mom said to Theia. "I will go make some coffee."

"Thanks, Theia. I guess I almost screwed up," Jazmyn exhaled. "Again."

"Fire is one of the powerful elements to try to control; it takes a while to master."

"I failed."

"In time, you will master all. I will let you get dressed," Theia said.

Jazmyn stepped into her bedroom to straighten it up a little more and to change her clothes.

When she went downstairs, she found Arion visiting with Theia and her mother.

"I was telling Arion what happened last night," Her mother said.

"Are you all right?" Arion asked, making his way closer to Jazmyn.

A spark lit Jazmyn's eye. "Yes, Thanks."

"He must be gaining strength if he is getting past the protection Abraham and I have put on this house," Theia said.

"Protection?" Jazmyn asked, sitting down at the table.

"Yes, after the first visit you had here, we put a spell on this house," Theia answered.

"Will he be able to harm my mother or me, physically now," Jazmyn asked.

"No, he will not be able to cross the spell boundaries. I know he not that strong yet," Theia answered." We can cloak your mother in a spell so he won't come for her."

"What can we do now that he can get past the spell and get to my daughter?" Gloria asked.

"The only thing we can do is to move her to the oak tree,"

Theia said.

"What?" Jazmyn questioned.

"I will show you after we have breakfast," Theia said, waving her hand to make food appear.

"Just wait, I'll make breakfast, I have to use up those eggs in there," Her mother said.

"Alright, then I will help you, I haven't made breakfast in years," Theia said, getting up from the table to go help.

"So, I hear you had a rough night," Arion said. "Are you alright?"

"Yea, I'm fine, thanks for asking," Jazmyn said.

"Your welcome. In a little while after you are settled, Do you want to go for a workout and I can teach you defense moves,"

"Sure, that sounds like what I need after last night," Jazmyn said.

After breakfast, Jazmyn changed into her workout clothes. Theia leads Arion and her to the oak tree.

"Are we going to build a house for me next to the tree?" Jazmyn asked.

"No, let us go in," Theia said.

They went down the stairs, and Allison met them at the doorway.

"Allison, we need to make room for Jazmyn, so Diomedes cannot enter her dreams and thoughts," Theia said.

"Alright? Something happened?" Allison said.

"Diomedes attacked her in her sleep," Theia said.

"Yes, this will be a safer place for Jazmyn," Allison said.

Allison walked over to the opposite side of the table. Standing in front of the blank wall, she waved her hand, and the wall opened up and made a door.

"Come over here, Jazmyn," Allison motioned.

"Ok," Jazmyn said as she walks over to the door.

"Open it," Allison said, gesturing at the doorknob.

When Jazmyn swung the door open, it was like she was walking into her bedroom at her mother's. Everything that was there now was here; even the window was the same.

"Anything you need, this old tree will give you," Theia said, joining Jazmyn and Allison.

"Thank you," Jazmyn said, walking into her new room.

She touched her bed and marveled at it like she had been gone for many years and just returned. She looked out the window and as if she was looking out her own. Another door also attached a bathroom.

"Wow," Jazmyn exclaimed.

Arion walked up next to her, and Jazmyn felt like a younger girl having a boy in her bedroom when her mother wasn't home.

"Nice room," Arion said.

Aw. Thanks," Jazmyn said, almost blushing. "Did you still want to work out?"

"Oh, yeah," Arion said, realizing he was staring at her.

"Arion, He is going to show me some moves-I mean defensive moves. Let's go," Jazmyn said to Allison as they passed them and headed upstairs.

Chapter Fourteen

They walked down Abraham's driveway, passing a little bus shelter next to the mailbox left there from the owners who used to live there before Abraham. Jazmyn and Miryssia used to use it as a playhouse.

The house seemed somehow different now that she knew that Abraham and the others had practiced magic here. It had three stories, painted white with green trim. It had a wraparound porch with a couple of rocking chairs on it. He had flowers all around the house, Abraham had a way with plants, Jazmyn could swear he had ten green thumbs.

She passed by Abraham's two-tone cargo van. She remembers times that he would take all of them into town on a hot summer's day; to have Ice cream. She climbed the stairs to the porch as she had done when she was a child coming over to play with her friends.

Arion held the front door open.

"Thanks," Jazmyn said, flashing a smile at him as she made her way in.

Abraham came from the study, where he would spend hours and even days there. That was also his makeshift classroom, where he would teach his lesson to his children. Now, Jazmyn understood what was behind the closed doors of that room; she was never allowed to open the doors when the kids were in class.

"Hello, Jazmyn," Abraham said.

"Good morning," Jazmyn replied.

"I thought we could use the gym, so I can show Jazmyn how to defend herself," Arion said.

"That would be fine," Abraham said and nodded his head, went back to his study.

Arion led Jazmyn to the kitchen, where the door to the basement was. When they got to the last step, the lights came on. It was bigger than the house above it.

There were weights and treadmills along half of one wall; there was a sparring area. The area after that was an obstacle course; there were climbing walls and ropes hanging from the ceiling.

At the far end was a massive wooden door with a lock on it.

"This is a big place," Jazmyn said.

Jazmyn always wondered what was down in the basement. When she would be in the house, he would say it wasn't safe to go down to the basement; she could see why all types of weapons were hanging on the wall.

"Yeah, it has everything we need to train you here," Arion said. "And more,"

"Really?" Jazmyn inquired.

"Yes, but later. Let's do some warm-ups,"

After they stretched, they both went to the sparring area and faced each other. Arion had a pair of punching mitts on.

"Let's start by see how hard you can hit," Arion said.

Jazmyn nodded her head; Arion held his hand out, she began to throw punches. Arion would move his hands around to test Jazmyn's strength and reach. After about five minutes, he put his arms down.

"You have pretty good reach, but the force of your punches could be more," Arion said.

"What?" Jazmyn said, catching her breath. "What do you mean? I was punching with all my strength,"

"There is away you can tie in your magic when you are fighting,"

"Really? How?" Jazmyn inquired while wiping some sweat

off her face.

"You learned to move an object with your mind, Right?" Arion asked.

"A little."

"The force you use to move things can be applied when you punch or kick," Arion informed as he took his mitts off.

Jazmyn followed Arion over to the large punching bags. They were well used.

"You need to focus your thoughts on where on the target at the same time as you hit it," Arion instructed her.

"Ok," Jazmyn said as she centered herself on the bag.

She started to throw some punches as she tried to focus, but she would either move the bag first, then miss it with her fist, or just hit it. Jazmyn tried a few times but couldn't make it happen.

"This is too hard," Jazmyn said, putting her arms down.

"Picture Diomedes's face on the bag, that might help."

Jazmyn formed a picture of Diomedes's face on the bag. She started to bash it.

She focused her powers, feeling the force going through her, out to her fists.

"Can you see him?" Arion asked.

She nodded.

"On go after him with everything you got."

Jazmyn started to feel anger towards what Diomedes had done and could do. Taking her father away from her, the taunting he has done to her. Her arms were flying punches harder and harder. She could feel her mind and body as one; then, she started to kickbox the bag. The thought of him saying she was no good and will never be.

"You, you bastard," She said as she kicked. "You are not better than me,"

Jazmyn whaled on the bag time and time again, the bottom chain snapped, and the stand with the bag on it smashed against the far wall.

"Whoa, tiger," Arion said.

"Sorry, my emotions got the best of me."

"That is good that you can feel them, but you need to learn to control them," Abraham said, coming down the stairs.

"Oh, sorry for ruining the punching bag," Jazmyn said, trying to pick it up and return it to where it was with the help of Arion.

"That is quite alright," Abraham said as he motioned with his hand and wrist, the punching bag lifted and sat back into its place.

Arion fixed the twisted bars with a touch, and the chain attached itself back to the floor.

"When it becomes time, you will need to be able to call on your emotions and you will need to learn to use them to your benefit. If you do not learn to control your feelings, your enemy can use them against you and you will be powerless," Abraham said.

"How can I control my emotions?" Jazmyn asked.

"I can teach you how to through meditation," Arion said.

"Ok, but for now, can we just go back to sparring?".

"I will excuse myself, I must do something," Abraham said as he made his way to the door at the far end of the basement.

"Where does that go?" Jazmyn half-whispered as Abraham got out of earshot.

"I have no clue. None of us have been in there," Arion said.

"Oh, curious," Jazmyn said.

Diomedes stood on a rocky outcrop next to the river, which overlooked the town, staring off into the distance.

He turned when he heard the warbling sound of someone about to appear.

"What are we doing here?!" Morzell said.

Ignoring Morzell outburst, "I want to create an army of foot soldiers to help take over this town."

"I already have an army and we should take the town now!" Morzell said.

Diomedes turned his head and glared at his gofer, "When these puny humans are under my control, they can die as my foot soldier, then my army."

"That little witch hasn't learned to master her powers, yet," Morzell got into Diomedes's face. "This would be the ideal time to attack, or are you too scared of the other weakling witches."

Diomedes picked Morzell up by his neck and squeezed. Morzell's panted, trying to get air.

A snap of Diomede's wrist sent Morzell flying through the air, the sound of bones cracking against a boulder echoed.

Morzell struggled onto his feet, wiping the blood that seeped from his nose.

"I am not scared of those witches."

Diomedes flew towards him and slammed him up against the boulder again. The pain seared through Morzell's body.

"I am getting tired of you telling me what to do. The next time will be your last," Diomedes raised his free hand and produced a red glowing energy ball. "Do you understand?"

Morzell nodded his head.

"This is what I need from you. Have my soldiers go to the fitness places, the high school and the park down there," Diomedes pointed down a path. "Have them take the strongest ones for my new foot soldiers and the weak ones I will use them for slaves."

Morzell got up, holding his ribs, nodded, and disappeared.

Diomedes once again looked out over the town and smiled, then vanished.

He reappeared at the opening where he kept Stephen, then strolled over to the cage; he stood there for the longest time just staring at this man sleeping in the corner of the cage.

"Wake up, Mr. Wolff," Diomedes said, rapping on Stephen's cage. "I got an offer for you."

Stephen slowly opened his eye; the other was beaten shut

by one of his guards, raised his head to look at his warden. "Wha?"

"I am going to set you free," Diomedes stated, and with a wave of his hand, the cage disappeared, and with a thud, Stephen.

He let out a scream from the dirt entering gashes on his back caused by being whipped for the past week. He has also been beaten and starved to the brink of death, he was sleep-deprived, and Stephen's lost his mind in some dark place.

Diomedes stood there looking at his prisoner; he could almost feel sorry for him but didn't.

"Didn't you hear me? I am going to set you free."

"You are not going to set-" Stephen winced in pain, trying to open his beaten eye"-me free. What is this offer?"

"I can offer you your health and freedom if you help me."

"I will not help you get Jazmyn's necklace for you if that's what you are asking."

"No, no, I don't want you to do that for me anymore. You have proven most stubborn for me to ask you again," Diomedes said.

"Then what?"

"I want you to help me with all these humans that I have working for me."

"Working, ya, right, your slaves, you mean. Why should I?" Stephen huffed.

"I am part human and I need you to be a liaison for me. I want them to see the world I want to creating will be much better placed than this one. I am tired of seeing you humans suffer from day to day struggles and crime, poverty and the list goes on."

Stephen knew that he shouldn't agree to his offer, but he was tired of all the suffering that he had been put through. There had been no rescue attempts; he felt like no one cared what was happening to him. His soul and his will teetered on the edge of an abyss, and so he pushed them.

"Yes, I will do this for you," Stephen sighed." But you must leave my daughter alone."

"I will not harm her," Diomedes smirked. "Follow me."

Stephen held the walls for support as he followed. He was led into a chamber with a few torches sprinkling the walls; the floor was covered with etched symbols. Opposite the door was a dais with a stone tablet in the center.

When Diomedes reached the center of the room, he gestures to Stephen to stop, making his way to the dais.

Stephen watched as Diomedes motioned his hands and arms in a circle, soon a thick black book appeared.

"Are you ready?" Diomedes spoke to a frail man standing in front of him.

"Please forgive me, Gloria and Jazmyn," Stephen whispered and slowly nodded.

Ghostly sounds filled the cavern as Diomedes paged through the book; his eyes widen accented with a smile when he found the page he wanted.

"What are you doing?!" Morzell yelled, startling Stephen when he appeared in the doorway.

Diomedes glared at him; with a movement of his hand Morzell was pulled to the alter next to him.

"What is that thing doing here?" Morzell asked.

"That thing has agreed to be my pet to command my slaves," Diomedes informed. "Now move out of my way I need to do something, first."

Diomedes spoke words out of the book in a language Stephen didn't know.

The floor surrounding Stephen began to glow red and soon pillars of light shot up; the smell of burning clothes filled his nose.

"OH, God, he's killing me," Stephen said, trying to move but was held by an unseen force.

A moment later, Stephen could feel his strength coming back; he looked down at his body; it began to fill out. He was no longer a skeleton.

"Stop!" Stephen screamed; he felt different. The word that

Diomedes spoke was no longer foreign.

Chapter Fifteen

After spending most of the day learning defensive moves, she was tired and sore. Jazmyn realized the defense courses she was taking before, for her mother's sake, were easy compared to trying to use her powers and muscles simultaneously. She felt as though she ran straight up Mt. Everest, backward.

Arion escorted her back to the tree, and Jazmyn watched him leave before she went inside.

Theia was sitting at the round table looking over dust-covered books,

"What are you do doing?" Jazmyn asked.

"Just looking up things. It looks like you need a shower."

"Yeah, I need to go back to my mothers to use the shower, so I need to grab some clothes...."

"You don't have to go anywhere, the tree will provide," Theia said.

"What do you mean?"

Theia got up and led Jazmyn toward her bedroom, "Just ask.'

"Tree?, I need to take a shower," Jazmyn felt like a fool talking to a tree.

The wall next to her bedroom moved farther back into the ground. Jazmyn watched as a door carved itself out of the wall; a sink appeared alongside a clawfoot tub with a showerhead popping out of the wall.

"Where's the toilet?" Jazmyn smirked.

A shape of a toilet came out of the floor; then, by the time the tank was full of water, it was a fully working toilet.

"Thanks," Jazmyn said.

"I will let you be," Theia said, then disappeared.

She let the hot water flow over her body; it felt so good. It was like the shower knew what to do to make her feel better, then she remembered that the oak tree would provide what she needed, and she wanted her pain to go away, and it slowly did. It felt like she spent hours in the shower, but it was only few minutes.

She stepped out of the shower and dried herself off, then change into her sweats and a t-shirt and laid on her bed.

Her phone buzzed on her nightstand; she turned over and saw a text from Izzie.

She thought of Izzie and how she would like to see her; she missed her friend. She started to message Izzie back, but all of a sudden, she was lying on Izzie's bedroom floor, looking up at Izzie.

"Holy shit! Jazmyn?" Izzie said, almost jumping through the roof.

"Ah, surprise," Jazmyn said, getting up off the floor.

"You scared the bejeebers out of me. What are you doing here?" Izzie said, feeling her heartbeat settling.

"I am sorry, I received your texts and then I thought of how I wanted to see you then poof, I'm here, I must be more careful next time."

"Well, I am glad to see you, of course, normal people would have come over in a car or walked," Izzie said, smiling.

"Haha, funny, glad to see you, too," Jazmyn said and hugged Izzie.

"So, what has been going on? I see that your magic is working."

"Yeah, we've learned that Diomedes took over the caves north of my mother's and he is using people as slaves," Jazmyn said.

"That's not good."

"No, it isn't. Diomedes also is working with another

demon named Morzell and his army of creatures."

"Weird. You know strange things are happening here." Izzie reported.

"Like?" Jazmyn said with a puzzled look on her face.

"You know, Bernie, that homeless guy that roams around town and collects soda cans."

"Yeah."

"He is missing. I haven't seen him lately anywhere."

"Maybe he is just sick." Jazmyn reasoned.

"Ms. Brown, the director of the homeless shelter, she came through my line the other day and she said she hadn't seen him either, plus he is not the only one is gone."

"What?"

"The sheriff came in today and I overheard him talking to Brad, his one and only deputy, that he was worried about all of the people that have been reported missing."

"Diomedes has taken people as slaves around the caves; he must be kidnapping people from the town also," Jazmyn said.

"We should tell the police," Izzie said.

"Tell them what? It not like we can tell them this evil demon is taking the people as slaves," Jazmyn stated. "Oh yeah, he is going to try to take the world over too."

"What's going to happen to them?"

"We are working on it," Jazmyn said.

"How?.... Never mind, you can tell me all about it when I come to see you this weekend." Izzie said, smiling.

"Sounds good, just be careful."

"I will, Mom," Izzie said, shoving Jazmyn a little. "But for now I need to get some sleep, I am working a double shift tomorrow, so I can take off early to see you."

"I should get back anyway. I am more or less on the house or tree lockdown. They don't want anything to happen to me." Jazmyn said.

"Yeah, I agree, I wouldn't want anything to happen to you either," Izzie said.

"Thanks, I will see you in a few days then. Jazmyn said,

hugging Izzie.

"Unless you think of me and show up unexpectedly again," Izzie said with a chuckle.

Jazmyn smiled; with a wink, she vanished and reappeared in her bedroom.

She sat on the edge of her bed, rested her arms on her legs, and took a look around.

I could go anywhere in the world, but I can't. I guess it's for my own good.

She crawled back into her bed, tried to fall asleep, but she couldn't get over the feeling of being trapped.

∞∞∞

Diomedes let out a loud yell as he sat on his throne; he slammed down his fist on the armrest, nearly breaking the arm.

"What is the matter? My Lord," one of his guards said, running up to him, that left his post at the doorway.

"How dare you speak to me without bowing!" Diomedes screamed as he stood up, and in an instant, his handed was around the guard's neck and lifted him off the floor.

"I apologize, My Lord," the guard gargled out as he struggled to breathe.

Diomedes stared into his eyes; the guard started to twitch and scream, then there was silence.

"Apology not taken," Diomedes said, throwing the lifeless guard's body against the far wall.

"It takes a lot of energy to create my soldiers," Morzell hissed; he appeared next to Diomedes and looked around.

"Don't make me kill you too," Diomedes said, clenching his fist at Morzell.

"Without me, you would have nothing," Morzell said.

Diomedes sat down and grumbled to himself; he knew Morzell was right. Morzell helped him regain his powers by taking powers from other demons and witches when Diomedes was weak.

"What is wrong?" Morzell said.

"I can't enter her dreams anymore," Diomedes said.

"They must have cast another protection spell," Morzell said.

"No, This is different, if it was a spell I could break through it," Diomedes said, then thought for a moment. "This magic is very ancient, I can't even find her."

"Should I send some soldiers out to search?"

"No, I will find a way to draw her out. Now go," Diomedes stated.

Morzell nodded his head, then walked out the door, but not before summoning another one of his soldiers out of the ground to replace the one killed.

Diomedes sat back and closed his eyes; he was trying again to find Jazmyn. He focused on the house of her mother and the land around it. Still, there was nothing, but he found that his thoughts couldn't touch in a particular part of the forest.

"That must be where she is. I must go take a look." He said, then disappeared.

Diomedes reappeared in the forest where he had lost her.

The moonless sky covered the trees with a shroud of darkness; he could seem as though it was daytime.

He held his hand up and waved it back and forth as we walk, using it as a guide to help him. He could feel the magic getting closer but could not feel anything.

Diomedes grew frustrated and was ready to leave when he noticed a rabbit scurried away, disappeared, then reappeared again as it ran farther into the woods.

"I know where you are hiding. You can't stay in there forever. I will find a way to get you." He said, then vanished.

∞ ∞ ∞

The sound of spring rain tapping at the window outside

teased Jazmyn out of her night's sleep. She looked out to watch the rain, especially when it was accompanied by lightning and thunder. She thought of the storm as a cleansing part of nature, washing the dirty snow left behind where the sun couldn't reach. It also gives the new growth a refreshing chance to grow.

She grabbed a pair of sweats and a hoodie to wear; she felt cozy in them and walked out of her door expecting to head downstairs but realized where she was and ran up the stairs out of the oak tree.

"Where do you think you are going?" Allison said as she appeared out of the book.

"I was going to go have my morning coffee with my mother," Jazmyn said, spinning around on the step.

"You need an escort, don't you?" Allison inquired.

"I think I can manage by myself today," Jazmyn continued up the stairs.

"You are not ready yet."

"I have learned more in the last few days from the book. Miryssia has taught me a bunch of stuff and the twins too. Arion is teaching me how to use my magic with defensive moves," Jazmyn explained, slumping her shoulders as she walks back to the table and sits down.

"Yes, I know you've learned a lot, but still, you need to learn more. I sensed that you left us for a short time last night," Allison said, sitting down next to Jazmyn.

"I am twenty-one years old; I don't need a babysitter. I feel like a prisoner here," Jazmyn said. "And now am I being spied on."

"No, when magic is used here, I can sense it. I do know how old you are, but you must understand that you are an essential part of what we are trying to do." Allison said.

"I know, but I didn't ask for any of this. Now I have to try to finish something you couldn't do 300 years ago." Jazmyn eyes angled in, and her nose flared.

"Yes," Allison stated.

"Yes, yes? Is that all you have to say. All you people, including my mother, dropped these bombshells on me about-" Jazmyn moved gestured wildly with her arms "-me being a witch, my father and this asshole of a demon."

"I admit that I couldn't stop him, but you have a chance to do what I was ready to do." Allison took a deep breath. "You have something I didn't have; you have us to help you learn. You see, I didn't have anyone, I had to make do with what I knew and that just wounded him."

Jazmyn bowed her head then looked at Allison, "What is it that I need to learn?"

"Soon, Theia will teach you how to used your stone to control the elements," Allison said.

"Sounds great," Jazmyn flashed a half-smile. "I still feel trapped, but I understand why. Sorry I blew up at you."

"That's quite alright," Allison said.

"By the way, it was an accident that I vanished last night. I am sorry, I was thinking of my friend Izzie and how I felt I needed to see her and found myself there."

"That's what I am talking about, you cannot control your powers yet, and that is dangerous.

Jazmyn nodded her head in agreement, "Izzie told me that people are disappearing from town and I think it is Diomedes is behind it."

"Let me summon everyone so we can discuss this; afterward, you can go visit your mother with an escort," Allison said, then closed her eyes for a few seconds then opened them up again.

"OK, but I need some coffee," Jazmyn said.

"They will arrive soon."

She moved her hand across the table. A steaming hot cup of coffee appeared. "That should tie you over."

Within a minute, Theia appeared first, then Abraham, Arion, and the others soon followed.

Miryssia was still half asleep, wiped the sleep from her eyes, "What is going on?"

"Jazmyn has something to tell us," Allison said.

"Hello everyone, I went to my friend Izzie's last night,"

Jazmyn put her palm down and waved it. "Before the lecture comes, I've been told already not to do that again. Izzie told me that people from my town are missing and I think Diomedes is behind it."

"That's not good," Miryssia said after a long moment of silence.

"No, it isn't," Arion said.

"We will go into town to investigate this," Theia said.

"I know, I will stay here," Jazmyn said.

"You know the town better than any of us, so you can come," Theia said.

"What!?" Jazmyn surprisingly said. "You lived with me as a cat and I am sure you know it too."

"Do you want to go or not?" Theia looked at Jazmyn. "Yes, I do know a little of what's in the town, but still, you could help us."

"Yes, I want to go," Jazmyn said, took the last sip of coffee and got up from the table, began to walk to the stairs. "But first, more coffee."

"I will walk you there," Arion said.

"I'll tag along. A cup of java is needed," Miryssia said, slowly getting up from the table.

"OK, We will meet back here in an hour," Abraham said.

Jazmyn held her thumb up as the trio went up and outside.

The rain clouds had moved on; the sun made the raindrops glisten on the branches and grass in the crisp morning air.

When they arrived at the house, they found her mother sitting at the kitchen table having coffee.

"Morning, Mom, Do you have some more of that?" Jazmyn said, pointing at her coffee cup and heading towards the coffee maker.

"Yes, I just made some more," Her mother said.

"Good morning, Mrs. Wolff," Arion said.

"Morning," Miryssia said.

"Good Morning," She said. "What you kids up to?"

"Going into town to in...." Arion stopped.

"To pick up some supplies, can't get everything by magic," Jazmyn interrupted as she brought three cups of coffee to the table.

"Yeah," Miryssia said, giving Jazmyn a bewildering look. "Just needed some go-go juice, thanks."

"Your welcome."

After they drank their coffees and some small talk, trying to avoid the real reason they were heading into town, they headed back to the tree.

"Why didn't you want me to tell your mother what we are going to do in town," Arion said.

"I don't want her to worry about us and to worry about the people who are missing from town, she knows a lot of people in town," Jazmyn explained.

"Oh," Arion said.

Jazmyn looked at the mighty oak tree that now had become her home and noticed some leaves on one low-lying branch that looked wilted and dead. In all the time she visited this tree, the leaves were always green and full of life.

"That's weird," Jazmyn said.

"What being asked to come along with us, it was just a matter of time," Arion said.

"No, this." Jazmyn pointed out the dead leaves. "I never have seen it do that before. is the tree dying?" Jazmyn said.

"No, I don't think so. Let me see." Arion said as he reached out and looked closer.

He closed his eyes and stood there for a moment, trying to heal the tree but couldn't.

"I can't heal it," Arion said.

"I am going to go get Theia," Miryssia said as she went for the door.

A minute later, Theia and Abraham, the twins, followed Miryssia up the stairs.

Theia slowly approached the branch and carefully reached up and felt the leaves. She pulled her hand away like a bee just stung it, "Evil has touched this tree."

"Diomedes was here." Jazmyn shuttered a little.

"Could have been him or could've been Morzell or one of his soldiers," Abraham said.

"They know we're here," Jazmyn said.

"Not to worry, the tree will protect us and it will heal itself in time. Evil can not enter unless invited." Theia said.

"We should go," Abraham said.

"Yes, but Tony and Tina stay behind to see if any evil returns," Theia said.

The twins nodded their heads at the same time, headed back into the tree. They gathered in a small circle and all at once disappeared but not before Theia looked back at the tree with a worried look.

Chapter Sixteen

The air crackled in the alley next to her old work. A flash of light announced the appearance of Theia and the rest. The streets seemed quiet as a few scattered cars cruised by.

"We will split up, Abraham and I will go to the police station to see if anyone else is missing and you three check around to see anything is happening," Theia said. "Be careful; call if you need help."

"Ok," Jazmyn said.

Miryssia watched Abraham, and Theia disappeared around the corner, "So, Jazmyn, where do you want to go too?"

"This is all new to me; I am not sure." Jazmyn shrugged her shoulders.

"Does anyplace stand out more than others?" Miryssia said.

Jazmyn perched her chin between her thumb and forefinger, "Maybe Onyx River park at the edge of town. It's kind of tucked out of the way, so I think it would be a good place to start."

"Yeah, if there isn't anything happening there, we could work our way back here checking out other places," Arion said.

"Ok, lead the way, Jaz," Miryssia said.

As they walked, Jazmyn pointed out places she had been in and when they passed by her old apartment. She saw some plants in the window.

Someone must be living there.

They passed by the bakery where she would buy donuts or maple-covered long johns. She was tempted, but just walked by.

When they arrived at the park, it was dotted with a few people. A man was sitting on a bench next to the river, feeding the ducks.

The clapping of feet on the tar path came from a few joggers. Over in the dog park section, there an elderly lady walking her miniature poodle.

"That's a small dog," Miryssia said.

"Yeah, that's Mrs. Spencer with her little dog, Snookie. She comes into where I work, or used to work with him in her cart." Jazmyn said as she waved at Mrs. Spencer.

"So, what should we be looking for?" Arion asked.

"Something strange, I guess," Miryssia said.

"You mean stranger than that guy jogging in that spandex outfit," Arion said with a bit of chuckle.

"Close, but yes." Miryssia burst into laughter, and the rest followed.

They walked around the park, observing to see if anything was out of place.

Stopping at a pavilion to rest, Miryssia sat on the top of a picnic table while the other sat on the bench.

The sound of a small waterfall caught Jazmyn's attention, "I would come here sometimes, on my lunch from work or just to listen to that beautiful waterfall."

"Beautiful," Arion said.

Jazmyn looked over to him and noticed that he was looking at her and not the scenery; she blushed a little, Arion turned away.

"Must be a good place to jog," Miryssia said as a woman jogger went by.

"Yes, I would come here to jog too," Jazmyn said.

"Um, Do you want to get some exercise in since we are here?" Arion said.

"Sure, no better way to see the whole park, besides I need it. Want to tag along, Miryssia?" Jazmyn said.

"No, I will just sit here, enjoying the view," Miryssia said, seeing a muscle-bound man getting out of his car.

"Grrr!" Jazmyn remarked, looking at the guy.

"Let's go," Arion said.

Jazmyn and Arion took off and jogged around the circle a few times, stopping back at where they started.

"See anything?" Miryssia asked.

"No, you?" Jazmyn said, sitting down.

"No, but that cute guy went into the restroom. He must have to go real bad; he has been in there along time," Miryssia nodded her head towards the restrooms. "I haven't seen him come out yet."

"I will check it out," Arion said.

They walked over to the restrooms; Arion walk into the men's.

"He isn't in there, but it stinks in there," Arion said as he came out, waving his hand in front of his face.

"It's a public bathroom," Jazmyn said, turned to Miryssia. "Are you sure you just didn't miss him when he came out."

"I kept my eye on that hunk of a man, so no," Miryssia said. "I'm going in."

All three of them walked into the restroom; it was spotless except for the smell.

"That smell, it's almost too much, it's making me want to gag." Jazmyn wrinkled her face.

"That's the same stink that the warhog have," Miryssia said.

"You're right, but how did he get in and out without you seeing it?" Jazmyn asked.

"Teleported," Miryssia said.

"I will call Theia and Abraham about this." Arion pulled his phone out, waved his arm in the air. "No signal, be right back."

Arion stepped out and walking away from the restrooms. Jazmyn and Miryssia looked around for clues.

"Find anything?" Jazmyn asked.

"Yeah, come here," Miryssia motioned to Jazmyn over to the last stall.

"What is it?" Jazmyn widens her eyes.

Miryssia pointed at an advertisement on the wall, "My favorite band is playing next month."

Jazmyn shook her head, "I thought it was something important."

"Well, it is to me," Miryssia said as they turned to walk out.

"What is that sound?" Jazmyn was tilting her head from side to side.

"Trouble!"

A warhog appeared and instantly lunged at them; they both jumped out of the way. Miryssia tore one of the doors from the stall with her mind and flung it at the beast.

The warhog flew against the wall, got back up, shoot a bolt of lighting at Miryssia, but Jazmyn picked up the door and defects it into the stall, exploding the toilet.

"Thanks," Miryssia said.

Jazmyn nodded and spun around and kicked the beast. It let out a squeal, stumbling, and landed against one of the sinks. When it came up, it ripped the sink off the wall and flung it at the both of them.

Miryssia stopped it in mid-air and flung it back at it, smashing it to pieces against the warhogs head. The beast fell to the floor, died then vanished.

"That's one good thing about killing demons; they clean up after themselves." Miryssia brushed herself off.

"Why is that?" Jazmyn inquired.

"The whole thing of keeping magic a secret, demons disappear when they die," Miryssia said. "Because I guess normal people can't handle the real truth."

"I am still getting used to all of this," Jazmyn said.

I was an average person not too long ago.

Arion ran in, "Are you guys alright?"

"Yeah, it's nothing us witches couldn't handle," Miryssia said, then blew on her knuckle and wiped them on her shirt.

Jazmyn smiled and winked at Miryssia.

Arion looked around and then held his hand out and

closed his eyes; the sink pieces assembled themselves and were put back on the wall, the door fixed itself. In a short time, it was like nothing happened.

"Wow," Jazmyn said, glancing at Arion; he just smiled.

"Let's go," Miryssia said.

As they walk out, a man walked in, giving them a confused look.

"When you gotta go, you gotta go," Miryssia said.

Theia and Abraham were waiting when they came out.

"Had another fight?" Abraham said.

"Yeah, it was one of those warhogs, again," Jazmyn said.

"Are you hurt?" Theia said to Jazmyn. "Should not have let you come."

"She kicked ass in there," Miryssia said. "She didn't panic, and she kept focused and helped out."

"Still, we should not take a chance like that," Theia said.

"Well, it wasn't the first one we fought and won. Besides, I am here and you need me here, and I am not going anywhere." Jazmyn stated.

"We have learned that most of the people are disappearing from this park at a place called Newman's Bluff," Abraham said, trying to change the subject.

"And in the biffy," Miryssia added, making Jazmyn smile.

"Could you show us where this place is?" Theia looked at Jazmyn.

"Yeah, sure. Newman's Bluff is just a mile or so up the river." Jazmyn said, pointing at a trail that followed the river bank.

"Newman's Bluff?" Arion asked.

"Its name came from one of the first residents of Oak Stone. His name was Harvey Newman; he went crazy after his wife mysteriously was killed. The townspeople accused him of doing it; he couldn't take it anymore and hung himself from a tree there. People go up there to make out. They say you can see him still today wandering around up there," Jazmyn told.

"He probably cannot find his way to the hereafter," Abraham said.

"Interesting to know, but getting back to the matter at hand, It took a guy from the bathroom. Damn, the guy was cute too," Miryssia said.

"It seems that Diomedes doesn't want to bring attention to himself; he is picking places that are far from people's eyes or in buildings," Theia said. "Abraham and I will cast a protection spell over these bathrooms and that pavilion, then we all will go to Newman's Bluff to check it out."

"Maybe you and Arion can have some alone time," Miryssia whispered to Jazmyn.

"Shut up." Jazmyn blushed.

Theia and Abraham face the restrooms and held their hands and arms out to their side.

Theia and Abraham spoke,

"We call the witches from the past. Protect this place until the last."

A blue glow came from their hands, and when it met, it formed a shell over the building then disappeared.

After doing the same to the pavilion, they followed the trail that led to the bluff. Jazmyn and Arion walked next to each other, with the others just ahead of them.

It was a beautiful walk with the water, slowly meandering downstream and the forest coming right up to the bank most of the way. Some snow hid, here and there, trying to hold its ground.

A squirrel began to chatter at Arion passing by to close, "A little grumpy?"

"It just mad about us being here," Jazmyn said, sensing the squirrel's emotion.

The terrain got a little steeper; the trail veered away from the river and headed into the woods.

"Almost have to be a billy goat," Miryssia said.

A clearing was just ahead; there were also signs that it was a party spot for kids.

"I hate it when people wreck a place of beauty," Theia said.

Farther up the hill, a fence guarded the bluff's edge. Just beyond it was a maple tree with some it roots hanging out from the hillside.

"Awesome view," Miryssia said.

"I always love the view," Jazmyn said.

"When you had time to look," Miryssia said, nudging Jazmyn.

"That tree looks like it ready to fall," Arion commented.

"That's where Mr. Newman hung himself; kids dare each other to go out to the end of that branch," Jazmyn said.

"That's stupid, it must be a one hundred foot drop," Arion said, stretching to look over the edge.

Jazmyn shook her head.

"Speaking of Mr. Newman, what was his first name again?" Theia asked.

"It was Harvey," Jazmyn said. "Why?"

Theia waved her hand; five lit candles appeared in a star pattern on the ground next to the tree.

"I asked the gods to summon Harvey Newman's spirit to come to us," Theia said with her head tilted back and eyes closed.

A gust of wind came up for an instant, blowing out the candles; from the smoke, a man's form faded in.

"Who called me here?" The spirit asked in an eerie voice.

"Harvey Newman, my name is Theia and these are my friends. We summoned you to ask you some questions," Theia said.

"I never knew ghosts were real," Jazmyn whispered to Arion.

"As you can see, they are," Arion whispered back.

Jazmyn was fascinated to see, what she thought were people's overactive imaginations right in front of her. A spirit of a man dressed in a turn of the century suit, with a small tie, he also wore glasses. He looked normal, but you could see what was behind him.

"Leave me alone," Harvey said, fading away.

"We won't take up too much of your time," Jazmyn said.

"Time, I have a lot of that, Jazmyn," Harvey said, turning toward her.

"How-how do you know my name?" Jazmyn inquired.

"Ever since you have moved to my town, I have been watching you," Harvey said.

"Why have you been watching me?" Jazmyn asked.

"On the ghostly plane, where I spend most of my time, I heard about you. I have been waiting for you to become a witch so you can help me."

"What can I help you with? You've been dead for so long," Jazmyn said.

"I need you to help me kill the demon that killed my beloved wife, Mary," Harvey said.

"Do you know the demon's name?" Theia asked.

"Yes, Morzell is its name. My wife and I were here on this bluff, enjoying the view of the full moon one night when this creature came out from the woods and attacked us. At first, I thought it was a bear, but the moonlight showed me it was a horrible beast. He went after me, but I hit him with a log, and then he went after my wife. She was petrified and could not run. I-I watched him as he slowly killed her. I tried to stop him, but I could not. Her screams will always be in my head." Harvey voice cracked. "He let me live and I slowly went crazy over it, I hung myself."

"Oh, my." Jazmyn gasped before she realized what she was doing; she reached for Arion's hand. "I am so sorry. We are on our on a mission to stop Diomedes and Morzell is working with him."

"I will help you then." Harvey paused. "I saw Morzell with this Diomedes here. Seeing him again made me feel the pain of losing her again and all I wanted to do is to rip him into pieces, but I can not since I am a ghost."

"I am sorry for your loss, what were they doing?" Theia said.

"They were making plans on where they were going to capture people. They decided to take them from here, in the park, and they were going to the high school and fitness buildings also."

"We knew that some of those, except for the last two. We will have to go and protect those places too, but was there anything else?" Theia asked.

"By next Saturday, my town will be turned into an army base filled with soldiers, made up of the townspeople and they will use them to attack the surrounding towns," Harvey said.

"We can't let that happen!." Jazmyn said.

"Some of the people will be enslaved," Harvey added.

"We must get back to the tree and figure out what do to stop this," Abraham said.

"Thank you, Harvey. We will do our best to help you now." Jazmyn said. "Do me one more favor."

"What?"

"Be sure to scare the kids away so they won't get captured here," Jazmyn said.

Harvey nodded his head and then faded away.

"All of you go back to the tree. Abraham and I will go and cast a protection spells," Theia said.

Jazmyn, Arion, and Miryssia appeared in front of the big oak tree; Jazmyn glanced towards the setting sun. It seemed to her that it was running to hide from upcoming evil. The three of them walked down inside and sat at the table.

"All those people are going to either die or be enslaved," Jazmyn said, as tears streamed down her face.

"We are not going to let that happen," Arion said, putting his arm around her.

"I know most of those people," Jazmyn stated, finding comfort with his arm about her.

"What has happened?" Allison said, appearing across the table from them.

"Diomedes and his sidekick are planning to take over the town," Miryssia said.

"Where are Theia and Abraham?" Allison asked, trying to push by the thought of Diomedes's plan.

"They are doing magic stuff. They will be back soon," Miryssia said.

"I have to tell my mother and Izzie," Jazmyn said, grabbing her cell phone.

"You can, but for now, wait," Allison said.

"Wait, we can't afford to wait. They need to know; especially Izzie, she lives there." Jazmyn stated.

"I know she does," Allison said.

"We will tell them as soon as we have something to tell them," Theia said as she came down the steps followed by Abraham.

"I need tell them about the people that are being kidnapped," Jazmyn said, turning her attention to Theia.

"First, we need to work on a plan to stop him. The spells we have cast will slow his progress down," Theia said.

Abraham closed her eyes for a moment. "I have called for the twins."

Tony and Tina showed up a moment later, and Theia filled them in.

Abraham, Theia, and Allison broke from the group and huddled in a corner, they didn't speak, but Jazmyn could tell they were discussing something.

"What do you think they are talking about?" Jazmyn asked.

"Probably the next move," Miryssia said, sitting down on the tabletop.

Theia walked over to Jazmyn after they were done, "You are ready to learn the true power of your necklace."

"Are you sure?" Jazmyn took a half step back.

"Yes, you are," Theia smiled.

"When?"

Theia took her hand and lightly pressed it in the middle of

Jazmyn's back, "Right now. We need to go outside."

"Ok," Jazmyn said, heading for the stairs.

The sound of heavy rain hitting the oak leaves echoed through Jazmyn's ears, "Might have to do this some other time."

"Why?" Theia perked her one eyebrow up.

"It's raining, hard,"

"Is rain part of nature?" Theia asked.

"Well, yeah," Jazmyn folded her arms in front of her and leaned against the doorway.

"Then it is a perfect time to learn," Theia smiled and walked out in the rain. "Come."

Jazmyn hesitated to step out from under the canopy; she slowly walked to join Theia. She hunched her shoulders and hugged herself, then stepped into the rain, and quickly, it drenched her.

"That necklace bonds you with nature closer than anyone else," Theia cupped the pendant in one hand. "Clear your mind. You need to hear nature voice all around you."

Closing her eyes seemed to enhance the fact the rain was freezing. She tried to ignore it to clear her mind, but every pounding raindrop brought made her body shiver, "I can't, I am too cold."

"Yes, you can. Concentrate"

Jazmyn looked at Theia, "How can you stand there like it was a nice bright sunny day?"

"I have learned to control my body. You just need to concentrate on finding your inner peace; then your body will take it from there."

"Ok, I will try, again,"

She closed her eyes again, her body objected at first, then as a sense of serenity came over her, the shivering stopped, and she began to feel and sense things she didn't know were around her.

The pounding rain seemed to fade away; she heard the bark on the oak tree crackle. Jazmyn opens her eyes and focused on a train of ants climbing up the tree. Far off in the distance, she could hear a herd of deer move through the forest. She turned to look but didn't see them, but she knew it.

"Can you feel nature?" Theia whispered.

Jazmyn closed her eyes tighter and could feel as though every creature, plant, tree, and element were present. It was almost like each one was something you could talk to.

"Now, rain the stop,"

Jazmyn nodded her head, "Rain, stop."

Nothing happened; the rain continued to pour.

"Why isn't it working?" Jazmyn opened her eyes and focused on Theia.

"You have to ask it in your mind, not out loud," Theia said.

Again Jazmyn closed her eyes and lifted her head to the sky, *"Please, could you stop the rain."*

The pendant began to glow in response.

"Thank you for asking nicely," a voice answered, and the rain let up, the clouds moved away, letting the sun warm her.

"I could hear it answer me."

A smile came across Theia's face, "Yes, as the animals have a voice, so does everything in nature."

Jazmyn sat down on one of the giant roots of her tree, "I never knew."

She closed her eyes again and focused on hearing all the voices. A few trickled in at; first, she tilted her head down. She focuses on a flower near her foot.

The flower's voice was garbled at first, then it became clear, "Sun, I love the sun."

A smile came across Jazmyn's face, "I can't believe it."

Voices began to flood her mind as if a dam had burst. Jazmyn covered her ears, trying to shield herself, but it didn't help. Her heart pounded wildly; it was hard for her to breathe.

She closed her eyes and shook her head back and forth, "I can hear everything."

"You need to concentrate on the here and now, focus."

Jazmyn could see Theia's mouth moving but couldn't hear her, "What!"

"Focus!" Theia yelled.

She tried to focus, but there were too many voices. She grabbed her hair by her ears and pulled.

"I-I can't!" Jazmyn screamed.

A voice faintly calls to her, "Focus on my voice."

The voice wasn't Theia's; it was someone else. She looked around, but no one else was around.

"I am here to help you," the voice said.

Jazmyn forced herself to listen to the voice, and it began to sing. Her pendant seemed to follow along with the song; all the other sounds one by one began to fade away.

Jazmyn arms began to relax; she let them fall to her side; she took a deep breath to help her heart settle.

"Are you all right?" Theia asked.

"Yes, I think so. I heard some woman singing; she helped me focus." Jazmyn said. "I have heard that voice before. Do you know who that could be? She has been there when I was in trouble."

Theia nodded, "I will tell you later, but first, we need to continue. Do you think you can carry on?"

Jazmyn took another deep breath, "I think so."

"You will learn in time to listen to one voice at a time or a group,"

"I sure hope so," Jazmyn rubbed her temple a little.

"Now, I will teach you the rest of the elements, earth, fire, and wind."

"Ok." Jazmyn said.

Chapter Seventeen

She looked at the clock; it read a quarter to twelve.

"Damn. I just want to stay in bed." Jazmyn said.

She still had a headache from her lessons from the day before, but forced herself out of bed.

When she walked out of her room, a smile came across her face when she saw Arion sitting at the big table with two cups of coffee.

"Good morning," Arion smiled back.

He stood up and handed her one cup of coffee.

"Smells good, thanks," Jazmyn took it and sat down; Arion followed.

After a few sips, her eyes widen; I must look like hell.

"I will be right back," Jazmyn got up.

"Where are you going?" Arion raised his eyebrow.

"To fix my hair." Jazmyn flashed a smile.

"You look great to me," Arion cheeks flushed a little, quickly taking a sip.

Jazmyn ran her fingers through her hair and sat down again.

"So, what did Theia teach you?"

"A lot, it sure takes a toll on a person,"

"Yes, it does. I remember when I began using my powers, I was tired all the time," Arion studied Jazmyn's face. "What's the matter?"

"Its nothing." Jazmyn looked away.

"Come on, you can tell me."

"It's just that-" ran her fingers through her hair, then looked at Arion. "-I am afraid."

"Of?" Arion leans in.

"Of what I can do now that I have learned to control nature," tears welled up in her eyes.

"Don't be. I know Theia, and she wouldn't have taught you if you weren't ready."

"It sure doesn't feel like I am ready." She wiped away a tear that escaped.

"I believe you are. You've handled everything so far."

"What if I make a mistake and somewhere in the world, I cause a flood or tornado."

Arion sat back in his chair and waved his hand, "Don't worry, you won't. Just trust in yourself."

I don't know if I can, Jazmyn thought.

The sound of the door to the tree opened, Theia and Abraham appeared coming down the stairs.

"How are you doing today, Jazmyn," Theia said, coming up next to her.

"Um, Just fine, I guess," Jazmyn eyed Arion then looked at Theia.

"I know you have doubts, but you will overcome them," Theia said.

"I hope so," Jazmyn lowered her head.

"We are going to discuss what we have learned about Diomede's plan," Abraham stated.

"Can I go get dressed first?" Jazmyn said.

"Yes," Theia nodded her head.

Jazmyn walked back into her room, rummaged through her closet and dresser, threw clothes on the bed, and went into the bathroom to brush her hair.

She stopped brushing her hair, leaned on the counter, and looked at her reflection.

"Am I ready for all this?"

"Yes, you are?" the strange woman voice said.

"Who are you?" Jazmyn said.

There was no reply, "Hello, are you there?"

She stood there for a moment but nothing happened; she finished and got dressed, walked back out to find everyone there besides her mother.

"So, what are we going to do about that asshole?" Miryssia said.

"Miryssia, we do not use that kind of language here," Theia glared at her.

"Sorry," She smirked, then looked at Jazmyn.

I think she does that to irritate her.

"I could see what Diomedes is up to," Jazmyn said.

"No, you mustn't, he can reverse the connection and take control over you and find out what you know," Theia said.

"He has been in my head, making me believe in things aren't real, why didn't he control me then?" Jazmyn asked.

"There are several ways of connecting with another. The way he has been fooling you is one way," Theia stated.

"Tony and Tina, can you see what will happen?" Abraham asked.

The twins nodded and turned their chairs to face each other and held hands and closed their eyes for a brief moment, then opened them again. Their eyes were glazed over and stared at one another; both of them mirrored the other one's facial movement.

It seemed to Jazmyn that she was watching them in fast forward; they would smile then move their mouths like they were talking, at times look like they were sleeping. They began to cry right before they came out of their trances.

"We are all going to die." The twins both said at the same time.

An eerie silence fills the room.

"Well, that's what I like to hear," Miryssia said, breaking the silence.

"What did you two see?" Abraham asked.

"Diomedes releases his army onto the town," Tina said.

"He has his army killing everyone," Tony said.

"You said we all die, how do we die?" Jazmyn asked hesitantly.

"You cause it. You fail us." Tony and Tina said sternly.

"How? Wh... What do you mean?" Jazmyn stammered; her body went weak. If she weren't sitting down, she would be on the floor.

"The future that Tony and Tina have seen is a future that has not been set yet. We have time to change it now." Theia said to Jazmyn.

"You give into Diomedes and give him your necklace," Tina said.

∞∞∞

"I would never." Jazmyn's heart thumped in her chest.

"The worst part is that you stand there and watch us die," Tony stated.

Jazmyn shot up from her seat and bolted up and out of the tree.

"Don't go, Jazmyn!" Theia yelled, which spurred Arion to get up and ran after her.

The full moon lit the night up, and it made it easy for Arion to see Jazmyn running toward her mother's house. She was halfway there before he caught up with her.

"Please stop!" Arion said, reaching out and grabbing her shoulder.

Jazmyn spun around with tears streaming down her face.

"Get away from me!" Jazmyn screamed, pulling out of his grip. "All I am going to do is to hurt you and the others."

"Theia said the future is not set yet, so don't worry about doing something that has not happened yet," Arion explained.

"You don't know that it won't happen someday. It might not happen soon, but it seemed to me that I have it in me to betray people." Jazmyn said as she shivered from the emotions.

"Maybe you were put under a spell or something, the

Jazmyn I know won't do that," Arion said.

"You've known me for what, a few days and now you think you know me. I need to leave!" Jazmyn turned away, then vanished.

∞∞∞

Jazmyn found herself in a place she had not been since she was a very young girl. She was standing just inside the entrance to the same zoo where she was with her mother and father for the last time, together and happy.

The crisp air made Jazmyn shiver as she aimlessly wandered around the zoo. She saw a few of the bigger animals enduring the cold in their enclosures. A polar bear was swimming around, enjoying the cold.

"Am I that type of person that could betray others?" She asked herself as she glanced at the polar bear; it shook its head in disagreement.

"Thanks," she said with a bit of smirk on her face.

She walked towards where the chimps were located and peered through the bars, but the chimps weren't there. They must be inside where it's warmer; she rubbed her arms and wished she was inside where it was warm too.

The door to the back room opened up by itself; it startled Jazmyn. She cautiously walked over and peeked in. She felt the heat flood her face, and stepped in and shut the door.

She looked and saw two chimps, a baby chimp, and her mother, the mother chimpanzee, reacted to her by coming closer, with the little one on her back.

"Hi, there," she said to them and felt that the mother chimp answered her back.

"What am I going to do?" Jazmyn asked.

The mother chimp reached out and touched Jazmyn's face. Jazmyn felt understanding from her. She looked at both chimps and realized that it wasn't just the humans she had to protect. It was also every living thing on this earth.

It would be easier to give in to Diomedes; then, I wouldn't have to deal with the responsibility of saving the world. I wouldn't have to learn to be a witch and leave the world to go to hell, literally.

Stop thinking that way. You are better than that.

Jazmyn shook her head.

You can't let those thoughts in. Allison told once you start down the wrong path, you will remain there. What could I do to prevent this all from happening

Jazmyn felt a cold wind; she shivered as it went down her back. When she turned around, she found an over-sized wolf standing there, staring at her.

"Ok, big fella, how did you get out of your enclosure?" Jazmyn held her arms out and backed up a little.

She couldn't feel what this wolf thoughts were as it came up to her. She got used to the idea that she read animals now, but this one was different.

"You must be the human called Jazmyn?" the wolf spoke with a females voice.

"How? You speak. Yes, I am," Jazmyn said in surprise.

"Yes, I can. My name is Syann."

"Where did you come from?" Jazmyn stated.

"From the forest farther north of Diomedes's cave," Syann said.

Jazmyn moved a little closer to Syann. "You came a long way; it must have taken days to get here. That brings me to ask, why are you here?"

"As you can travel distances in a blink of an eye, I can, too," Syann replied.

"You are magical too? I never knew animals could use magic."

"I have evolved to use magic. The gemstone that you wear awakened the magic of my ancestors. My pack and I can use magic," Syann said.

Syann looked around and sniffed the air, "We must go. Come with me," Syann said, walking up next to Jazmyn.

"Why? Where…" Jazmyn voice traveled off as they disappeared.

A moment later, Diomedes appeared and found himself alone with the animals.

"Damn!" Diomedes looked around, then vanished.

Jazmyn found herself in the middle of some dark woods with only the moonlight to see. She realized besides Syann, several other wolves were surrounding her. She felt like she stepped into a nightmare.

"Don't be alarmed, this is the rest of my pack, "Syann explained.

Jazmyn felt like prey, "H-Hello."

"This is Daymeeun, my brother, Ismaria, my sister, and these are my last year's pups Isyia, and Hawthorne," Syann announced; she looked around. "Where is Wen?"

Hawthorne turned his head and pointed to a wolf walking away, "Father is over there."

"Wen, come back and introduce yourself," Syann said.

"Why should I," Wen said and continued walking.

"We hear that Diomedes is back," Hawthorne snarled a little. "He has been killing animals of the forest."

"Yes, but why did you bring me here?" Jazmyn asked.

"We are willing to help you," Isyia said.

"I am not going go up against him," Jazmyn stated.

"We know that you are just learning your craft, but when you do, we will help you," Daymeeun said.

Jazmyn hung her head, "I will just betray you so you will have to fight without me, I am not fighting,"

"What?," Ismaria said. "Why?"

"I am getting out of this before I get anyone killed," Jazmyn said and turned, walked away.

The circle of animals looked at each other. Daymeeun caught up to her and sat down in front of her.

"What do you mean to betray us?" He asked.

"When Syann found me at the zoo, I was running away. I was told that in the future, I would give Diomedes the necklace and all for whom I care for would die," Jazmyn said. "I am not someone that anyone would want to follow into battle. I am not a leader."

Syann came up behind her and brushed her leg. "Don't let what has not happened, stop you from doing what is right."

"I am not strong enough to go up against him," Jazmyn said.

"You don't need to be," Syann said.

"What do you mean? Yes, I do. I need to be strong, or the future will come true."

Jazmyn noticed that Isyia was walking around her, and she stopped.

"You have a lot of courage, you just are scared to use it," Isyia said.

"How do you know?" Jazmyn asked.

"Call it animal instinct. You just have to overcome your fears. Now that someone told you that you are about to betray everyone, it is easier for you to give in to that than to stand your ground," Isyia said.

"We have heard that you have already stood up to demons and won. That took courage," Daymeeun added.

"They were easy to take care of, plus I had help," Jazmyn said. "When Diomedes first attacked me when he was Luc, I was terrified."

"That was before you knew you were a witch, now that you have magic on your side, you can do it," Daymeeun said. "You are stronger than you know. When you have learned all there is to learn about your craft, nothing can hurt you, not even Diomedes."

"Your fears will pass as you become more and more confident," Syann said.

"Are you sure, right now I don't feel a lot of confidence," Jazmyn said.

"Believe me, it will come," a faint voice said from behind her and when Jazmyn turned and saw Theia standing there.

"How did you find me?" Jazmyn asked.

"I received a message from your new-found friends," Theia said. "Hello, Syann, Daymeeun and the rest of you. It's been some time since our last meeting."

"Greetings, Theia," Syann replied.

"Where is Wen?" Theia asked.

"Over there. He is still holding a grudge against Jazmyn," Daymeeun said.

"Grudge, I just got here, I didn't do anything," Jazmyn stated.

"No, dear, you are not the one Wen is upset with," Theia said.

"You mean my ancestor?. What happened?" Jazmyn asked.

"Long ago, when your ancestor took on Diomedes," Syann said. "She thought that Wen helped Diomedes kill her parents. Wen tried to tell her that he was there to help to protect her parents and to defeat Diomedes. In an angry rage, our ancestor refuse to listen and tried to kill Wen, but Wen escaped and she paid for it with her life,"

"Oh, my, I thought she said that she severely wounded Diomedes," Jazmyn said.

"She did, when she casted a spell to kill Wen the necklace lashed out, Diomedes was hurt and it killed your ancestor. The necklace can not be used to hurt or kill those who are innocent," Theia said.

"So, if Allison would have just listened to Wen, I probably wouldn't be here feeling guilty about something that has not happened yet and I wouldn't be here right now," Jazmyn thought for a moment, "How would Diomedes be able to use it for evil then?."

"There is a couple of ways it can be done," Daymeeun said.

"If Diomedes takes it and turns it evil through using a spell on it," Syann explained. "Or If it's given to him freely."

"So, the only way for him not to use it is to destroy him," Jazmyn said.

"Yes, it is," Syann said.

"If I go back, would you and the rest of the animal friends

help me in ending him?" Jazmyn said.

"We will…" Daymeeun started.

"NO! we will not," Wen said.

Everyone turned and looked at Wen as he walked up to them.

"Why not, she will need all the help she can get," Daymeeun stated.

"Don't argue with me! I am the leader here and do as I say!" Wen growled.

"But…" Daymeeun started.

"Just let it be," Syann said.

"Why did you bring me here if you won't offer your help?" Jazmyn asked.

"To let you know that the animal world believes in you and what you can do," Syann said.

"Let us leave and go back home," Theia said.

"I apologize for what my ancestor did to you," Jazmyn said, turning towards Wen.

"It is not your place to apologize to me, it is hers," Wen said.

Theia and Jazmyn disappeared.

Wen stood there for a moment and thought then faded into the woods.

Arion rushed to meet Jazmyn as she walked down the staircase of the oak tree, and the others were excited to see her.

"Are you alright?" Arion asked.

"Yes, I just need a little more time to process somethings," Jazmyn said as she looked at Allison.

"Where did you travel off too?" Miryssia wondered.

"I went to the zoo where my family and I used to go the. Never mind I will tell you later I am tired and I need to get some sleep," Jazmyn said.

"Let us leave and we will talk tomorrow," Theia said.

They all got up and left, but before Arion disappeared up the stairs, he glanced back at Jazmyn, caught his eye, and just smiled, then he left

"Was there something you wanted to say to me?" Allison inquired.

Jazmyn debated with herself about the knowledge of the feud between Allison and Wen. Should she get in the middle of this or leave for now. She could see the benefits of the help from the animals, but she didn't want to make Allison mad at her for sticking her nose where it doesn't belong.

"No, I-I guess not," Jazmyn stammered

"Alright, then have a good rest."

With that, Jazmyn went to her room and shut the door.

Chapter Eighteen

Jazmyn was lying in her bed when she could hear someone talking.

"Jazmyn, wake up," A voice said.

She sat up and looked around her room, but it was empty, "Abraham? I must have been dreaming."

"Jazmyn, Come see me at my house," Abraham said.

She looked around again, "Where are you?"

"I am telepathically linked to your mind." Abraham said." I am sending Miryssia to get you."

"Alright," Jazmyn felt kinda silly talking to no one, but she figured it is nothing different than seeing people walking down the street talking into a Bluetooth earpiece.

She stretched the night stiffness away and got ready for the day. She went out and sat at the big round table, wishing there was coffee, and before she knew it, there was a steaming cup of coffee in front of her. "Thanks."

She picked it up and blew across the top and took a few sips when opening up and sparkling orbs came out of it, then Allison appeared, "Good morning."

"Ya,"

Allison seemed different now that Jazmyn knew the whole story of what happened and how Allison really died trying to kill an animal, not Diomedes.

"Is there something wrong?" Allison asked, walking over to Jazmyn.

Jazmyn balled her fist up and felt her face flush; instead of blowing up at Allison, she got up and grabbed her coat, and went outside to wait for Miryssia.

When she open the door a rush of cold air made her gasp. She zipped up her coat, flipped up her hood, propped herself up against the root of the tree. The weather helped to temper her anger by the time Miryssia showed up.

"How's it going?" Miryssia asked.

Jazmyn glanced at her as she walked by, "Good."

Miryssia stood there for a moment and then caught up to her. "Did I miss something?"

"No, I don't want to talk about it."

"So, I did miss something? What is it?" Miryssia lightly grabbed Jazmyn's arm to stop her.

Jazmyn turned to her, "Not now."

On the way to Abraham's, Jazmyn tried to calm herself by listening to the birds sing, now that she can understand the animals. She could hear them arguing about finding food, a couple of them were in the middle of a mating ritual.

"Damn it!."

"What?," Miryssia wondered.

"I can hear all the birds," Jazmyn informed, pulling her hood over her ears.

"It's a beautiful sound, all chirps and peeps."

"Not when you can understand what all the chirps mean."

"Sorry, I forgot you could talk to animals. Must be cool to do that," Miryssia said.

"I wish I could just hear their songs," Jazmyn said, then pointed at a couple of birds sitting on a limb just above them. "They are not singing; they are trying to figure out where to build a nest. He wants to use that birch tree over there and she wants the bigger oak tree they are sitting because it withstands the weather better."

"It just sounds like a typical relationship to me."

Jazmyn smirk a little, "And that one...."

"What's wrong with that one?"

"Shh," Jazmyn held her finger up; she strained to hear

voices in the distance, she couldn't make out all of the words, but she listened to her name, "Two squirrels are talking about me."

"And?" Miryssia inquired, trying to listen too.

Jazmyn moved a little closer, "They are saying that I am going to be the one to save them."

"I guess news travels fast, even in the animal kingdom."

"Yes, it does."

Miryssia and Jazmyn both jumped then turned to find Abraham standing there.

"Hi ya Abe," Miryssia said.

"Hey," Jazmyn said.

"Good morning, Ladies," Abraham bowed a little and proceeded back towards his house.

When they arrived at the house, Miryssia went up to her room. Abraham leads Jazmyn to his study.

After Abraham closed the doors, the room seemed to come alive. The lights came on just enough to see. Jazmyn looked around; a giant fireplace built with oversized boulders made up most of the face in the middle of the far wall. Moss covered most of the chimney rocks with tiny flowers growing from them. Next to it was a small table with a book laying upside down, marking the page. The chair next to it looked like it was growing out of the floor. Her eyes followed it up until she noticed branches with leaves on them.

"Is it real?" Jazmyn asked.

"Yes, Theia helped me with this room. The tree was her touch to the room.

Abraham motioned Jazmyn over towards a table off to one side. It had a few bottles filled with herbs and other things. She didn't want to know what was in them. A small cauldron sat on top of a ring of stone. Under the cauldron was a fire burning from thin air.

"I've been in this house a lot of times when I was younger, but I don't remember seeing any of this," Jazmyn said, still looking around.

"Until you became a witch, All of this remained hidden

from your eyes and now that you are one, there are many things that will become visible to you," Abraham said. "It is now time to teach you about potions."

"I have read about potions from my book, but I don't see the purpose of them. It seems to me that you can do everything with just magic itself."

"Yes, It does seem that you can do anything you wanted with magic, but you can not," Abraham informed her. He picked up a block of wood and placed it on the table. "Turn this into metal with a spell."

"Okay, let see," Jazmyn pondered. "Take this chunk of wood and turn it to metal where it stood."

The piece of wood rose up, floated in the air and spun around, and settled back down, with a metallic shine to it.

"See," She boasted.

No sooner as she said that, the wood returned to its normal state.

"What happened?"

"Magic can not solve everything," Abraham answered. "You need a potion to make it stay that way."

Abraham picked up a vial of a green solution and poured it on the piece of wood, and it burst into flames with a green hue; within a few moments, a solid piece of metal shaped as the wood replaced it.

Jazmyn reached over and picked it up, "It's heavy."

"Yes, it is. You see, you can't use magic all the time. Potions have many uses. A witch can mix up one to heal wounds, help a person sleep at night," Abraham explained as he walked around. "Use of potions can reveal unknown truths. You can even mix a potion to mimics powers like molecule manipulation of time or even teleporting."

Jazmyn picked up a container labeled dried Dragon's liver, making a weird face, "Why would need a potion to copy a power?."

"When a witch is too weak or for non-magical witches that have practice for many years," Abraham answered, moving over to a bookcase. He pulled out a small black book.

"This is my potions book. Please turn it to the first potion," Abraham handed the book to Jazmyn.

"It's empty," Jazmyn explained when she flipped through the pages.

"Look again."

She turned to the first page; the ink faded in, revealing the words.

"You should have all that you will need to make the potion."

'Wood to Metal.' was the title on the page. It read almost like a regular recipe, but ordinary people wouldn't cook with most of these ingredients.

The first thing on the list was Beryllium dust; the dust was black with silver flex. She poured the amount called for into the small cauldron; next, she added a few dashes of Crystallized Ocean Water.

"When you add the next ingredient, be careful," Abraham warned.

"No problem, I helped mom cook when I was younger," Jazmyn stated, confidently looking at Abraham.

She reached for the Acetic Acid, glancing at the worn page; it said to add three drops the size of tears. She took the dropper out of the bottle and put it over the cauldron, and squeezed it; she watched every drop. With the last one, she sighed with relief nothing happened; then, without warning, the potion exploded, knocking her on her butt.

"What happened?" Jazmyn shook her head to get the ringing out of her head.

"You must be precise with your measurement; your last drop was a little too much," Abraham explained, helping her up.

She looked into the cauldron; it was empty. Abraham smiled and instructed her to try it again. After a few minor explosions and restarts, she was getting more frustrated with every try.

"You must clear your mind of distractions."

She closed her eyes to clear her mind, but her thoughts raced back to the reason why she even had to do all of this, Allison.

"Is there something the matter?" Abraham asked, seeing Jazmyn wincing her face.

"Nothing," Jazmyn snapped.

After a few seconds, when her thoughts cleared, "Ready."

This time she got through the whole process without it exploding. She was ready it try her potions on a block of wood. She grabbed the wood and poured her potion on it, and nothing happened.

"I can't do this," Jazmyn hung her shoulders then sat down next to the fireplace.

"Yes, you can, it just takes time and reading the potion to the letter," Abraham said.

"I did."

"Reread it," Abraham brought the book over to her.

She reread it and realized that she needed to turn to the next page with the last step, "Let sit for at least five minutes before using."

She got back up, remixed everything, then tried it, and this time it worked.

"I knew you could do it, now move on to the next potion," Abraham instructed.

Jazmyn worked at making potions until the afternoon sunlight up the west window.

"That will be all for today," Abraham informed. "Potions are an important part of the magical world."

"I know that now, Thank you." Jazmyn hugged Abraham and then noticed Arion standing in the doorway, "Hey."

"Hi," Arion said, moving into the room.

"Hello, Arion." Abraham said, "Would you like to escort Jazmyn back to the tree?"

"Ah, sure."

"See you later, Abraham," Jazmyn walked out the front door.

Arion grabbed Jazmyn's coat and helped her put it on, "Thanks."

"No worries, mate," Arion said, trying to do his best Australian accent.

Jazmyn noticed that the spring-like weather was taking more and more snow as the sun's rays were getting warmer as the two of them walked.

"Did you learn a lot, today?" Arion wondered.

"Yes, It's just like baking but a little more intense, I learned that the hard way," Jazmyn rubbed her backside. "Did you have to learn to make potions?"

"Yeah, I learned by landing on my ass too, "Arion leaned in. "Personally, I think Abraham gets a chuckle out of it. I only learned a few of the basic ones."

"Why only a few?"

"Not sure, they concentrated on learning about healing and fighting skills."

They walked a few paces down the trail before Jazmyn turned to Arion.

"Speaking of fighting, you and I should spend more time together, I mean with you-I-fighting stuff. You know what I mean." Jazmyn stammered, then looked away.

"Umm-okay," Arion said, running his fingers through his hair.

Jazmyn and Arion walked the rest of the way in silence; Glancing over at each other every once in a while.

∞∞∞

A knock came on her door that startled Jazmyn from the little sleep she had received. She tossed and turned all night. She didn't think if she dared to continue with this mission.

"Jazmyn, it's Miryssia. I have someone here that would like to see you," Miryssia said.

Who could that be?

Jazmyn jumped out of bed.

What if it's Arion? I must look hideous.

She stood in the middle of her room, not knowing what to do first. Her heart beating like crazy, "Give me a minute."

She quickly threw some clothes on and ran a brush through her hair, adjusting her clothes once more before promptly open the door with a smile on her face.

"Nice smile, Jaz," Izzie said, smiling back, walked through the door.

"Hey, Izzie, Miryssia," Jazmyn said, her smile slowly fading.

"This is crazy. How did you move your whole room here?" Izzie asked, looking around.

"She didn't, Allison did it," Miryssia said.

"What are you doing here? You shouldn't be here; you should leave," Jazmyn said.

"Why should I leave?" Izzie inquired.

"She means she would like to leave with us to go do some shopping," Miryssia stated from behind Izzie's back, shaking her head at Jazmyn.

"How did you know I was here to take you shopping? Oh, never mind you're a witch you probably saw the future or something," Izzie said.

"Yeah, that's it, you caught me doing witchy stuff," Jazmyn lowered her eyes.

"I'll join you if you guys don't mind," Miryssia said.

"That's fine with me," Izzie looked Jazmyn up and down, "I bet you have another pair of socks like that."

Jazmyn looked down at her mismatched socks, "Damn."

"I will let you get ready; I will go check out this tree," Izzie said.

"K," Jazmyn said as Izzie went out the door.

"I need to tell Izzie about what's going to happen. I can't let her go back to that town," Jazmyn said as she fixed her socks.

"Look, Theia and Abraham said they didn't want anyone to know what's going to happen."

"How am I going to act like nothing is going to happen when literally all hell is going to break loose."

"You're going to have to until we can come up with a plan," Miryssia said.

Against Jazmyn's better judgment, she was forced to agree, with a nod of her head, then grabbed her boots and forced them on and threw her jacket on suddenly stopped.

"I thought I had to stay here because of it the safest place for me," Jazmyn said.

"There is a way around that, I am going to teach you," Miryssia said.

"How?" Jazmyn wondered.

"Glamour," Miryssia said.

"You are going to put makeup on me, and that will what, fool everyone," Jazmyn scoffed.

"In away. Come closer," Miryssia said. Jazmyn moved toward her.

"Glamour is a magical way of projecting the illusion of a person or animal."

Jazmyn tapped her finger on her chin, "That must of been Theia who warned me, at my work."

"Nope. That was me. Theia and Abraham protected you at the theater from dumb ass."

"So, all of you guys have been watching out for me for a while."

Miryssia cracked a smile and nodded, "Yeah, let me show you."

A glow surrounded Miryssia, then suddenly, Abraham was standing in front of Jazmyn.

"Just simple as that," Miryssia said.

"Weird, but you still sound like yourself," Jazmyn commented.

"Yes, I was showing you can glamour into anyone you want, male or female. I haven't been able to change my voice yet, but it's possible." Miryssia said, changing back to herself. "So, I usually turn into some girl.

"How do you do that?" Jazmyn said.

"Just clear your mind and then think of someone you want to look like and then say to yourself. I picture in my mind who I want to be." Miryssia instructed.

Jazmyn nodded, took a deep breath, cleared her mind, pictured her mother, and recited the incantation. She could feel her body shiver a little, and she looked down at her hands; the veins popped out, a few age spots peppered her hands.

"Weird, I have my mother's hands," Jazmyn's voice cracked.

She went to her mirror; slight wrinkles appeared, gray highlights interlaced with her hair, and her eye color changed from green to blue. Jazmyn blinked; her mother was staring back at her.

"Wow, how do I look," Jazmyn said but with her mother's voice.

"You even sound like her," Miryissa commented. "You're a natural."

"How do you turn back?" Jazmyn asked.

"Just think of yourself, then repeat the spell."

"OK, let's go," Jazmyn said.

"Aren't you going to turn into some else?" Miryssia asked.

"Just wait," Jazmyn said as she walks out and looks for her friend Izzie and found her admiring the meeting table.

"Oh, Mrs. W, I didn't know you were here," Izzie said.

"Hello, Izzie there is something I want to talk to you about," Jazmyn said, not trying to let out a giggle.

"What?" Izzie inquired.

"I want to tell you that you are a bad influence on Jazmyn,"

"What do you mean?" Izzie surprisingly said.

"Got ya," Jazmyn said as she turned back into herself.

"That is so cool, talk about a major makeover," Izzie said.

"I see you learned another skill," Allison spoke as she materialized out of the book. "Hello, Izzie."

"Whoa, she could be your twin," Izzie stated. "Hey."

"This is Allison, she is Jazmyn's ancestor," Miryssia said

after realizing Jazmyn wasn't going to say anything.

"I see you are ready to go somewhere, where are you off to?" Allison asked.

"Shopping," Jazmyn said sharply. "Let's get going."

"What was that all about?" Miryssia wondered when they stepped out of the oak tree.

"Nothing," Jazmyn said.

"OK, then. Before we leave, you should change," Miryssia said.

"What's wrong with what she has on, she looks so cute in that outfit," Izzie said.

"She means to change my looks to someone else," Jazmyn said.

"You change into someone famous, like Angelina Jolie or that one girl that plays Supergirl um... Melissa Benoist," Izzie said.

"We can't draw attention to our selves," Miryssia said.

Jazmyn stood there and thought of someone that she knew that she could pretend to be. She remembered a high school friend, she spoke the words, and she turned into a blond-haired girl who wore glasses and was shorter.

"Who are you suppose to be?" Miryssia asked.

"A friend I knew from high school, her name is Amy," Jazmyn said.

"OK, Amy, let's go," Izzie said.

They all climbed into Jazmyn's old car and headed to town. She sat there most of the time, thinking about what had happened the night before.

How could Allison be so cold towards Wen, especially after Wen tried to explain he was trying to help not hurt her family.

Jazmyn was getting upset with her ancestor. "How are you so stupid!"

"What do you mean, stupid? I am only a few miles over the speed limit," Izzie remarked.

"What?, oh sorry, I wasn't talking to you," Jazmyn said.

"So, where is your mind at?" Miryssia asked, peeking through the space between the front seats.

"Last night, when I disappeared on you and the others, I met a wolf named Syann, and she took me to talk to her wolf pack," Jazmyn explained.

"You met who now?" Izzie asked.

As they continued down the road, Jazmyn filled them in on what happened the night before.

"So, what are you going to say to Allison?" Miryssia wondered as they got out of the car at the department store.

"I am not sure, yet," Jazmyn said. "Let's just forget it for now."

$$\infty \infty \infty$$

Miryssia and Izzie shook their heads, and then all of them aimed towards the clothing department in the store. They spent most of the morning trying on clothes and joking around. Jazmyn tried her best to forget what was happening around the town and not warning Izzie about it.

"Now that we have some outfits, we should consider accessories," Izzie stated and led them to the jewelry department.

As they walked there, they saw Arion trying to find some jeans and decided to see him.

"Hi, Arion," Jazmyn said.

"Hi?" Arion said with a shaky voice.

He looked at Miryssia, and Izzie with a puzzled look.

"Hey," Miryssia said.

"Do we know each other? Who are you? and have you ladies seen Jazmyn?" Arion asked.

"It's...My name is Amy, I am a friend of Izzie's," Jazmyn said.

"What?. But you are...," Izzie said.

"Nice to meet you," Jazmyn interrupted, giving a glance at Izzie.

"Same to you, Miryssia, could I talk to you, in private. Excuse us," Arion said as he ushered Miryssia into the next aisle.

"Why didn't you want Arion to know it was you?" Izzie question.

"I was going to trick him as I did you, but now I wonder what they are talking about," Jazmyn said.

Jazmyn stood there and thought for a bit and then looked around, then suddenly morphed into a man.

"I will find out," winked at Izzie and walked into the next aisle.

"Miryssia, You have known Jazmyn for a long time, Right?. Um. I want to ask her out, but I don't know-how," Arion said.

"That's easy, just ask her?" Miryssia asked.

"It's easy for you. I think I like her," Arion said.

"Yess!" Jazmyn said.

Arion and Miryssia looked at this man standing next to them; both shared the same look of 'What the.'

"Oh, Sorry," Jazmyn cleared her throat and tried to add some bass to her voice. "I got a little excited; this store finally got the underwear I like." Jazmyn picked up a package off the hook and then disappeared around the isle.

Jazmyn returned to her form and ran up to Izzie with a big smile on her face.

"What happened?" Izzie asked.

"I just found out he likes me," Jazmyn said, trying to hold herself together.

"That's awesome," Izzie said.

"What am I going to do now? He was asking Miryssia if should he ask me out," Jazmyn said.

"And she said?" Izzie wondered.

"I don't know. I was too excited to stick around to find out,"

"Well, change yourself again and go find out," Izzie stated.

"I guess I could do...." Jazmyn started to say.

She looked out the department store window and saw someone with a hood looking in the window at her. She looked closer, and it was of Diomedes's warhog.

"Shit!" Jazmyn yelled when she realized that she didn't morph back into Amy.

"Jazmyn?!" Arion said as he and Miryssia came around the corner.

"What is it?" Miryssia asked, then looked in the same direction as Izzie and Jazmyn was and suddenly saw the bad news.

"Did he see you? Kinda weird for them to show themselves out in public," Miryssia inquired.

"I don't know if it saw me, Diomedes is probably getting desperate," Jazmyn whispered. "Let's get to the fitting rooms and get out of here," Jazmyn said.

"Where is that friend of Izzie, Amy?" Arion wondered.

"Ah, she left already," Jazmyn said.

"Why the fitting rooms, we should head for the back door and what about my car?" Izzie stated.

"We'll come back later. Just trust us, let's go," Jazmyn said.

They all crouched low and worked their way to the fitting rooms, and rushed in. Jazmyn took Arion into one, and Miryssia and Izzie went into the other.

"Excuse me, Only one at a time in the rooms," A worker said as both doors slammed shut.

They all teleported back to the oak tree. Izzie stood there for a while, trying to find the horizon again. Her body found it, but her head didn't, so she stumbled to the bushes and threw up.

"You could have warned me," Izzie said, coming back out.

"Sorry, there was no time," Miryssia said.

They all proceeded down the stairs; Theia was standing next to Allison, talking.

Theia turned and looked at them, "Where were you? You are supposed to stay here and study."

"Izzie and I took her shopping," Miryssia said. "I taught her to glamour, so she wouldn't be seen."

"You were there the whole time?" Arion wondered.

Jazmyn shied away and nodded her head. She felt a little guilty now.

"Did you hear...," Arion began.

"Aw, we saw a warhog, so we ran," Jazmyn piped in.

"Was anyone hurt? I thought you were in disguise?" Theia wondered.

"No, and Yes, I was, but I turned back into myself, but I don't think it saw me," Jazmyn said.

"That's good," Allison commented.

"Yeah, as you if," Jazmyn said under her breath and glared at Allison.

"What?" Allison puzzled.

"Nothing," Jazmyn said, Miryssia looking at her.

"It is time for Jazmyn to learn some more of her craft," Theia said.

Chapter Nineteen

Jazmyn sat on her bed, slumped over her book, trying to concentrate. She had an uneasy feeling. She looked to see Theia standing in the doorway. "Can we talk?"

"About?" Jazmyn asked, shifting farther into the corner of the bed.

Theia strolled over and sat on the edge of the bed, "What you learned from Syann."

Shutting her book, Jazmyn let a short huff of air, "I don't want to talk about it."

"I know you are upset," Theia sympathized.

"Upset!" Jazmyn could feel her anger rising.

Her necklace began to glow, the room responded by coming to life, the bed started to shake, her alarm clock flew across the room and smashed against the wall, the dresser tipped over.

Theia could hear an eerie cracking sound; she shot up from the bed and looked out of the window, and saw a rift in the shroud of magic protecting the tree. She turned, "Jazmyn, please calm yourself." Theia said with a silky smooth voice.

Jazmyn took a deep breath, "Sorry."

"You will need to learn to control it more," Theia said, looking back at Jazmyn as she waved her hand and the room fixed itself.

Abraham rushed into her bedroom, "I felt a disturbance, what happened?"

"Jazmyn lost control of her magic and it cracked the shroud," Theia answered.

"I did what?" Jazmyn panic and went to the window and saw the damage she did, "I didn't mean to do that."

"I know you didn't, but you need to learn to control your temper. Anger is a potent emotion, and our magic comes from our emotions." Theia informed.

"I know." Jazmyn agreed, "How are we going to repair the crack?"

"We will figure out that later, I do not think it's big enough to worry about," Abraham inserted. "Why are you so angry?"

"We were about to discuss that," Theia said and gave that look that Abraham knew well enough, and he excused himself to leave them alone.

Theia waved her hand and everything went back in its place in the room. She sat down on her bed while Jazmyn strolled a few paces and leaned against her dresser, fidgeting with her assorted lipsticks she collected that she never wears anymore, awaiting Theia's questions.

"I understand how you can be upset with Allison, but you need to forgive her," Theia explained.

"How? My life was my life before I learned of all of this," Jazmyn stated, picking up a comb to use it as a pointer. "Now, I am here to clean up after someone that failed to do it right in the beginning."

"You are part of a line of witches that have died protecting that necklace from evil," Theia stated as she walked over to Jazmyn and pointed at the necklace.

"Yes, I know, but I can't forgive Allison."

Jazmyn felt her anger flaring; she walked over to the window and opened it to help her cool down.

"Do you see that out there?" Theia asked, joining Jazmyn at the window.

Jazmyn looked around, "What?" she snapped.

"Nature, without your forgiveness, you are committing this land to die. We all need to work as a team to make sure nature lives on."

"What do you mean?"

"A team must trust each other. If you keep holding on to this anger for Allison, you will doom us to fail like the vision the twins seen."

"I am supposed to be this all-powerful witch, so I don't need her help," Jazmyn stated. "Besides, she is not even alive, how much can she help when she is stuck here."

"She might not be of this world anymore, but she has knowledge that she can share with us, and can guide you with that knowledge."

"All I need to do is read my book," Jazmyn paused and looked back to her book. "Everything I need to know is in there."

"That book is, in a sense, Allison," Theia went over and grabbed her book and brought it to Jazmyn. "Forgive her and learn from her."

Theia placed her book in Jazmyn's hands, and with a smile, she left.

Jazmyn looked down at the crest on her book then looked back out the window.

She fought with herself.

Allison does know a lot, but why wouldn't she accept help when it was offered to her.

"Kinds sounds like me," Jazmyn bit lip, "a little."

A movement caught her eye, she turned her head to see Arion jogging by, and it was like all her thoughts went silent.

He must have been on the trail for a while; he was drenched in sweat; she could see his t-shirt conform to his body.

Heat rose from somewhere deep inside; she looked down to see her hands on fire, and she let out a little scream.

Arion stopped and looked up at her. Her face felt it was burning, and tried to act cool and just waved at him while her hand still were on fire.

"Are you alright!" Arion yelled up, wiping his forehead.

Jazmyn shook her and hands violently try to extinguish them, "YA!, I..., I am good, just practicing."

"Need a break? Want to join me?"

Her hands flared up again as she felt hot again, "Ah, ya,

give me a minute," She turns and concentrated on her hands, and they finally went back to normal.

She darted to her dresser, looking for her workout clothes, and realized they were dirty. "Now what am I going to do?"

Her eyes lit up, and she imagined herself with her workout clothes cleaned, and on her, with a wave, she was ready to go, "Nice."

When Jazmyn opened the door, she found Arion sitting on the root of the oak tree, "Hey."

"Hey," Arion said. "How's it going?"

"Just fine," Jazmyn lied and turned and put her leg up on a root to stretch.

"Studying hard?" Arion said, moving in front of her.

"I was until I was interrupted," Jazmyn stated.

"I didn't mean to take you away, I..."

"No, no, it wasn't you," Jazmyn interjected, putting her head down. "It was someone else.

"Are you alright?" Arion reached and cupped her chin and lifted her head. "What's bothering you?"

Jazmyn took a deep breath and opened her mouth to say something but stopped, "Are you ready? let's go."

She took off down the path leaving Arion standing there.

"Ya, I guess," Arion said and went after her.

Arion jogged next to her for about a quarter of a mile before opening his mouth, "You know you can talk to me and I won't say anything to anyone else."

"I know," She agreed. "Not here, not now."

It was silent except for the thumping of their feet on the ground.

"OK, Let's get back."

They continued with their jog when they arrived back at the tree. Her mother was heading towards the door carrying a basket.

"Hey, Ma," Jazmyn said, running up to her.

"Oh, I thought you would be studying. Hello, Arion."

"Hello, Mrs. Wolff," Arion said. "I will let you two talk. See you later, Jazmyn."

"K, Bye," Jazmyn wave her hand a little and smiled.

"You can call me Gloria, you know. Bye."

Arion smiled then nodded, "Ok."

Gloria watched her daughter's face, seeing a gleam in her eyes, "He is such a nice young man. It looks like you two are getting along well."

Realizing she was staring at Arion as he left, Jazmyn snapped back and looked at her mom.

"Yeah, I guess. What's in the basket?" Jazmyn asked, looking down at her mother's hand.

"I brought you some of my chicken soup and couple of biscuits," her mom said.

"Thanks, Do you want to come in and see inside of the tree?"

"No, I don't want to bother, I just brought this for you."

"K, thank you," Jazmyn said and reached for the basket.

It fell out of her mother's hand and stopped it in mid-air. Jazmyn looked around and saw a bird, caught in mid-flight, hanging in the sky.

"Mom?" She said, seeing her mother froze with a funny look on her face.

Jazmyn realized she stopped everything; she reached and grabbed the basket, and the world began moving again.

"OH. My," Her mother said. "Glad you were fast enough to catch that.

"Yeah," Jazmyn smirked a little. "Bye."

Jazmyn walked down the stairs and found the main room empty and spread out her meal on the table and found that her mother even packed silverware. She loved her mother's chicken noodle soup; it was made with homemade noodles. She had tried to make them a few times but never got them right.

∞ ∞ ∞

After eating, Jazmyn paged through her book of shadows, reading about demons and how they have all sorts of different powers and ways of doing evil. The rest of the gang left, but Allison was sitting down at the head of the table reading.

Some demons will possess humans to kill other humans, so the demon world stays hidden. Others like to steal powers from witches and or other afflictions.

Jazmyn shook her head at all the different kinds there are.

"Is there something wrong?" Allison inquired.

"It's just...never mind." Jazmyn flared a glance at Allison.

Jazmyn grabbed her book and went into her made-up bedroom, sat on her bed.

Moments later her door suddenly opened, and Theia stood there with a strange look on her face. "Come quick!"

"What's going on?" Jazmyn asked as she closed her book, tossed it on her bed, and headed out the door.

Theia said nothing, leading her up the stairs and out towards her mother's cabin.

A dreaded feeling came over Jazmyn, "Is there something wrong with mother?"

She didn't wait for an answer; she rushed past Theia and busted the door open.

"Mom?!"

Her stomach felt as though rocks were tumbling in it, and tears started to flow from Jazmyn's eyes when she saw Arion standing over her mother; she was lying on the couch. Her mother's face was sunk in; her eyes were glazed over with a black film.

"What's wrong with her?" Jazmyn questioned as she knelt next to her and held her cold, clammy hand.

"We don't know," Theia said.

"I have tried to heal her, but my powers can't touch this," Arion said.

"How did this happen?" Jazmyn inquired.

"I came over to talk to her," Theia said. "I found her on the living room floor convulsing. I put her on the sofa to she make her more comfortable."

"Jazmyn?" her mother's weak voice spoke.

"I'm here, mama, I am here."

"I saw your father, is he still here?" Gloria strained to talk.

"No, Dad isn't here. He is not here," Jazmyn said, looked up at Theia.

"I saw him. He hugged me and kissed me. He told me he was going to go find you to tell you he got away," Gloria said.

"Are you sure he was here? Maybe you thought you saw Dad," Jazmyn said.

Gloria raised her head a little. "He was here! Your father was just as close to me as you are now. Believe me."

"We believe you, Gloria, rest now," Theia said.

Gloria laid her head back down and closed her eyes, and fell asleep.

"I have to go find my Dad!" Jazmyn said.

She sprang to her feet with the spark of hope in her eyes.

"I really don't believe he was here," Theia noted.

"You heard her, what she said. I have to tell him about Mom."

"I believe Diomedes had a hand in this," Theia said.

Hope vanished from her eyes. "That son of a bitch!" then turned to see Abraham, Miryssia, and the twins suddenly appeared.

"Abraham, I believe Gloria was poisoned," Theia said.

Abraham went to Gloria's side and bent down to examine her.

Jazmyn began to pace the floor to do something. Arion went over to her. "Are you alright?"

"Do you think I am alright? I am pissed off! He attack my mother; he has my father! I want to get that piece of shit!" Jazmyn exclaimed.

"I understand," Arion said, not knowing what to say.

"No, you don't!" Jazmyn glared at him.

"Have you found anything, Abraham?" Theia asked to break the mood.

"One moment," Abraham said as he carefully looked at Gloria's lips.

Abraham produced a vile out of thin air and pressed it against the corner of Gloria's mouth, and collected a single drop of yellow liquid.

"What is it?" Theia queried.

"Not sure, I need to take this back to my house to try to figure it out," Abraham said, then turn to Jazmyn. "I know that you are angry, but you have to control your emotions. Diomedes is trying to get to you and you must not let him."

Jazmyn nodded her head. "ok."

"We will find out we can," Abraham said. "Tony, Tina, come with me so that you can share your vision."

"Arion and Miryssia, you stay here with Jazmyn, but don't take too long," Theia said, put her hand on Gloria, and with a glow, she and her mother were gone, then Abraham and the twins disappeared.

"Where did they go?" Jazmyn said.

"Probably to Abraham's," Miryssia said.

"Without me."

"I am sure once they get some news they will let you go," Arion said.

"I am going," Jazmyn huffed.

"Just stay here for a bit," Miryssia said.

Jazmyn nodded, and got up and wandered around the house. She stopped to look at the crystals; her mom likes to hang to cast rainbows on the walls, but it was like they knew something was wrong, no rainbows.

"You guys were so worried about me, making sure I was safe," Jazmyn stated as she entered the living room again. "Not letting me warn my mother and Izzie about any of this!"

"We didn't know this would happen," Miryssia countered

"We are trying to protect everyone, "Arion said.

"Protect! If this is how you protect people, it's not working!" Jazmyn disagreed.

A bright light illuminated the room coming from

Jazmyn's necklace; things around them were moving, disappear-ing, and reappearing. The house started to shake.

"Jazmyn, you need to cool it," Miryssia said, trying to keep her voice calm.

The couch lifted off the floor, headed towards Arion; he ducked out of the way. Miryssia deflected the TV away from her. The floorboard's nails were loosening.

"Arion, you got to do something!," Miryssia yelled over the radio that is now blaring.

"What?," Arion blurted. "You are a witch."

"Yeah, But I don't know what to do," Miryssia glancing over to Arion.

Arion went over to her and grabbed her shoulders, "Jazmyn, do you want to go out with me!"

Jazmyn looked at him with confusion, then all the furni-ture stopped and dropped to the floor.

"I am sorry," Jazmyn pinched her brows together and shook her head. "What?"

"What?" Miryssia echoed.

Jazmyn looked at Arion. "My mother has been poisoned and she might die and you ask me that."

"I panicked."

Miryssia glared at Arion, then turned to Jazmyn, "Are you good?"

"Yeah, I guess." Jazmyn answered, walking out of the living room.

"We should clean this place up," Arion added, trying to for-get the awkwardness of what just happened.

"'We? There is no we, not after that, you can do this your-self." Miryssia shook her head and left the room.

She found Jazmyn sitting at the table, staring at her mother's coffee cup with tears flowing down her cheek. She slowly sat down across from Jazmyn.

"Everything will be fine. Abe is good at what he does; he'll figure out about your mother." Miryssia reassured.

Jazmyn shook her head, then raised her eyes, wiping the

tears away, "I'm sorry for blowing up in there."

"It's all right to get mad, but in our case, the emotion we feel can and will influence our magic. You need to learn to curb it a little."

"I know, this isn't the first time my emotions got the best of me. I would like to see my mom," Jazmyn said.

"Ok." Miryssia agreed.

They both got up from the table, "Let's go, Romeo!" Miryssia yelled.

Arion came in, flashed a glance at Jazmyn, and she held out her hand; he took it; then, they all vanished.

They reappeared in Abraham's house and found him in the library, looking through a stack of books.

"Where is my mother? Is she upstairs?" Jazmyn asked.

"No, she is in…a special place," Abraham announced, looking up from his book.

"What special place," Jazmyn threw her arms up. "I want to see her!"

Abraham got up and walked over to her. "I know you do. Miryssia and Arion, could you excuse us?"

Miryssia and Arion went upstairs; Abraham led Jazmyn towards the basement.

Jazmyn hesitating before she took each step. A tears fell, soaking her cheeks, looked around, expecting to see her mother, but she wasn't anywhere.

Abraham looked at Jazmyn; he guided her to the mystery door. He paused at the entrance and spoke a spell that Jazmyn couldn't understand; the door then opened.

Both twins stepped out and headed for the stairs; they both looked at her, "Everything will be fine."

Jazmin found little comfort in that; she hesitated to step through the threshold; the room was dark except for the glowing shell over her mother.

"I put your mother in a state of deep sleep to slow the poison," Abraham said. With a wave of his hand, the whole room lit up.

She shuffled her feet, fidget with her hands to her mother's side; her mother looked so peaceful, like Jazmyn remembered standing by her bedside as a child watching her sleep before she would wake her up to make sure she wasn't leaving her like her father.

Jazmyn scanned her, "Is she going to be ok?"

"She will be fine as long as she stays here. Until I find the cure for your mother," Abraham said as he went over to his work table, which was full of vials and books opened and stacked.

"Can she hear me?" Jazmyn slowly turned her head.

Abraham nodded and turned to his book.

"Mom, If you can, hear me. Please don't leave me. I need you to be a part of my life." Jazmyn sobbed. "The soup was good."

Chapter Twenty

Jazmyn emerged from the basement. The daylight didn't help her to find her way out of the darkness that shrouded her mind. Wandering outside, tears falling off her cheeks. The world around her didn't exist; the only thing she could see was how everything was going wrong.

She found herself at the shore of the lake; she sat down, wrapping her arms around her knees, she rocked back and forth, staring out into the water. She thought back to when she made her mom mad, and all the arguments they used to get into now seem trivial. She would take them all back if it meant her mom was going to be alright.

A buzzing of her phone startled her; she took it out of her pocket and seen it was Izzie. Jazmyn hit the ignore button.

Not now, Izzie.

A few moments later, her phone notified her of a new voice mail; She just shut her phone off.

Something across the lake caught her eye. She wiped them clear; it was a man peeking into her mother's windows.

She made her way around the lake; the ground resisted her footfalls with a snapping of twigs and leaves. The man pauses as if he heard the noise; Jazmyn crouched down behind a fallen tree.

A few heartbeats later, she produced an energy ball. She peeked up.

"Dad?"

The man turned to face her; a shot of excitement went

through her. She extinguished the energy ball, jumped over the log, launching herself towards him, wrapping her arms around him, and hugged him with everything she had. Her tears flowed once more.

She pushed him away at arm's length and stared, taking a moment in, "Your here, now, aren't you? This is real?" Jazmyn smiled.

"Yes, Jazmyn, it's me," Stephen said.

She hadn't heard his voice in such a long time; she barely could remember how comforting it was. She sat a log before her knees gave into their weakness.

"How-how are you here? What are you doing here? I thought you were locked up."

"I was locked up, but Diomedes wanted me to help him with all the captured people, I led him to believe I would," her dad sat next to her. "At the first chance, I slipped away."

"I am so happy that you did. My life has changed so much since you've been gone. I am a witch now, and I guess always have been."

"I know, you are," Stephen said.

"How?" Jazmyn arching one of her eyebrows in interest.

"Your mother told me all about it when I went to see her."

"OH, mom," She shot up. "Mom is very sick. We think Diomedes poison her somehow. Was she alright when you seen her?"

"She was fine when I was there."

"He must have done it after you left. I will take you to her, let's go."

Grabbing his hand, she pulls him along back to Abraham's house.

When they arrived, Abraham met them at the threshold, "Stephen?"

"Yes, who are you?" Stephen inquired, sizing him up.

"Hello, I am Abraham," he said as he offered his hand. Stephen was hesitant to reach for it; he glared at Abraham then shook his hand.

Abraham felt a slight jolt of energy as their hands separated. He mumbled to himself, "That's odd."

"We want to see my mom," Jazmyn gestured with her hand to guide her dad down to the basement.

Abraham stepped in front of them, "I must apologize I put a spell on her to help me find out what is making her sick and you will interrupt it."

"How long?" Jazmyn said, wrinkling her brow.

"It shouldn't take more than an hour or two, it's hard to tell." Abraham slowly turned as he closed the door.

"We should go back to Gloria's house and get to know one other again," Stephen said.

Jazmyn scratched her head, "Gloria's house? you mean mom's house."

Stephen lowered his eyes and paced a few steps, "Sorry, It's been hard on me being away so long," clearing his throat, "It feels like I hardly know her."

She peaked her eyebrow up and looked at him.

I guess it has been a while.

The way back around the lake was quiet except for a whisper of wind through the leaves. Every once in a while, the wind blew hard as if it was saying, "Watch out."

It spooked Jazmyn; her hand instinctively went for her dad's hand, like a little girl seeking comfort, but he just pulled his hand away.

When they arrived back at the house, Jazmyn went for the coffee maker; she needed some caffeine, "Hey, Dad?." Her eyes widen a little; a smile came across her face; it seemed forever ago since she said those words.

"Yes?" Stephen looked up at her from the kitchen table.

"Did you want some coffee? I bet it's been a while," Jazmyn stated, getting a filter for the machine.

"A while for what?" Stephen answer with a blank look.

She turned to face him with the filters in her hands, trying to separate them, "For coffee. Are you alright?"

"Of course, I am alright, just trying to adjust," he smiled, then look down. "And yes, I will have some coffee."

Once she had the coffee maker up and running, she took down a couple of cups and placed them on the counter.

"I have missed you so much. For the longest time mom told me that you were dead," Jazmyn lowered her eyes a little. "Only after I was told I was a witch, she told me that Diomedes captured you."

She turned to see if the coffee was made, biting the inside of her lip, "I saw you when you in that cage and how they were treating you like an animal."

His mouth fell open, then glared, "How?!"

Jazmyn snapped her head back around.

"I can look through other people's eye," she squeaked out, then cleared her throat and spoke a normal. "To see what others see."

"I am sorry for that," Stephen said with an offset smile, and his voice cracked. "What did you see?"

Grasping the pot's handle when the bell went off, Jazmyn bought it over and poured the black liquid into the white cups.

Jazmyn glanced at her dad when she came back to sit down, "Just you sitting in a cage with bony knees."

Her dad just looked at her with a blank stare. That uneasy feeling came back; chills teased her spine on the way up to her head. Leaning forward in her chair with her cup in front of her. Her necklace peeked out from under her shirt, "How did you get so healthy it wasn't too long ago I had my vision?"

Stephen took a sip of his coffee and covered his mouth, "That's taste horrible!." He pushed the cup away and sat back.

Eyes widen, Jazmyn, looked at the cup, then him then back again, "Sorry, did you want some sugar or cream?"

"No," averting his eyes to her necklace.

Jazmyn followed his gaze to her necklace; she pulled it out and displayed it between her fingers, "Yeah, this is mine, this is where all my powers come from."

Stephen almost yanked it off her neck but slowed his hand down and reached for it; it began to glow. Jazmyn glanced at the pendent, "Must be something wrong with this."

He quickly withdrew, the glowing ceased, he sat back again, pushing himself a little farther away.

Jazmyn focused her eyes on the pendant.

Why would it do that?. Maybe he isn't my dad. Ah, of course, he is.

She noticed his forehead glistened with sweat.

Or isn't he?

Everything in her was trying to warn her, but she ignored it. She did want to give in to her thoughts.

This is my dad. He got to be. I have waited so long for this to happen.

Her mother lay what could be her death bed; her emotions couldn't take much more of this crazy roller coaster ride she's been on since her birthday.

Her dad sat up straight, saying, "There is something I-." A knock on the kitchen door startles them both. Jazmyn got up, cleared her mind, and headed for the door.

Jazmyn opened the door to see Arion and Miryssia standing there like children waiting for candy on Halloween.

"Hi, guys," Jazmyn beamed. "I want to introduce you to my Dad." She outstretched her arm in the direction of the table.

"Dad, this is Arion and Miryssia. They live with Abraham," Jazmyn said.

Stephen just looked at them and didn't say a word.

"Hey," Miryssia said.

"Hi, Mr. Wolff," Arion said with an outstretched hand.

There was still no response; they all stood there in silence.

"Have a seat. Do you guys want a cup of coffee?" Jazmyn said.

"Yeah, sure," Miryssia said, keeping an eye on Stephen.

"No, thank you, Jazmyn," Arion answered and cleared his throat.

Jazmyn pours a cup, sits in front of Miryssia, and sits back down, "What are you guys doing here?"

They both looked at each other, and Miryssia said, "You are

not supposed to be alone, remember."

"Oh, yeah, that's right," Jazmyn shifted her view to her dad. "That asshole, Diomedes, is trying to get this necklace."

Stephen got up and finally spoke, "I am tired. I had a long day."

Jazmyn shot back up, pushing her chair back with her knees, "Do you want to go lay on the couch or in the spare bedroom upstairs?"

"I will go upstairs now," without another word, he disappeared out of the kitchen.

"He's a joy to be around," Miryssia scoffed.

"He's not himself," Jazmyn paused, feeling there was more to that statement than at its face value.

"I get a bad vibe from him," Miryssia said.

"Maybe as he said he's had a long day and needs to recharge," Arion piped in.

Jazmyn bit her inside of her cheek," Maybe."

∞∞∞

"Are you in possession of what I want?" Diomedes stared with soulless eyes at a floating vision of a creature.

"No, getting close, my master," the creature replied.

"I will wait for your success," Diomedes said. With a wave of his hand, the vision vanished.

He shot up from his throne and put his hands behind his back, strolled out into the tunnel; both of his guards snapped to attention as he passed.

The loose pebbles covering the cave floor cracked under his feet as he made his way down to where his prisoners are kept.

Diomedes peered over his newest prisoner as they were paraded by him, "Hold up!"

His warhogs did his bidding and stopped the group of prisoners.

"What are we doing here, you creep?!" a feisty woman

screamed, struggling against the steel grip of her captor.

He approaches the woman, and with his ruff claw of his finger, he slowly brushes her cheek. The young woman tried to shy away from his assault, but he snatched her face in his hand and squeezed.

"I have plans for all of you humans, your all are going to serve me," Diomedes spoke as his eyes fell on the woman releasing his grip a little.

"We are not going to serve you, asshole!" the woman yelled.

"Yes, you are!" he slapped the woman, and with a thud, she fell to the cave floor and didn't move.

The prisoners flinched, and some turned away when blood trailed from the woman's face.

"Take this one and throw her in my special cell," looking at the lifeless form on the ground. "Get rid of the rest of them."

As Diomedes walked the caverns, He entered a room where several prisoners and a few guards were.

He approached the warhogs, clasped his behind himself, "How are my guests fairing?"

The warhogs didn't answer; they knew better.

They tortured them; screams of pain echoed through the caverns. A few of them were shackled to the wall, their backs covered with blood from being whipped.

After a few hours of this, they were bound by their hands and feet by chained, lying on stone tablets.

A living black ooze is poured on their chest; it crawled all over their victim's body. It seeked to find ways in; when it does, it infects the mind. The infection caused them to lose their sense of self, opening them to become slaves to Diomedes; they will do whatever he asked.

He paused to look at the ones that had been processed; their faces had no emotion, and the infection caused their skin to turn gray.

Happy with what he was doing, Diomedes left, but when he passed one of the side rooms, he stopped and watched Morzell in animated talk with one of his warhogs.

"Morzell, come."

Morzell jumped a little and let out a low growl.

I am not your dog.

He quickly waved the warhog away, "Um. Yes."

Diomedes continues his walk, Morzell, by his side.

"What were you talking to Kor about?"

"We were... discussing battle plans," his eyes coward away. "My Master."

Diomedes raised an eyebrow, "Walk with me."

Morzell nodded his head and followed behind him as he continued on his way.

"Morzell? Do you know why I despise humans?"

"No,"

"They are the worst creatures that crawl on this earth," Diomedes snarled his lip. "They are just a waste of space."

Morzell came up along the side of him, "Yes."

"We are stuck in the underworld, while the humans are up here living their carefree lives."

"We need to attack her now and get that necklace so that we can take this world from them." Morzell stepped in front of Diomedes, stopping him.

"Don't worry. I have a plan in motion." Diomedes pushed Morzell out of his way, then put his arm behind him and continued.

"You are doomed to fail with that plan."

The walls and the floor began to shake as Diomedes turned, "What!"

"I am sick of you wasting time," Morzell folded his fingers into a fist. "You have been cuddling that witch, you need to attack and you need to do it now!"

Diomedes' eyes began to glow red. Holding his hands out, a plasma ball burst into existents, "You have argued with me for the last time."

He threw the ball at Morzell, but he ducked, producing a plasma ball himself, and hit Diomedes with it.

Diomedes fell back against the cave wall, causing a crater; he flew towards Morzell and knocked him off his feet without hesitation.

With his foot on Morzell's throat, he pressed down, struggling Morzell could feel his life and his neck being crushed.

"I would like to thank you for your service," Diomedes smiled as he forced his foot down.

Morzell grabbed a small knife and stabbed it into Diomedes leg. Diomedes screamed in pain, lifting his leg; Morzell thrust Diomedes off of him and shimmered away.

Diomedes pulled the knife out and tossed it away and let out a nightmarish scream, and took off down the hall out of the cave and took to the air.

"That insolent fool!. I am not cuddling that witch, what is that idiot thinking? I know what I am doing. She is playing right into my plans."

Diomedes looked around far above what was left of the forest. Smoke filled the air; the trees were chard or burning as far as can be seen. Forest animals littered the ground; some were still alive, others their fur and skin were burnt off, the lucky ones were dead.

A commotion caught his eye; a group of prisoners was rebelling, "This should calm me down."

"Settle down! You are my permanent guest now. There is no need to fight; there is no place for you to go." Diomedes floated down.

"Go to hell!" a man from the crowd yell up at him.

"Aw, yes, home. I decided to expand, home improvements you know," Diomedes landed and sashayed over to the man, the rest of the prisoner backed away. "What is your name?"

"What is it to you?" the man croaked.

"Just want to know the name of the brave man." Diomedes smiled through narrowed eyes.

"Bert Albertson." He stood there at attention, but his eye shifted nervously.

"Nice to meet you, Bert Albertson." Diomedes laid his hand

on his trembling shoulder, then turned and stepped a few paces away.

"This Bert Albertson is an example of a man that can take charge." He slowly faced Bert.

Bert stood there with a crooked smile and feeling as though he was just given a prize.

Diomedes raised one hand and threw it down to his side as he did a bolt of lightning and struck Bert, killing him.

"I am sick of you humans thinking you rule here. I do!. Don't be like Bert Albertson," Diomedes said hissed.

One of his soldiers picked up the chard body, tossed it aside, and then turned towards the rest. A loud screeching pitch came from the mouth of the creature, causing them to cover their ears.

"Now, all of you will dig a hole here," Diomedes pointed to the ground. "I need somewhere to bury the ones who defy me."

Women, men, and children faces grew dark, and hopelessness filled their souls; without objection, they picked up picks and shovel and began to dig.

Chapter Twenty-One

"Are you hungry?" Jazmyn snapped up from the kitchen table as her Dad as he entered.

"No, I am not," Her Dad growled. "What is she doing here?"

"I stayed the night to protect your daughter," Miryssia said, then cleared her throat and got up, went over to Jazmyn.

"What are you doing?, Miryssia?," Jazmyn let out an awkward laugh then, with eyes wide, looked at Miryssia.

Miryssia slowly moves back to her chair, "Just doing what they asked me to do."

"This is my dad, I don't your protecting." Jazmyn scuffed.

"It sounded like you had your doubts yesterday," Miryssia said, shifting in her seat.

"I thought about it last night, and I change my feelings."

A darting glance at Miryssia stopped her from saying any more.

"How are you doing, Dad?" Jazmyn asked, turning back to him.

"I am sorry for yesterday, I wasn't myself," Stephen said, rubbing the back of his head.

"Don't worry about it, I understand. Are you sure you want nothing?" Jazmyn asked, and her heartbeat increased a little. "Some milk, tea, water, anything at all?"

She paced a little, feeling like her Dad's little girl again. She wanted to make him feel at home.

"No, I don't," Stephen flared his nostrils.

"We could show you my tree," Jazmyn moved her hand,

pointing at Miryssia and herself.

"No, we can't." She glared at Jazmyn, "Can I talk to you, in private."

Miryssia yanked Jazmyn out of her chair almost before she had a chance to get up.

She was guided Jazmyn into the living room, "What do you think yours do? Are you crazy?"

"What is your problem?" Jazmyn crossed her arms.

"I have a bad feeling about your 'Dad'," Miryssia said, creating air quotes.

"I know he was acting strange, but he has been locked in a dark dingy cage for years," Jazmyn huffed. "What do you expect?"

"How do you know he is your dad," Miryssia gestured toward Stephen.

"I know he is. You never met him, so how do you know he isn't?"

Miryssia softens her voice a little, "I am just looking out for you."

"I think I can do that myself, I am a witch," Jazmyn walked away, leaving her friend standing there.

Jazmyn linked her arm with her Dad, "Let's go."

The sunlight hid behind the dark looming clouds, and the forest seemed a little quiet as they walked.

Jazmyn tipped her chin down, "Sorry for how Miryssia was acting."

Her Dad looked down at his daughter, "Don't fret about it, now where is that tree."

"Just up here."

"Where?" Her Dad asked.

The grandeur of the oak tree soon came into sight, Jazmyn still awed at the sight of it. She tilted her head when she noticed the tree turned all its leaves out, forming a shell.

An invisible force stopped Stephen, "What's going on, I can't go any farther."

That's strange, it let mom in. The only reason it wouldn't let someone see it or let anyone in is.

Jazmyn slowly looked up at him. *If that person is evil.*

Stephen ran his hand throws his hair; his heart raced, "I'm not evil, I am your Dad. You know."

Jazmyn's eyes widen a little; her heart thump hard in her chest, her mouth went dry.

At that moment, Theia appeared next to Jazmyn and grabbed her arm, and pulled her inside the shield protected the tree.

"What are you doing?" Jazmyn choked out.

Theia cuddled her in close, "This isn't your Father."

Jazmyn skin turned pale, "Wha- what do you mean?"

"The tree senses the evil in him," Theia jerks her head towards Stephen. "Who are you?"

"I am her Father," Stephen lowered his shoulders and held out his hand. "Tell her who I am, my daughter."

Jazmyn felt her stomach turn. She looks at her Dad, then back to Theia, then back again.

Theia raised her arms slowly, and the wind churned. Then she closed her eyes, moved her hand to waist height, moved them in a ball shape, a bright white appearing in between them. "Now, tell me who in the hell you are!"

Stephen steps back a few steps. Sweat formed on his brow, "Jazmyn?" he began. "When you were little you used to like bringing your dolls in with you when we're taking a bath. Remember?"

Jazmyn's eyes darted from side to side while her mind sorted through her memories.

Is he my father, or isn't he? Why is Theia so dead set that he isn't? Maybe the tree is picking up on that he just escaped from evil.

The look in his eyes was telling her it was her Dad.

Theia was ready to throw the energy ball at him when Jazmyn pulled at her arm; Theia turns to her.

"Wait! Let me prove to you he is my father. Which doll was my favorite?" Jazmyn found words, hoping that he answered right.

"That easy," said matter-of-factly. Stephen's eyes widen, "It was your Rubba Dub Dolly. You always insisted that she take a bath with because she was always dirty as you."

A smile covered Jazmyn's face, "Yes! That's it, Dad."

Theia lowered her arms, and the energy ball vanished. She had a terrible feeling, "If you feel that he is your Father, then I will believe you." Theia said, then slowly faded away, monitoring Stephen.

Jazmyn cocked an eye to Theia, turned to her Dad, "Come on in."

With that, the tree dropped its shield; Jazmyn took the lead, followed by Stephen, then Theia.

Before the door shut, Jazmyn looked back and saw a single leaf drop.

She followed her Dad down the stairs, but it seemed the tree still didn't approve. The candles didn't light when they went past.

Funny, Jazmyn thought, then waved her hand to light the candles.

She watches her Dad from the last step; he roamed around, looking at everything. He walked up to the podium, and her book closed itself and flew into Jazmyn's hands, almost knocking her over.

"I was just going to look at it," her father said.

"I-I don't know why it came to me," Jazmyn creased her eyebrow and looked at her Dad.

She stepped off the stairs, carried the book back over to her Dad, but it flew out of her hands and landed at the far end of the table.

"I am sorry, my tree and book don't like you," Jazmyn said. That sounds funny to say.

Her stomach twisted. She took a few steps back and faced the stairs.

Stephen stood, his eyes wide, then turned away, "Maybe all this is happening because I have been close to evil too long."

"Maybe," she said, taking a deep breath.

Take him out of the tree, an angelic voice spoke in her head.

"What?" Jazmyn looked around.

"Did you say something?"

She shook her head and then closed her eyes, and This is my father; why should I take him outside?

Trust me.

She felt that she should do what the voice told her, "Aw, that's enough let's go back outside."

"I want to see more," her father scolded.

She grabbed his hand and led him up the stairs, "Later, please."

When they emerged from the tree, she took him into the woods.

"Show me what you can do?" her Dad stopped.

The feeling of worry seemed to disappear, replaced by an excited little kid wanting to show off.

Jazmyn's stomach fluttered. She looked towards her Dad, and a smile came across her face. "Do you really want to see what I can do?"

Her Dad smiled back, "Yes, my sweet daughter."

She shook excitedly like a child showing her parents a drawing. She held her hands out fingers up, twisted her wrists, a good size log shook, it lifted off the ground. She spun her hands, and the log mimicked the motion. She looks back at her Dad to see his reaction. His smile on his face wasn't there, no emotion.

Thud went the log as her heartfelt heavy, "Maybe this."

She motioned to get his attention then disappeared. Within a blink of an eye, she appeared behind him.

He turned, "I've seen better."

It felt as though a building was pressing down on her chest, "What do you mean?"

Stephen crack a half-smile, "Being trapped, I have seen a lot of magic performed in front of me. What you are doing is nothing."

A lost look came over her, and she couldn't even think and just stood there.

"If you are planning to defeat Diomedes, do better."

Her brain churned, trying to think of something to impress her Dad, to get his approval. She put her hands together, closed her eyes. A green glow seeped out between the cracks of her fingers. Moving her hands apart revealed an orb was radiating brightly. Jazmyn aims at a dead tree then threw it, but it vanished feet before it hit.

"What was that?" her Dad asked.

Jazmyn's eyes filled with tears, "I don't know what happened."

This isn't the Dad she knew; he wouldn't put her down; he was so supportive of her when she was younger.

Stephen stood rigid, almost like on cue Morzell appeared behind him.

"Dad, Move!"

Jazmyn raised her hand in front of her and produced another green ball.

Her Dad turned to see what was behind him. Morzell reached out to grab him but was repulsed by a flash of light.

"Diomedes is not going to like this," Stephen spoke in a different voice.

Jazmyn let her arms fall to her side. The plasma ball disappeared and she just stood there. Her eyes did not believe anything she was seeing.

"I am not falling him anymore," Morzell pushed Stephen aside and looked Jazmyn right in the eyes, and pointed at her. "I am here to rid this world of that witch and gain the power of the necklace for myself.

Stephen convulsed, and a mysterious smoke force itself from Stephen's mouth. Stephen soon fell to the ground, his lifeless body laid in a heap.

"Daddy!" Jazmyn yelled out. "No, not again!"

She fell to her knees and put her head in her hands, trying to stop the river of tears.

The smoke convalesces into a shape of a beast with four legs like a bear, but its top half was human with arms.

"Grahamopheles will not allow that," the creature grabbed Morzell and threw him against a tree. The tree snapped and toppled to the ground.

Morzell picked himself up looked at the creature, "Grahamopheles, I never liked you. You're just a parasite demon."

Grahamopheles let out an ear-piercing scream and charged Morzell.

Morzell jumped out of the way and picked up the fallen tree, smashed across Grahamopheles's back, making the creature's legs give out, it crashed to the ground.

Jazmyn cleared her eyes and ran towards her father; Grahamopheles picked himself up and saw Jazmyn running and, with one monstrous arm, picked up Morzell with one hand and waved his other, causing Stephen to vanish.

"No!" Jazmyn screamed.

She stopped and faced the two creatures battling. Her emerald glowed. She lifted her head towards the sky and spoke.

"From the skies above, lightning hear my call. Give me your power. Give me it all."

The clouds grew dark; the wind swirled around; the lightning crept through the sky, gathering in one spot above Jazmyn.

She held her hands up above the head, and the lightning came down, filling her hands with a blinding light; she had them there gathering the lighting than a swift move, she put her hand out in front of her and shot it at the two creatures.

They both let out a scream that could barely be heard over the thunder.

Then silence.

Jazmyn stumbled back a few paces; weakened, she forced herself to walk over. The two creatures were dead. The stench of their burnt bodies fills the air.

After a few moments, they turned to dust, and the wind carried their ashes away.

"Dad!" Jazmyn yelled and looked for him, but he had gone again.

∞ ∞ ∞

Jazmyn's hands trembled bringing them up to her face. Tears streamed down her cheeks.

What is happening?

Her mind reeled,

First, my mother is poisoned. I get my father back then find out he isn't my father, just an asshole of a demon. What else?

She felt that someone was behind her. She jumped up and turned and with a plasma ball in her hand.

"Whoa, it's just me, "Arion said, holding his hands out.

"How do I know it is you? I was tricked before," Jazmyn tossing the plasma ball up and down. "Tell me something stupid you've done, that I know about."

Arion paced a bit, "I asked you out at weirdest the time."

Satisfied with his answer, she clinched her first and extinguished the plasma ball, sat back down, "I would like to be alone, please."

"Ok, Just wanted to know if you were ok. Just to let you know that I am a good listener, if need one," Arion informed, slowly turned, and walked away.

"Yeah, Thanks," Jazmyn answered.

Her thoughts rushed back; she wanted the images to stop going through her mind, picturing her mother lying there, her dad; it felt like her world was ending.

"No, wait!"

Arion turned back around and walked up to her, "Do you want to talk?"

"I think I need a distraction. Were you serious about what you ask me?"

Arion looked down and then raised his head and look her straight into her eyes, "Um, Habit if you are not up to it with all that is going on, we can wait."

"I need this, I will go crazy otherwise." Jazmyn exclaimed.

"All right, when?" Arion asked.

"Now," Jazmyn stated.

She grabbed his hand. Before he could say anything, she closed her eyes, opened them again. They were standing in the alleyway next to the Oak Stone Cafe.

"I guess that would be fine then." Arion smirked.

She guided him into the cafe and sat in her spot next to the windows. Jazmyn looked over behind the counter, trying to catch the waitress's attention, but it seemed that she was too busy to notice them.

"Kinda looks like they are shorthanded," Arion said.

"Yeah, as long as I have been coming here they always have enough people working," Jazmyn informed.

"Weird," Arion said. "It's a nice place in here, I've been here once."

"Yes, it is."

Jazmyn was fidgeting with her napkin, folding it and undoing it again.

"I know this will be a stupid question, but how are you doing?" Arion asked.

She looked out the window, watched a few people going by.

"I think I will be... Ok." Jazmyn let out a sigh.

"That's good."

"Sorry, for the wait," a voice said, putting down two menus on the table. "My one waitress is running her ass off here."

Jazmyn turn to see it was Helen, "Why? You usually have enough people."

"I try to, but my people are not showing up. What can get ya to drink?" Helen said, noticing Jazmyn's look. "What the matter, Hun?"

Jazmyn struggled to keep her tears from falling. Helen was almost like her 2nd mom.

She moved to talk, to tell her what was going on, but she couldn't.

"Nothing," Jazmyn lied, then turned back to the window.

"Did you want something to drink?" Helen asked Arion.

"Just water, please."

When Helen left, Arion moved over next to Jazmyn, "Everything will be all right."

"How do you know?" She said, not turning to him.

"Abraham is good at what he does, he will figure it out and your mother will be herself again." Arion said.

Jazmyn faced him with teary eyes and wrapped her arms around him, "I'm scared."

Arion hugged her back, "I am here for you."

Jazmyn pulled back a little, a rush of emotion to over, pressing her lips to his.

Her body relaxed, her tensions melted away, then she panicked and pulled away, "I'm sorry."

"Whoa," Arion said, trying to catch his breath. "Don't be."

"I don't know why I did that, sorry." Jazmyn said.

Arion moved out of the way as she made her way to the restroom.

She leaned up against the sink. Her heart was beating fast, her thoughts raced, "What am I doing?. I shouldn't be doing this it not the time for it."

She faced the mirror, with bloodshot eyes, stared back. Her thoughts landed on Izzie; she grabbed her phone and dialed her friend's number. The rings couldn't go fast enough. She realized that Izzie wasn't picking up. "Dammit, Izzie, where are you? You never let it ring more than once."

Jazmyn felt that something was wrong. Then she remembered that Izzie called earlier. She pressed on the voice mail icon.

"Jazmyn, Jazmyn!," Izzie screamed. "Some bat ugly creatures are trying to get me outside my work. Help me!. Oh no, they saw me. Let go of me!"

The sound of the phone hitting the ground, Jazmyn's heart jumped.

The message ended with Izzie screaming; the phone went silent.

Jazmyn catapulted out of the bathroom, looked at Arion, dashed out the door.

"What's wrong?" Arion yelled, trying to catch her.

"Izzie, something happened to Izzie!" Jazmyn turned her head and continued running toward her old work.

Jazmyn rattled the handles, but the doors were locked, "Come on, open up!, Dammit! I can't lose you too."

Jazmyn's eyes widen. "Maybe she is in her car."

She dashed around to the alley. The car was empty, but the driver's door was opened.

Arion found her standing next to the dumpster hold a blood-soaked phone, "What happened?"

"This is Izzies phone," Jazmyn held it tight against her. "They took her, I knew I should have warned her and you people didn't let me!" Jazmyn temper exploded; she flung her arms out, Arion tumbled through the air, slamming against the wall.

"Please, Jazmyn, calm down," Arion stumbled to his feet.

"Why?!" She blurted out, running to the end of the alley, hoping her friend was there; she wasn't.

"I will call Theia, She'll know what to do." Arion stated.

By the time he hung up his phone, Theia, the rest and were standing next to him.

"Jazmyn, please come back here," Theia said.

Jazmyn turned around to see Diomedes standing between her and the rest.

"This was a trap? Diomedes," Abraham said.

"I told you they'll show, Kor," Diomedes chuckled, turning his head turns a warhog standing next to him.

With a wave of his hand, an army of warhogs surrounded Theia and the rest.

Jazmyn ran towards them but was grabbed from behind and held tightly.

Diomedes raised his arms high in the air and said a foreign spell, and a ball of energy engulfed Jazmyn's friends.

He held his hand out and began slowly make a fist, causing the ball of energy to grow smaller. Theia and Abraham shot streams of energy out of their hand, trying to crack the shell, but it just continued to crush them.

"I can stop this if you just give me what I want," Diomedes said, slithering towards Jazmyn.

"No, I won't!," Jazmyn screamed.

The clouds stirred in the sky grew darker, the wind picked up, blowing debt all around. Lightning ran across the clouds; it filled the air with electricity, then a bolt of lightning came down and almost stuck Diomedes, but he defected it, a scream came from one of his warhogs. The lightning coursed through his body, the smell of burnt flesh stung Jazmyn's nose, a final squeal came, a charred body laid motionless on the ground.

"Impressive," Diomedes smirked. "By the way thank you for deposing of that imbecile, Morzell for me, I didn't like him anyway, But I liked Grahamopheles, he was one of my loyal companion. If try to hurt me again, they will die."

"I will not give this to you," Jazmyn looks to see her friends being crushed.

"I believe," His eyes widen. "Izzie is it?, she wanted me to tell you goodbye, or at least I think she would have before she died."

Diomedes smiled at her as he slowly walked around her.

Jazmyn went limp. Her body felt like it was shutting down. Everyone she cared for or love was being torn from her life.

"Hand it here," Diomedes reached his hand out.

Jazmyn looked up to him with tears running, "Ok, only if release them."

"I will do that for you once I have that necklace. Then nothing will touch me."

The creature holding her step back and Jazmyn slowly move to take the necklace off. The necklace glowed and fought against her sensing what would happening. She looked at the faces of all of her friends and stared into Arion's eyes with a final tug; the necklace relinquished its hold.

Diomedes took his prize, "It almost wasn't anticlimactic

but thanks anyway, now let's have some fun."

Like a kid with a toy, Diomedes proudly showed it off. He held it high into the air and recited a spell. The sky darkens, the wind picked, upbringing in a rush of freezing air. A green glow shot out in all directions; it seems to fight off an orb of dark red light surrounded the necklace; with the final word of the incantation, the pendent flickered back and forth from green to red, with the last flicker of green light, it dimmed then turns red.

Jazmyn could feel her magic being ripped from deep within her, and it was like someone had ripped her soul from her body.

Diomedes turns toward his group of captives, and with one jester of his hand closing, the ball collapsed.

Just before the ball disappeared, a sliver of white light shot out, it illuminated the whole night sky, then exploded.

"Come now, we are done here. Thanks," Diomedes vanished along with the rest of the demons.

Jazmyn fell to the ground, alone.

Chapter Twenty-Two

"Arion?, Theia?, anybody?" She called out.

The only thing she heard was the echo of her voice. She looked around, crawled to the department store's wall and used the wall to help her, and pulled herself up.

The weight of the world was pressing down on her, and now she had to bear it alone. She couldn't believe everyone she knew was gone, and tears fell again,

Will, I ever quit crying?

Her stomach felt hollow; she felt ashamed for what she had done, "How can I do this on my own without my necklace."

She staggered to the street when the sounds of screaming made her lookup. It was like stepping into a war zone, people running in every direction seeking shelter from the onslaught of an army of warhogs.

Something hit her from behind, knocking her off her feet; she got back up to see it was Bernie, the pop can collector, but he was different. His skin was green with warts and blisters, and his face was sunken.

"Bernie, its me Jazmyn," She announced, her heart raced.

Bernie ignored her and swung the board he was wielding; Jazmyn rolled out of the way and got back up.

"I don't want to hurt you," She advised and raised her hands, and she couldn't stop him by freezing him; she tried again, "What's wrong?"

She took a step back, almost tripped over a board on the ground. She picked it up and, with all of her might, swung it at

Bernie, knocking him hard against a building; he slunk over and stopped moving.

The once peaceful town was now full of chaos; there were fires everywhere, raged unchecked, jumping from building to building, eating its way through the town.

Jazmyn couldn't take much more of it as she tried to teleport but couldn't.

"Damn it!" she screamed.

I have lost everything that I could help me take Diomedes out. What use am I now?

An overwhelming urge to panic came over her; she felt her head spin, her legs didn't want to carry her anymore.

Leaning against a building, she looked around, warhogs were grabbing people. Others from the town acting like zombies marching alongside them, causing mayhem.

She knew she had to hide somewhere, forcing herself to move; she knew that it wasn't safe. A window in front of the thrift store was smashed in by a zombie. Her heart jumped, giving her the push to run.

She searched for a safe place to go; she ran down an alley then came across a rundown building, untouched by the destruction going on around her. Quickly hurried to the front door, crushing an ornamental bunny before jumping the steps of the porch. She burst through the door. The place was dark; she stumbled over furniture, stopping for a few moments hoping the sound didn't attract attention, but the only thing she heard was her heart thumping hard in her chest.

She found a closet, dashed in, shuffled a few things aside, and settled in the corner. She pulled down the coats to cover her; they smelt musty.

She sat alone in the dark, hearing small explosions off in the distance. They almost sounded like a heartbeat. It seemed like every moment took years to go by, but she slowly drifted off to sleep.

∞∞∞

The smoke in the air hung heavy, almost blocking out the sun. It choked Jazmyn as she cautiously walked the streets of Oak Stone. The small town was lifeless. None of the buildings that stood were on fire or destroyed.

She had betrayed everyone that she cares for. Now they are all are dead, just as the twins had predicted. A deep feeling of guilt and disappointment in herself made her feel useless, and she wishes she could turn the tides back, but she couldn't.

She looked above the bar where she used to live, found that the wall was gone. Her old living room was exposed. She remembered the day that she talked to her mother about her birthday, where all this had started.

The sound of paper flapping in the wind drew her attention to a notebook hanging out of the side of the building. Jazmyn recognized it as hers, the one she thought she had lost. She tried to float up to retrieve it but remembered she couldn't anymore; she looked at it again, and it seemed to beckon for her.

Jazmyn made her way up the stairway avoiding the missing stairs; when she arrived at the upper floor, she found the path to the door was almost not there. She shuffled across the railing until she was in line with the threshold. Jazmyn jumped and landed next to the door when she heard a loud crack. The floor disappeared from under her. She quickly grabbed hold of the door, hoping that the hinge holding it wouldn't give out. Swinging the door, she found part of the floor that was solid and stood up.

You better be worth it, notebook.

Jazmyn worked her way to the opening and reached for the notebook as she did. Part of the wall gave way, and she realized how far up she was from the sidewalk below. She finally got it and pulled herself back in and sat down on the couch that was there, shoving aside tons of pillows.

A few of the page edges were burnt as she went through it. She hadn't touched it in years; her thoughts and feelings came back to her. It gave her a sense of normalcy in this chaos that has happened. Her dirty fingers left smudges on each page she flipped.

"What am I going to do," She spoke out loud, half expecting Onyx to listen to her, but her cat or Theia couldn't hear her anymore.

Tears streamed down her cheek, soaking the pages of her memories. When she came across a poem she wrote a few years back to the day, and it was a strange poem when she wrote it, the words made sense now it wasn't a poem; it was an incantation.

Her face lit up for just a second, "What am I going to do with this, I can't- I don't have my powers."

A huff of air escaped her lips as she ran her fingers through her hair, stopping on her neck; she looked around, "Now to figure away down."

Jazmyn pushed the couch out the side of the building, and luckily it landed upright; the pillows fell all over the ground.

Here goes nothing.

She jumped and landed on the couch, looked around, hoping the noise didn't draw attention to her from Diomedes's slaves. Jazmyn cautiously walked the streets, trying to find a vehicle that wasn't damaged.

She heard a voice that caught her attention. She followed it to find it was coming from a car's radio that was still running.

The voice was of a newscaster; she listens to it.

... the weather around the world has set a new president. Mass of thunderstorm cloud has covered the entire planet. Flooding rains are happening everywhere, and it is not letting up anytime soon... Breaking news has come across our desks.

Climbing behind the steering wheel, Jazmyn turned the volume up a little more.

It seems an army of... (is this right?) zombies have gathered in every city across the nation. They are taking over the cities, and there seems no way of stopping them.

"Holy shit, what have I done? I got to do something." Jazmyn reached over, shut the radio off, shut the car door, and grabbed the steering wheel. "What am I doing, I can't steal this car."

The decision to take the car was made for her when a warhog smashed the car's rear window.

"Shit!, shit," Jazmyn screamed and shoved the car into drive and forced the accelerator peddle to the floor.

The beast crawled partly through the window and grabbed Jazmyn by the shoulder; she let out a scream. The car swerved all over its clipped cars as she tried to wiggle free, but the creature dug his claws into her skin. Without thinking, she twisted her head around and clamped down on its dirty finger, and it let go.

Jazmyn turns the car sharply to the right around a corner, and the beast flew back out the window and went through the thrift store window.

∞∞∞

She drove to her mom's cabin as fast as she could. But, unfortunately, the landscape on either side of the road was on fire. The farther she went, more and more of the flames had already eaten the trees and grass.

When she arrived at the cabin, it was almost entirely reduced to rubble. A sick feeling in her stomach almost made her puke, knowing she did this, but she slowly got out of the car and crept closer. She shuffled through the debris to see all of the mother's things were destroyed. Almost like it was displayed for her, the sweater that her mother made for her hung from a broken post. She picked it up and carried it through the back door and sat curled up, hugging it.

Tears ran freely down, soaking the sweater; she raised her head to look across the lake to see Abraham's house untouched; it stood there like a beacon.

Jazmyn wiped her tears with the sweater. She darted around the lake, her feet seeming never hitting the ground. Rushing up to the house, she realized that a protective shield was put around the house.

How is this possible? Abraham is dead, and his magic should be?

She went up to the front door and slowly opened it. The creaking floors echoed throughout the house, and she made her way down the stairs to see if her mother was still there. She held her breath until she saw her still in that protective room.

A single light cast a halo of light around her mother. Jazmyn almost tiptoed up to her, not wanting to wake her as she did when she used to stay up late at night walking around the house, but it didn't matter. Her mother was in sleep that she would never wake up from again.

She laid her notebook on a little table next to the bed, stood there for a long time before she spoke, "Hi, mom." Half expecting a reply, but the silence was all there was. Jazmyn pulled up a chair next to her and reached out and gently took her hand, and it was cold.

"I'm here, mom. How are you doing?" Jazmyn spoke softly.

She rubbed her mother's hand with her fingers, occasionally wiping a tear from her cheek that escaped her eye.

"Mom, I-," she mustering the courage to speak, "I have failed, I gave up my necklace, and I have gotten everyone killed. The world is ending."

Jazmyn put her hand over her mouth, not believing the words she spoke. It made it more real now. The knots in her stomach wrenched tighter, making her bunch over. The horrifying sight of them being killed flashback into her mind.

Jazmyn bowed her head, the tears let loose again, "Mom, I wish it was me lying there instead of you."

Never knowing she could ever feel this much suffering, pain, and loss made her end it all. To join them wherever they are.

It was like someone slapped her; she snaps up straight in

her chair, wiped the tears away, "Dammit, I am better than this."

A kernel of hope sprouted somewhere deep within her. She could feel the strength of the confidence coming back. Her body reacted to the warmth she was feeling all around her. It invited her in a tingling feeling stirred from the same deep place spreading out to the tips of her head, toes, and fingers, "What the?"

A glowing light trickles through Jazmyn's body, and it travels from her into her mother's body.

A movement caught her eye. She looked down, her mother stirred, her eyes slowly opened, then focused on her daughter followed by a smile.

"Jazmyn," a meek voice came from her mother's mouth.

"Mom?!" Jazmyn stood up and held her mother's hand up next to her face, and hugged it. "How?"

Gloria cleared her throat a little and spoke louder, "Jazmyn, what happened?"

"Dad who wasn't really dad, but he had a demon that took over him, poisoned you" Jazmyn stopped. "Too much info, sorry."

"You were poisoned," She finished.

"Did you find the cure?" her mother asked, trying to sit up.

"No, I didn't. Don't get up," Jazmyn eased her down onto the bed again.

"Then how?" her mother search for the answer in her daughter's eyes.

Jazmyn remembered what Arion told her, that on an infrequent occasion, a witch could do both. Her eyes widen, "I healed you. I don't know how I did it, but I did."

A weak smile came to Gloria's face, "I knew you had more to offer, I am so proud of you."

Jazmyn could see the color coming back. She gave her mother a real hug this time.

"Thanks, mom."

The tears she cried this time were of pride, not sorrow.

She stepped back and straightened her shirt as her mother sat up.

"Take it slow, mom."

"You said your father poisoned me?" Gloria's eyes widen.

"It wasn't dad, his body was taken over by a demon," Jazmyn explained.

"Where is he now?"

"The demon took him," Jazmyn said. "I don't know if he is dead or alive, he's probably dead."

Gloria's eyes filled with tears, "I always held on to the notion that you would find him and bring him home. I had hoped when I saw him standing in front of me," her voice cracked. "But it wasn't even him."

"I know, when I saw him I thought it was him also, I even defended him from everyone," Jazmyn shook her head. "I guess he, I mean the demon fooled me. I was so stupid."

"You are not stupid," Gloria disputed.

"I was told that I wasn't even a witch that Theia just lead me to believe I was."

"That's terrible."

Jazmyn knew she was and wasn't stupid, but talking about it made her feel just as bad, "How are you doing?" changing the subject.

"I almost feel back to normal. How did," Gloria saw that her necklace wasn't around her neck. "What happened?" pointing at the space around Jazmyn's neck.

Jazmyn lowered her eyes, not wanting to make eye contacted. She was swallowing the lump that formed in her throat.

"I was forced to give it to Diomedes."

A flash of anger crossed her mother's eyes, "What do you mean?, Why?"

Jazmyn paced the floor, hugging her arms, eyes still lowered, "He captured all of them, even Izzie," pain welled up in her eyes. "He-he killed them all."

"I am so sorry, Honey," a softer voice came out, wrapping her arms around her daughter.

"And you were gone, I didn't know if you would live, I didn't think I had anything or anybody." She tried to justify her actions.

Her mother slowly walked over to her daughter, "What are you going to do about it?"

Pulling away, Jazmyn tucked a few strands of hair behind her ear, "I don't know, I found an incantation in my poem notebook, but I can't do anything with it.." Slowly gesturing her head towards the little table.

Gloria walked over and took the notebook and placed it into Jazmyn's hands, "Go to your tree maybe something there can help you, maybe you find a way."

"What's the sense?, I have lost all of my powers, I am not a witch anymore."

Jazmyn tossed the notebook and walked away.

Gloria blocks her way, "Give up, you always gave up, it's easier isn't it?"

Jazmyn could see the flames of anger in her mother's eyes; she turned her head. "I can't do anything, I am useless."

"People put you down making you have believe that your worthless for most of your life, make it up by sacrificing your life by helping people with this or that, to what end," Gloria gestured wildly. "To make you feel better about yourself."

What her mother said hit a cord inside of Jazmyn, "Yes, that's all I know how to do."

"It's about time you learn something new," Gloria grabbed Jazmyn's shoulder, turning her head back to look. "It's time for you."

Jazmyn walked out of Abraham's house and slowly headed for her tree, clutching her tattered notebook. She took a deep breath, "What the hell am I going to do?" she spoke to an empty forest.

There weren't any animals; the ones that could escape did, but the ones that couldn't litter the ground. The smell of burning wood woke her up to the fact that there was no tree or any plants that weren't charred or on fire, "Did my tree survive? I'm sure it did, it's a strong tree, it will be there waiting for me."

She walked a few more paces and stopped and looked

around, "This is all my fault, I am sure once Diomedes got his hands on my necklace he laid waste to everything in sight."

A pile of rocks caught her attention. She reached out her hand and tried to make them move, "Damn it!"

She shoved the pile of rocks over with her foot. Jazmyn sunk her hands into her pockets, lowered her head, and continued.

As she rounded the corner, her heart sunk when she saw her tree, it was still standing, but it seemed dead, all the leaves were gone, and the once-proud noble branches bowed in defeat, its twigs scattered the ground. She could feel its life was almost gone, "I am sorry for this."

Jazmyn pushed the door open and walked down the staircase. Leaves crunched under her feet echoed through the tree. The usual torches along the wall just laid dormant. She had to use the light on her phone.

The last few steps were smashed; she jumped down to the floor, landing on broken glass. Light from her phone showed that the table splintered into many pieces.

Jazmyn slowly made her way to where the podium was and found it was lying on the floor. Her foot kicked something on the floor; she used her phone to find her book of shadows, ripped, torn, and burnt. There weren't any pages left in it.

Jazmyn sat up against the wall, holding what was left, pulled tight to her chest, "Allison?" she squeaked.

The silence was her answer.

Jazmyn glanced over to where the tree had made room for her, but that was gone too.

Her phone's light faded, "No, come on, not now."

The dark crept closer and closer to Jazmyn; she banged her phone in her hand, attempting to coax it to work, but it died.

Jazmyn sat alone in the blackness.

"Heal me."

Chapter Twenty-Three

"Who's there? Jazmyn strained to see into the dark.

"Heal me."

"Where are you? Who are you?"

"Heal me," the voice was fading. *"Hurry."*

"How can I heal you when I can't see you," Jazmyn said.

Her chest glowed; Jazmyn looked down to see the cover to her book was emitting a dull light.

She laid the book down on the floor and placed her hand on it. Warmth filled her body, and her hand glowed with a green flame. The book grew brighter and opened up; all the pages lost grew from the binder.

Jazmyn stood and watched as the room filled with the light from the book. Finally, the table assembled itself; chairs flew together and placed themselves under the table.

The podium stood up, the book lifted, settled on it. A brilliant glow came from the symbol in the middle of the table. Jazmyn felt the ground vibrating, and it was almost sounded as if it was singing. A green light up from the table and up the trunk of her tree.

"What the?"

She marveled at how the tree was repairing itself.

How's the outside?

Dashing up the stairs, bursting through the door, and watched as the branches stood proud again and the leaves instantly grew; it was alive again.

"How?"

"You, Jazmyn."

Jazmyn jumped and turned around to see Allison standing there.

"How are you here? I thought you were gone like the rest of them. How are you outside of the tree?"

"You," Allison enlighten. "Deep within you always had the power to do great things, and that's how you brought me back to life."

"Is this real? Are you?" Jazmyn's eyes widen trying to comprehend what was happening.

"Yes, I am real, Jazmyn. Follow me." Allison motion Jazmyn to return down into the tree.

"I am sorry for how I have treated you lately," Jazmyn said.

"That is aright. I understand."

Allison escorted Jazmyn over to the book of shadows.

"Touch it." Allison nodded towards the book.

Jazmyn reached her hand out, hesitant at first; she laid her hand on the book. When she did, she could feel the electricity flowing from the book to her; it almost like she felt the first time she touched the book but, this time, it was more intense.

Volumes of knowledge from the book flooded her mind. It was almost too much for her brain. Then, after what seemed a lifetime, the flow stopped. Her body responded; she could feel everything around her. She could feel every living creature, every plant, and every tree. It was like the whole world of nature, and the universe was one in her.

Jazmyn felt a little weak and steadied herself by holding onto the podium.

Jazmyn stood there trying to find some words to say, "What was that?"

Allison walked to the front of the podium, "The book and you are one now."

"What?" Jazmyn asked.

The book was gone.

She walked over, sat down at the big table, "Why did this happen to me? Why didn't this happen sooner?"

"You weren't ready. Rage and wanting revenge on Diomedes for what he had done. It block you from excepting what the book could offer you." Allison sat next to her and lowered her eyes.

"I feel the...," Jazmyn stopped. "All that I have lost; what had transpired ever since my birthday. I wanted to set things right to somehow return everything back to the way it was. But, I-I guess I don't feel the same."

"You can set things right."

Jazmyn's eye's widened; her hand went to her chest. Feeling for her necklace; it wasn't there, her heart raced.

"My necklace, how am I suppose to defeat him without it?"

Allison smiled a little and nodded her head toward the chair across from them, "Move it."

Jazmyn eyes widen as she swept her head from Allison to the chair then back, "I can't. My magic is gone. I need my necklace."

"No, you never needed your necklace. The magic is still there. Its deep within you. Can you feel it?" Assurance entered Allison's eyes. "You always had it within you."

The memory of when she was angry at the vending machine at work gave back her money. She felt it then.

She turned to the chair and reached her hand out, picturing the chair in the air. A meek feeling stirred deep inside of her. It grew until her whole body was filled with a tingling feeling.

The chair shifted at first, then slowly lifted off the floor, then suddenly dropped.

Elation shined from her face, "Why did I need the necklace then?"

"To help you focus."

"It was my destiny to use the necklace to destroy Diomedes. You said it in the book the first time I opened it."

"No, you needed to learn more than I knew to defeat him and the necklace would help you to do so."

"You mean I can do everything I could do before?" Jazmyn asked.

Allison nodded, "And more."

"What do you mean more?" Jazmyn perked an eyebrow up.

Allison just smiled.

∞ ∞ ∞

Diomedes was about to pick through his herd when he felt something different, something happening somewhere else. He closed his eyes and stretched his mind out to find the disturbance.

"No," Diomedes scowled, then vanished.

He reappeared deep in the woods; he looked around and found the oak tree to be healthy and strong as ever. "How could this have happened, I destroyed this infernal tree," Diomedes bent his eyebrows in anger.

"You know I love this tree and I couldn't bear to see it die," Jazmyn confidently spoke as she came out from behind the tree. "So I healed it."

"But how?" Diomedes questioned. "You can't heal, you're a useless witch."

"Let's just say I gained a new talent," Jazmyn cracking a sideways smile as she stepped away from the tree.

"You might have found a new talent, but can you heal yourself?" Diomedes raised his arms; his necklace glowed an eerie blood-red glow, the clouds created darkness covering the whole sky, lightning erupted from the clouds and stuck at Jazmyn.

Jazmyn waved her arms, and a blue shield encased her, protecting her from the bolt. Then, with a loud crash, the shock wave forced Diomedes back a few steps.

"I have your necklace," He grabbed the necklace. "How can you do magic?"

"Oops, I forgot to tell you." Jazmyn smiled, then she spun her hands around and around, causing the wind to pick up. A cyclone of wind lifted Diomedes off the ground, and it forced him through the air repeatably splintered trees as he flailed about.

He stopped himself and dist pursed the cyclone, "Impressive." Brushing himself off.

He held his hand out palm up, a fireball appeared, "Let's play with fire, shall we."

With a quick flick of his wrist, the fireball launched at Jazmyn, striking her. She held her arms up to protect her; the smell of burning flesh filled her nose. She thought of water; the surrounding air gave up its moisture, a drenching deluge of water covered her. The flames went out.

She fell to the ground; the pain was too intense for her to bear.

"Don't give up," a voice somewhere deep within her spoke, and it wasn't hers.

"Wha..," before she could finish, a moss-covered log rose from the ground, striking her, causing her to fly, colliding against a tree. The bark shattered, she heard a snap, then her head hit, stars filled her vision.

"Get up!" The angelic voice cried out.

She laid there for a few seconds; her head felt like it was ready to explode. She tried to shake away the enormous headache but it hung on. Finally, she pulled herself up, but pain shot through her weaken left arm; she knew it was broken. She inched her way up the tree. The taste of blood filled her mouth.

Jazmyn shook her head to clear it, holding her arm as she stood straight up and glared at her opponent.

"Are you going to cry?" Diomedes snickered.

"No, I will not," that she raised her good arm and commanded a lightning bolt to strike, but Diomedes put his hand up and deflected it back at Jazmyn.

She leaped out of the way, landing on her back; she cried out in pain when her arm slammed against a sharp rock.

"You are no match for me. Do you think these past few months of training could prepare you to fight me?" Diomedes informed.

He strolled up to Jazmyn, still laying on the ground; he placed his foot on her broken arm and stepped down. Jazmyn bit her lips, trying not to give him the satisfaction of screaming.

"I have been around for over 300 years, I think I know a little more than you." He steps back, raising his hands skyward, clenching his fingers towards his palms. The ground trembled all around Jazmyn. Without warning, tree roots wrapped her in a suffocating grip.

The pressure on her body was unbearable; she could feel the wind being forced out of her lungs.

She tried to scream, but there was no air left. Her surroundings were going dark.

"This was too easy," was the last thing she heard before passing out.

Chapter Twenty-Four

Jazmyn felt herself floating. When she opened her eyes, she looked up and saw a clear blue sky. The sun was rising above the far-off horizon; she could feel the heat bathing her body.

She looked down to see the tops of the trees and ground far below, "Am I dead?" Her voice sounded as far off as the horizon was.

"No, you are not," the angelic voice said.

"Who are you? You've been haunting me." Jazmyn saw a glowing form in front of her; it had no shape, just a mass of sparkling lights.

"We never met me in this form before," the voice singing.

"What do you mean?" Jazmyn wondered, her eyebrow pinched downward. "Theia?"

"No, look down."

Jazmyn followed the instruction and saw a glow surrounding her tree.

"Hello Jazmyn, I am the spirit of your tree, Alva."

"It was you all along, speaking to me." Pulling her eyes from the tree.

"Yes, Jazmyn,"

Out of the formless spread of light came a woman; she wore a green leaf-colored flowing dress. "Come."

Alva held her hand out Jazmyn hesitated but finally took the invite. They floated back down to earth next to her tree. Jazmyn looked around to see the forest was alive again; birds filled the air with their beautiful music, a small herd of deer meandered in and out of the trees eating on the luscious green grass that replenished the ground.

"How is this possible?" Jazmyn finally spoke, watching a rabbit scurry around.

"It's not," Alva harshly said.

Jazmyn snapped her eyes back to Alva's. "What?"

Alva sprawled her arms out, "All of this will never exist unless you stand against evil.

"I tried, I can't!" Jazmyn confessed. "He is too strong for me."

"You have all the strength you need inside of you," Alva said.

Jazmyn looked at Alva and turned away. She shook her head a little. All of her life, she put others first, never her. She believed it made her strong inside; it always made her feel like she didn't need to help herself. The strength came from helping others.

As though Alva was reading her mind, "It is time to help yourself." She reached out and touched Jazmyn's shoulder.

The beautiful forest no longer surrounded Jazmyn, but she found herself lying on her back inside a cage. The pain of her burns and broken arm reminded her she was still alive. The smell of rotting flesh penetrated her nose. She turned her head and squinted her eyes to see where she was. Cavern walls all around her lit only by the firelight coming from the opening.

She grabbed a bar to hoist herself up. Pain shot through her whole body, "Shit."

She struggled to upright herself; she held her breath against the pain.

She finally rested her back against the bar opposite the entrance; then she realized that she wasn't alone.

A snap echoed through the darkness; one by one, the torches along the walls ignited, making a loud popping noise.

The smug face of Diomedes appeared from the dark, "Glad to see your alive."

Jazmyn's looked around to scope out the cave and found

several dead animals littering the ground.

"You should clean up more often, a guest like me could take offense," Jazmyn retorted, trying not to show that her insides were quivering.

A nasty smile came across his face and just leered at her as he strolled closer to the cage.

Jazmyn leaned forward and lifted her good arm, and tried to use her magic to shove him away, but it caused a backlash, it propelled her to slam up against the back of the cage; pain coursed through her body, almost causing her to blackout.

"Don't bother, You can't use your magic as long as you are in there," Diomedes peered through the bars as someone looking at an animal in a zoo.

"Why don't you just kill me, like you killed the others?"

Jazmyn's mind flashed to Arion for the last time, causing a tear to escape from the corner of her eye. She quickly wiped it away.

"I never wanted to kill you. Oh, did in the beginning, but now I will keep you like I kept your daddy," He said. "I love to stay here just to see you suffer, but I've been told that your mother is alive, and I can't..."

"You bastard!" Jazmyn screamed, launching her arm through the bars at Diomedes, trying to reach him. "You leave her alone!"

"Now, now, Jazmyn, you shouldn't interrupt someone who was speaking. Where was I? Oh, yeah. I can't have your mother around to suffer the loss of her child and husband; that just won't be right; Diomedes strolled out and turned. "Have a nice stay, and I must go now."

Jazmyn curled up in a ball in the corner, "I have all these powers and I can't, again, save my mother." She thought as the tears began to flow down her cheeks.

A sound caught her ear; She looked around, she saw one of the legs move of the dead animal, shifting to the other side of the cage to put some distance, "What the hell?"

A person's head came out from under the pile of animals.

It was a young woman with blood in her blond hair.

"Izzie?!" Jazmyn screamed.

Izzie put her finger up to her mouth, "Shh." Then duck down behind the pile when she saw a guard poke his ugly head in.

They both were silent as the warhog guard crept in to check things out. After what seemed like forever, the warhog went back to his post.

Jazmyn couldn't believe that she was alive.

"Hey, Jazzy." Izzie whispered.

"I thought you were dead, asshole said he killed you." Jazmyn said.

"He knocked me down and I just played dead and those beasts threw me in here on that pile, I am glad to see you." Izzie smiled with streams of tears cutting a path down her cheek through the dirt. "I've been running around helping others to escape."

"Way to go, Rambo woman." Jazmyn said.

"Let's see if we can get you out of here, by the way you look like shit," Izzie said, grabbing the lock on the cage.

"Thanks, you too," Jazmyn smiled a little." Go, save yourself, Izzie."

"I am not going anywhere without you. Besides, you and the others need to kick Diomedes's ass and save your mother."

Jazmyn lowers her eyes, "The others are dead, except for Allison, she has become a real person."

Izzie shook her head, "That's sad. Lets get you out of here. The guard has the key on his hip."

"How are you going to get it?" Jazmyn asked. "It's too dangerous."

"Dangerous is my middle name," Izzie snickered and headed for the opening.

When Izzie was almost to the threshold, she saw the shadow of the warhog grew closer. She quickly put her back against the wall and held her breath. She picked up a stone next to her foot and raised it above her head. As the warhog passed her, she had to jump up to hit the creature with the stone. The warhog fell to the ground motionless; Izzie dug for the key, "Damn, it stinks."

"Thanks, you're my hero," Jazmyn said, springing from her confines.

"No worries," Izzie hugged Jazmyn, causing Jazmyn to flinch. "What's wrong?"

"My arm is broken, battling Diomedes." Jazmyn said gingerly, rubbing her arm.

"Wow, you when up against him? Where is your necklace? Did he take it?" Izzie acted like a child.

"I don't need my necklace anymore. I will explain later.

Jazmyn places her hand on the broken part of her arm; her hand glowed with a golden light. After a few moments, she could move her arm with no pain.

"I didn't know you could do that too," Izzie expressed.

Jazmyn smiled, "That's another thing to explain. Do you know the way out?"

"Yeah, My Dad brought me here many times camping, and I used to explore these caves, lets go."

They both peeked around the opening and made a run towards the back of the cave.

"Kinda getting dark," Izzie said as they entered a tunnel. "You wouldn't happen to have a flashlight?"

"No, but let me see what I can do," Jazmyn thought for a moment and swirled her hand in circles.

Sparks raised from her hand and floated up into the air, then gathered all together to form a small sun lighting up the darkness.

"I still can't believe you can do all of this cools stuff," Izzie said.

Jazmyn never thought she would do all is cool stuff, either, but it is becoming second nature to her, and she felt a belonging. She just nodded at Izzie, and they continued with her little sun glowing brightly.

The tunnel had many twists and turns, growing narrow in

some part and opening into grand caverns. This part of the caves was never opened to the public.

In one of the cathedral caverns, Jazmyn's light grew to show them a sight that took their breaths away. The spires coming from the ceiling crowned a deep blue lake; the sound of water dripping was the only sound that could be heard besides their breathing.

"This is so beautiful," Izzie said wide-eyed. "I knew this was here, but my old flashlight never showed me this."

"You are right about that, with all the destruction happening outside, places like this will be harder and harder to find."

Izzie looked at Jazmyn; her forehead wrinkled, "Will you be able to fix all of this?"

Jazmyn flashed a look at her friend then turned away. A moment of silence followed.

"I don't know, Izzie. I need to make sure he doesn't hurt my mother first."

"I believe you will," Izzie smiled and motioned Jazmyn to continue. "This tunnel will lead us out."

The night air was refreshing as they emerged from the tunnel, soon the smell of smoke stung their noses; far off, they could see a fire burning wildly through the trees.

"I need to get to my mother." Jazmyn said. "Give me your hand."

"Ok," Izzie stated.

As soon as Izzie grabbed her hand, they vanished and then reappeared near Abraham's house.

"Whoa." Izzie then held her hand to her mouth and ran to a nearby bush, and threw up.

Allison greeted them, "I am glad to see your two still alive. I saw Diomedes take you."

"How are you here?" Izzie asked, looking at Allison after she returned and rested against Abraham's truck.

"It is because of Jazmyn," Allison said.

"I need to see if my mother is all right, Diomedes said he was going to...."

Allison held her hand up, "She's fine, I thought he would try something like this so I brought her back to your tree."

Jazmyn felt a weight had been lifted off of her, "Let's get back there then, before ugly gets here."

As they ran back to her tree, Jazmyn noticed some green returning to the forest. Hope was creeping back into her.

A sound made all of them stop, Jazmyn waved her hard arms in a half-circle, and a dome of golden light surrounded them.

A figure of a wolf emerged from the dark. It was Wen, followed by the rest of her pack.

"Are they going to attack?" Izzie asked.

Jazmyn shook her head and waved her hands, and the dome vanished.

"Hello, Jazmyn, it's been a long time." Wen said, looking at Allison.

"Yes, it has," Allison said.

"They can talk," Izzie's eyes widen. "Why shouldn't I be surprised."

"Wen, What are you doing here?" Jazmyn moved closer.

"We are here to help you with the threat," Syann said.

"The forest that we call home has been destroyed," Daymeeun stated.

"All the animals we hunt have vanished or have been killed," Hawthorne added.

Jazmyn shook her head and looked around, "Where is your daugther's Ismaria and Isyia?"

Syann lowered her head, "They perished in the flames."

When she raised her head again, tears soaked her fur.

"A fireball caught us off guard and Ismaria and Isyia were hit," Daymeeun told.

"So, we are here to take revenge and kill Diomedes," Hawthorne glared his teeth and stood in attack position.

"Hawthorne!" Syann snapped. Wen gave a glare at his son.

"Jazmyn, we need to talk," Wen walked away Jazmyn followed. "I mean the other Jazmyn."

"Oh, sorry, we call her Allison to avoid confusion."

The other stood in silence as Allison and Wen disappeared around the backside of her tree.

"Hi, I am Izzie, best friend of Jazmyn's," Izzie finally whispered.

"Hello, Izzie, I am Syann," she said, then introduced the rest of the pack.

Izzie waved timidly.

"Diomedes must have the necklace to do all this damage," Syann said.

"Yes, I gave it to him but I don't need it to do magic," Jazmyn said.

"You have grown since the scared girl I found in the zoo," Syann smiled.

Jazmyn thought back to when she first met her and the rest of the pack. She just nodded.

Wen sat facing away from Allison, "I am here to kill that demon."

"It was terrible what happened to your daughter and Ismaria, I am sorry," Allison lowered her eyes.

"Yes, it was. My heart is heavy with sorrow," Wen turned his head his fur caught a tear. "Since that happened I had time to think."

Allison focused on his face as she came around to see him clearly. "Thinking of?"

"I know how you felt," Wen paused. "When that demon killed your family."

Allison's eyes welled up, and she lost a tear down her cheek, "I am sorry for not believing you when you said you were there to help, I was not in my right mind."

"The moment I heard that they were killed I want to seek vengeance on Diomedes," Wen showing his teeth, "I searched the woods trying to find him. As I would come across one of his warhogs I'd tear them apart."

Allison held her hand against her mouth as she watches Wen act out what he was saying. She watched him gnaw on a branch that laid on the ground like it was a beast's leg. After snapping it into two, he turned his attention to Allison. His eyes glowed red, his teeth gnashing together. She let out a scream that was answered first by the rest of the pack.

Syann and Daymeeun jumped in between them and Hawthorne went behind his father; they all growled loudly, the hair on their backs rose to meet the sky.

"Settle down, Wen!" Daymeeun warned.

"Please, Wen, save your anger until we meet our enemy," Syann pleaded.

Jazmyn stopped by her tree and raised her hands, causing lighting to travel between her fingers, waiting for her to release them, "Stop!"

Wen looked at Jazmyn; his eye returned to normal; he sat down again, "I am sorry. My anger took control but I am in control now."

"Is it safe to come out now?" Izzie said, peeking around the tree.

"Yes," Syann said.

Jazmyn walked up in front of everyone, "We need to come up with a plan. It would be easier if Arion, Theia and the rest were here."

She paused with her head lowered. It would be easier, and I wouldn't have to do this. Then raised it slowly.

Jazmyn cleared her throat, "First of all we need to find him."

"We can find him," Wen began "We can fan out and search the woods."

"How are you going to let us know when you find him?" Izzie asked with a raised eyebrow.

"Telepathically," Allison said.

"Oh, Duh," Izzie hit her forehead with her hand.

"When you do, I will join you," Jazmyn said.

"Hey, wait, I can help too," Izzie said.

"So can I," Allison added.

"It will be far too dangerous for you two. Izzie, I don't want you to get hurt, I thought I lost you once I don't want to lose you again. Allison, without the book can you do any magic?"

"I can still do some magic, I will need to mix up some potions to do the rest." Allison stated.

"Jazmyn, I can take care of myself," Izzie paused "besides maybe Allison and I can help the rest of the people out of the caves while you keep creepy busy."

Jazmyn smiled and nodded her head.

"Do you think you can kill him?" Syann stared at Jazmyn with weight the of the world. "Can you?"

Can I end him? I killed no one before. I know he defiantly deserves to die for all that he has done. He killed Arion and the others, Allison's family, and he killed Ismaria and Isyia, not to mention all the destruction he has caused.

Jazmyn stood up, clenched her fists, took a deep breath, "Yes. I can"

∞∞∞

Jazmyn thought she would have more time to prepare for what she had to do, but when Wen contacted her that they had found him, her pulse began to race.

She looked around the inside of her tree, sitting at the big round table, her hands began to sweat, rubbing them on her pants, trying to dry them off, but it wasn't working very well.

The last time I went up against him, I thought I could beat him, but he was too much. I made a stupid mistake; I underestimated him. I have all this power, and it went to my head; this time, it will be different.

Jazmyn got up and went into a room that the tree made for Allison to mix some potions. Izzie was there watching like a wide-eyed little child watching her mother cook.

"It's time," Jazmyn said.

"Don't make it sound so final," Izzie said, popping her head up.

Jazmyn just raised her eyebrows and nodded her head a little, and walked back out.

"She has a lot on her mind," Allison said.

"I know."

Izzie helped Allison pack a small leather satchel with the potions and went out and joined Jazmyn.

"Ready?" Jazmyn sighed.

"Cheer up, Buttercup," Izzie smiled.

Jazmyn cracked a half-smile, "Now you two need to head back to Abraham's so you can borrow his cargo van.

She paused a moment,

I am sounding like he's going to come back to use it.

"The keys are under the second rock from the front steps, on the left."

"Thank you and good luck, Jazmyn," Allison smiled.

Jazmyn nodded her head and then looked at Izzie. It almost felt like this would be the last she would see her friend; tears filled her eyes.

Izzie wiped the tears from her eyes and gave her best friend a big hug.

"Come back, you're the only person who can put up with my shit." Izzie said.

"I know. I will come back," Jazmyn said, pulled back. She wiped her face and smiled. Then she was gone.

Jazmyn appeared at Onyx Park, next to the restrooms.

Jazmyn looked to see the whole pack there except for one, "Where is Wen?"

"He is just up the trail, on the look out," Daymeeun said.

"He is keeping an eye on Diomedes," Syann said.

Without warning, the sky lit up in that direction, followed by a loud crack of thunder. Out of the woods, Wen came running with half of his back burnt.

Wen collapsed next to them, "He saw me, he is on his way."

Syann came to his side and began to lick his wounds, "You fool, I should have been the one up there."

"It is my job to protect you," Wen managed to push out of

his weakened body.

The other wolves surrounded him.

"Hang in there, Dad," Hawthorne said.

Jazmyn knelt next to him and laid her hands on him; they began to glow.

She closed her eyes, letting the power flow through her and travel out of her hands. The skin healed, and his fur grew back.

Wen jumped up and shook, "I didn't know you could do that."

"Come out, come out, puppy dog," Diomedes cried.

"Thank you. Stay here, we will attack first," Wen said.

The wolf pack darted out from behind the restrooms on both sides surrounding Diomedes.

"Oh look more puppies to play with." Diomedes laughed.

Jazmyn covered her ears when she heard a loud howl coming from the pack. She peeked around the side to see all of the wolves grow five times their size.

They all ran at Diomedes, he tried to move out of the way, but Syann grabbed his leg and whipped him back and forth, letting him go, making him soar through the air snapping treetops as he went.

"Two can play that game."

A thunderous boom shook the ground, causing them all to stumble. Emerging from the woods was a giant. Diomedes towered over the wolves.

The pack let out a growl that made Jazmyn shiver and they went after him again.

Diomedes bent over and picked Daymeeun up and threw him like he was nothing. Hawthorne latched onto his leg, ripping the flesh off.

Diomedes let out a scream and then kicked Hawthorne; a series of loud cracks came from his body as he flew and hit the ground with a thud and didn't get up.

Wen and Syann looked, and Hawthorne quickly turned back, gnashed their teeth, and attacked him.

Diomedes jumped up and floated out of the way, then circled his hand, causing the wind to pick up; hurling the wolves into the air.

The restroom couldn't hold against the onslaught of the wind and broke apart, exposing Jazmyn.

Jazmyn follows Wen and Syann until they were out of sight.

"Hi, Jazmyn, I've missed you," Diomedes said as he shrunk back down to normal size.

Jazmyn turned back and raised her hands to strike him down with lighting, but he acted first, swiping his arm up then down, and Jazmyn's body followed the action slamming her to the ground; the air escapes her lungs; Jazmyn gasped.

Diomedes calmly walked over to Jazmyn, "I think we were in this position before."

Chapter Twenty-Five

Izzie and Allison crouched behind a pile of rocks just outside the entrance to the caves. The scene made Izzie's stomach turn several times, there were people aimlessly walking around with death in their eyes; others were working as slaves.

Pictures of the holocaust filled Izzie's mind, "I can't believe this is happening here were I live and grew up."

"Everything will turn out," Allison whispered matter a factly.

Izzie just looked at her, "How can you act like that with all this going on?"

Allison turned her attention back to the entrance and counted several warhogs on guard.

"Well?" Izzie's voice cracked trying to keep her voice low.

"I have seen this thing before along time ago, it still bothers me but I can not let it effect me."

The sound of a woman's screams sent sparks of electricity down Izzie's spine; not far from the opening, people were being made to carry stones that a muscle-bound weight lifter would have trouble moving.

Allison pointed out the woman; she was crawling across the ground, wearing nothing more than a ripped blood-soaked shirt; a man was standing over her with a whip.

"Son. Stop! I am your mother, please stop." the voice of the woman weakened.

Izzie gasped, "Holy shit, We have to do something."

Allison dug in her satchel and pulled out one of the vials of potion, "Follow me."

They made their way closer to the group of people. Izzie realized that the man that was whipping the woman was one of her regulars at the department store.

"I know that guy, you can't hurt him," Izzy panicked.

"Don't worry I won't hurt him," Allison remarked.

Allison stood up, and with a flick of her wrist, she sent one of the vials into the air, landing at the man's feet; breaking with a puff of smoke the man froze.

The two women quickly shot from the tree line. Izzie went to the woman on the ground, Allison attended to the others.

Izzie didn't know how to touch her; it looked like she was as fragile as a dried-up leaf, "Can you turn over?"

Tears rolled down the woman's face turning to Izzie and nodded her head.

Izzie tied her tattered shirt together, "Let me help you, we need to get out of here."

"Thank you," the woman managed to squeak out.

They lead the people back to where they stashed the cargo van; Izzie carefully helped the battered woman into the seat.

"My son," the woman pleaded.

"Do not worry. He will be fine. We will be back," Allison announced to the frightened people.

∞∞∞

Jazmyn raised her hand and sending Diomedes through the air, "It's not going to end up the same."

She got up and threw both of her hands out in front of her creating a blizzard of ice shards hurdling at him. He let out a scream when they hit their mark.

A smile came to Jazmyn's face, but it was short-lived as he sent his own arrows made of ice. She raised her arms, a shield of fire melted the arrows.

Her foe moved one of his arms, causing a gale-force wind,

hitting Jazmyn from the back, sending her through the air like a rag doll. Her body slammed to the ground; Diomedes approached freezing her arms down.

"When will you learn? I will win over you every time," He said.

The sting from the cold made her arms ache, she tried to break free, but it was no use, "Dammit!"

She was trapped, nowhere to go, heart and her mind began to race as he approached. Jazmyn turned her head from side to side looking for something, anything; then it came to her

Jazmyn closed her eyes to concentrate, to let words flow through her, then spoke,

"I call on the earth to defend me,
Rise earth, rise I say let it be."

The earth began to shake, a mound of dirt exploded into the air surrounding her, producing a high wall. The vibration caused the ice to crack about her wrist freeing her.

She stood up and rubbed the soreness from her wrist and arms; a series of dull thuds caught her attention. She turned to see a part of the wall began to give way.

Butterflies tormented her stomach as Jazmyn paced inside her makeshift shelter.

Ok, Jazmyn, settle your shit down. I can't do this on my own. I wish Theia was here she would know what to do. Damn, I wish Arion was here too. Well they aren't here so it up to me, but how?

Off in the distance, she could hear explosions then the pounding stopped. She waited a few minutes then raised her hands and the walls around her dissolved back into the ground.

She stood ready to attack but Diomedes wasn't anywhere to be seen. She scanned the woods until she saw him off in the distance in a clearing fighting something or someone that she couldn't see.

Is he fighting the wolves again?

Jazmyn ran up to see who he was fighting, ducking behind a tree, peeking around the tree.

The wolves again but there were others there too helping. When she realized who they were she couldn't believe it.

It was Theia, Abraham, and Miryssia unleashing all kinds of magic at Diomedes.

"Jazmyn!"

Jazmyn turns to see who was calling, it was Arion, her heart raced.

"Arion is... that really you?" Jazmyn stumbling over her welling emotions.

"Yes, its me."

Her body and mind swam with emotions and thoughts, she launched herself at Arion and gave him strong hug, and stained his shirt with tears.

Arion pulled her away and with his deep blue eyes staring at her, grabbing behind her head, he pulled her close and kissed her.

The world and all its troubles faded away, she lost herself in the kiss. Not wanting that moment to end, a bolt of lightning struck a nearby tree and snapped back.

Arion took Jazmyn by her hand and ducked behind a fallen tree, "Are you alright?"

Jazmyn shook her head, "How? I-I saw you all die."

"Abraham and Theia transported all of us out just before Diomedes could collapsed his bubble."

"What took you so long to come back?"

"They had to gain their strength back."

Jazmyn could ask him more questions but she turned her attention back to the battle, "I need to go help them."

A confused look struck Arion's face.

"Trust me," Jazmyn flashed a smile at him and darted out and ran a few paces and stopped raising her hand she called for the lightning, it hit Diomedes directly in the chest knocking him back.

The others stopped and looked at Jazmyn. Theia and Abraham gave a knowing smile at her.

"Way to go!" Miryssia yelled.

Without skipping a beat the wolf pack jumped at Diomedes, he hit the ground hard. They began to shred his clothes and ripped at his skin.

"That is enough!" Wen said his teeth dripping with blood.

The other wolves back down leaving a pile of flesh that once was Diomedes.

"Is he dead?" Miryssia asked.

"I don't know," Jazmyn said flashing a glance at Miryssia.

Their question was answered, Diomedes's body began to repair itself, and before any of them reacted his eyes opened, and stood straight up.

A deep growl filled the air followed by a burst of light, blinding them and then a hurricane-force wind threw all of them out in every direction.

Diomedes floated up above the ground, "You think it would be that easy to kill me, think again."

The necklace around his neck shined with bright blood-red color, the sky seemed to come to life with lightning. He motioned his arms down and the hail size of boulders began to plunge towards the earth.

"This world is mine and none of you can stop me!" Diomedes said.

Theia threw up a shield to protect them, "Jazmyn, come seek shelter."

Jazmyn just stood alone, turning her gaze up at Diomedes, "I will!"

Diomedes floated back down and landed right in front of Jazmyn, "You've tried and failed so many times, my young one. I can see a future together, you have become a very powerful witch. This world would bend to our rule, join me."

"I'd rather die than do anything with you," Jazmyn stared him right into his eyes, "asshole."

"Oh ouch, that hurts."

Diomedes reached around and grabbed her hair and yanking her down to her knees, she struggled against him but her legs gave out and her knees cratered the ground. Diomedes caused the stones around her to become her shackles.

Diomedes turned to Abraham and the wolves and spoke,

"I Diomedes commander of nature,

Take your magic now and into the future."

Jazmyn watched as the magic ripped out of her friends one by one, collapsing as through there life was taken away. Diomedes waved his hand he caused the earth to split apart, the chasm grew deep, movement of his fingers caused it to split apart.

"Now watch your friends truly die this time." Diomedes exclaimed again he waved his hands like he was conducting a symphony. The pillars that they clung to shattered underneath their feet and Jazmyn watched them plummet out of sight.

"No!, not again," She screamed.

The last thing she heard was the howl from one of the wolves, her head went limp and fell to her knees, tears puddled on the ground.

Who am I fooling, I just can't do this anymore.

Deep within her mind, a voice spoke, "Believe."

"Believe in what?" Jazmyn raised her head, her face stained with dirt and tears.

"You will join me now or you can join your friends," Diomedes reach his hand out and pinched her chin.

"Believe, hope is coming."

"Why should I," Jazmyn said turning her eyes to Diomedes, "I will…"

A sound off in the distance stopped Jazmyn she turned to see a truck barreling towards them, Izzie, Allison, and her mother were in the cab.

Diomedes swiftly moved out of the way before the truck hit him, he raised his hands and the truck followed suit and sprang into the air and flew towards the giant hole in the ground.

The last look in Izzie's eyes sparked a fire within Jazmyn, Her body and soul was filled with life and she remembered what she read in her notebook and yelled it out,

> **"I call on upon the all nature's power,**
> **from every animal and every flower,**
> **To rid this world of this blight,**
> **So we all can again see the light"**

The ground shook all around her, she felt a surge of strength flow through her. She easily broke free from her shackles and she stood up and held her arms out wide letting the magic flow through her, directing it at Diomedes.

Jazmyn could feel every cell in her body come alive with magic, it burst out of her emitting a light that was so brilliant it lit up the whole sky as the power hit Diomedes. His clothing was ripped apart. The flesh began to peel off his bones finally he was gone.

Jazmyn fell to the ground, too weak to move it felt like she hadn't slept in years all her strength was gone. As she lay there she could feel her life leaving her body.

"Jazmyn, Jazmyn!" was the last words from her mother she heard.

Her mother knelt by her side as Jazmyn took her last breath.

Chapter Twenty-Six

"She can't die like this," her mother said as she picked up her daughter's lifeless body.

Arion's eyes widen then shook his head, "No!"

He rushed to her side, grabbed her limp arm. He closed his eyes and focused every ounce of his powers trying to bring her back from death.

"Come on!, Dammit," Arion yelled he tightened his eyes. "Come back to us!"

Izzie looked at Theia with tears in her eyes, "There must be something you can do, Theia."

Theia pointed to something in the grass not too far from where they were standing, "Get the necklace for me.

"Isn't the necklace evil?" Izzie said with confusion in her eyes.

"As long as Diomedes is dead the necklace will become neutral," Theia explained.

Without another word, Izzie dashed to retrieve the necklace, but someone got it first.

"Who are you?" Izzie questioned.

Gloria snapped her head around, "Stephen, our daughter needs that necklace."

"I know," Stephen said carrying it back to the crowd.

Wen and Syann growled at him and block him from getting any closer.

"Once Diomedes died, it freed me from his evil that was inside of me."

"Let him pass," Abraham said.

Stephen handed the necklace over to Theia and took a step back.

"Gloria you need to lay her down on the ground," Theia said.

"No, I don't want to, I need to be right here," Gloria sobbed.

"Come, Gloria, I know it's hard but you need to let Theia help Jazmyn," Stephen lay his hand on Gloria's shoulder.

Gloria's face was covered with tears when she turned to her husband. She looked into his eyes and saw her love had come back into his eyes. She nodded her head and slowly laid her daughter back on the ground and stood up and moved to her husband.

Everyone stepped back, Miryssia flashed a glance at Stephen and with a little hesitation took him by the hand.

"Your cool, right?" Miryssia said.

Stephen just smiled and nodded his head.

Theia looked at the pendant, the red was gone replaced with a dull gray color, "It is ready." She put the pendant over Jazmyn's heart.

Theia raise her arms high and spoke,

"Alva, the power of life is your gift,
Remove the shroud of death and set it adrift."

A burning glow ignited in the air above them and slowly descended and landed as a circle of bright green light, around Jazmyn's body. The ground trembled, a low vibration traveled through the air, everyone took a quick breath as the wave passed through them. Vines encircled Jazmyn, wrapping around her, with pulses of green light following the path of the vine.

After what seemed like an eternity the vines stopped glowing and retreated back into the ground. Jazmyn laid motionless, her face had a grey tone. Blood from her wounds stained the grass.

Arion knelt down next to her and just above a whisper, "I love you."

Jazmyn's body twitched, with a quick breath air filled her

lungs then she exhaled. The necklace on her chest returned green again.

Slowly she opened her eyes, Jazmyn smiled when she focused on Arion, "I love you too."

The surrounding crowd broke out in cheers hugging each other. Arion bent his head lower, she propped herself up to meet him halfway, and they kissed.

"Is he really gone?" Jazmyn pulling back a little. "Yes, he is gone," Arion said.

Jazmyn looked around, "What happened?"

"You died, girl," Izzie said.

"I what?" Jazmyn eyes widen.

"Yeah, but I am tickled pink that you didn't remain that way," Izzie said.

She smiled at her, feeling her strength coming back she tried to lift her body but she fell back.

"Let me help you,"

"Dad?" Jazmyn eyes focused on a person kneeling on the other side.

"Yes, it me, Jazmyn," her dad took her arm and slowly helped Jazmyn to her feet.

Jazmyn gave him a hug, crying, her mother joined them.

∞ ∞ ∞

The clouds of smoke had cleared from the sky, by the time Jazmyn woke up the next morning. She sat up in bed and felt a familiar weight around her neck.

"It is good to have you back."

The necklace responded with a flicker of green light like it was glad to be back.

She got out of bed and walked over to the window and slid the curtains aside, letting the sunlight fill the room. She realized she hadn't seen the sun for a while and it seemed a lot brighter.

A bird landed on a branch just outside her window. She

watched for a while, happy that some normalcy was returning. She focuses on the bird. She gasped at the sight of what the fires had done to the forest. There wasn't a tree that wasn't charred as far as she could see.

"There is a lot of damage out there," a voice spoke from behind her.

She turned to see Arion standing there, "Yes there is."

"I am glad to see you up and out of bed. You have been there for 4 days." Arion said, approaching her.

"Four days?" Jazmyn exclaimed.

"You died after all," Arion lowered his head. "I tried to heal you, but it was too late. I didn't think I would ever see you again."

Jazmyn stepped closer to Arion and wrapped her arms around his neck she looked deep into his eyes and move her lips within an inch of his, "I am glad you tried."

He moved the other inch, and they kissed.

Her body came alive, she felt as though the world was gone around them and at that moment the feeling of magic will never compare to what she was feeling now.

"Jazmyn and Arion sitting in a tree," Izzie said, standing at the door.

"Take that somewhere else," Miryssia added.

"Shut up you two," Jazmyn said and gave Arion another kiss.

"You were supposed to just check on her, not make out with her," Miryssia said.

"Glad to see you are ok," Izzie said.

"Let's go see the others," Arion said, leading Jazmyn out the door.

Everyone was gathered around the table, the twins, Theia, Abraham, Allison, and the whole wolf pack was sitting next to the table.

"I am happy to see you are well, Dear," her mother said giving her a hug, then her father.

Tears welled up in her eyes to see both of her parents standing in front of her. "I love you both."

"We love you too," her dad said.

Theia stood up and made her way over to Jazmyn and took her hand in hers as a smile came across her face.

"You did well."

"Thank you for your help," Jazmyn said and gave her a hug then faced everyone else. "Thank you all, you all had helped me to become the witch I was meant to be."

Jazmyn walked around the table hugging everyone and over to Wen and Syann, "I am happy you joined us, it was a big help."

"You are welcome," Syann said. We will help you whenever you need us."

"Jazmyn and Allison you will always be a part of our pack," Wen said looking over to Allison.

Allison smiled, "Thank you."

"We must be on our way, we need to get back to our home," Wen said.

"Enough of this mushy crap, I am hungry," Miryssia said.

"Your right, I am sure Jazmyn is famished," Theia said.

The ache in Jazmyn's stomach and the low growling sound it made agreed with Theia.

"My treat," Jazmyn said, motioning her arm over the table, filling it with foods of all kinds.

"I hope you can cook better this way than the normal way," Izzie said making a funny face.

Jazmyn smirk, "Shut up."

Jazmyn sat down next to Arion. As she looked around the table she saw her friends and family laughing and joking. Seemed like a few days ago none of this would have happened if her fears and lack of confidence had their way.

"I wonder how long it will take for everything to return to normal or close to it?" Gloria asked.

"Not long, Jazmyn will fix everything," Tony and Tina spoke together.

'What? How?" Jazmyn said, almost choking on her food.

"We have seen it," Tina said.

"Everything will go back as they were," Tony said.

"How am I going to do that?" Jazmyn asked.

"With some help from nature," Theia said. "But more of that after we finish our meals."

"The town, the forest and the people who have died. How am I going to be able to fix everything? I can't bring people back to life with all the power in the world I wouldn't be able too. Can I?"

After their meal, Theia and Allison led Jazmyn up and out of the tree. The smell of smoke still lingered in the air, the crackle of dying embers echoed from everywhere.

"This is hopeless, I won't be able to 'fix' everything," Jazmyn held up her hands and aired quotes.

"Trust in yourself," Theia stated.

"I can't bring people or even animals back to life," Jazmyn shoulders sunk.

"You will do anything you want," Allison said, placing her hand on Jazmyn's shoulder. "Now call for your book."

"OK," Jazmyn signed and held her hands out.

Her book appeared, and she almost dropped it, "Why is so heavy? It looks different. It's not tattered or worn."

The book responded and lifted itself and floated in front of Jazmyn.

Allison smiled, "Yes, it is different. This book is truly yours. Everything you went through, every spell you said is now in your book. The book will grow with you."

"Really? Everything?" Jazmyn said.

"Yes, Dear," Theia said.

Jazmyn waved her hand, and the book flipped open and showed her what it had learned. Jazmyn watched as the last few weeks flashed by on the pages. Every spell she spoke was there, even the time she teleported to Izzie's by mistake.

The book stopped on an empty page and Hovered as though it was waiting for something.

"Now reach deep inside of yourself with everything that makes you," Theia said. "Then find the words."

Her necklace glowed as if it was warming up for the moment. Jazmyn closed her eyes and held her arms out wide. Her mind and body came together as one. Words slowly formed from somewhere deep.

Her whole body glowed, and an aurora formed around her, then she spoke:

> **"To what was taken from this world,**
> **For every unwanted wind that had twirled.**
> **With all the power I have been given,**
> **I ask for all to be forgiven."**

A burst of energy exploded from Jazmyn, and the wave spread out in every direction. The trees all around them turned from charred black to their normal healthy colors, leaves sprouted on the branches. The birds rang out in song celebrating the return of the forest and flowers and grass sprung from the ground adding a multitude of colors to the picture.

Jazmyn felt weak but stood there and just smiled, not really believing what she had done. She never knew she had it in her.

The rest of them emerged from the tree and spread out to look around.

"We are so proud of you, Jazmyn," her mother said walking with her father.

"Thanks," Jazmyn said.

"Yeah, I taught her everything she knows," Miryssia stated with a smirk on her face. "You did well."

Jazmyn wrapped her arms around Miryssia and gave her a hug, "Thank you for all you did."

Miryssia gave her a wink and went towards the twins.

"Can you believe that?" Izzie said.

Jazmyn turned around to find Izzie sliding her phone into her pocket, "What?"

"That was work, they ask me to fill in for someone."

"That must mean everything is back to normal in town," Jazmyn stated.

"Yeah, I guess your right," Izzie said. "That doesn't mean I still need to go to work."

"I think you deserve at least one day off," Jazmyn laughed.

She spotted Abraham talking to Theia and Allison as she made her way over to him, "I am glad you moved in next to mom."

"I am happy to be your neighbor," Abraham said.

"Thank you all for believing in me and teaching me what I needed."

"You are welcome," Theia said.

"Bless it be, Jazmyn," Allison said.

"Um, Allison, what are you going to do now that you are alive again?"

"I do not know. I have never thought of it," Allison paused. "Maybe find my own little town far away and live out my life there."

"I wish you luck," Jazmyn smiled then thought for a bit. "Everyone I would like to get a picture of all of us, something to remember this day."

Agreements came from everyone as they gathered around.

"Who will take the picture if everyone one's in it?" Izzie asked.

Jazmyn smirked, "Magic."

Arion stood next to Jazmyn and then her parents on either side, followed by the rest.

"Hey," Arion whispered. "I think we should finish our date, don't you?"

"Yes," Jazmyn gave him a hug and a kiss.

Epilogue

"You can't get rid of me that easy," Jazmyn said.

Jazmyn placed a card on the discard pile, "Draw four, and I pick the color of green."

"I could have gone out." Arion said.

"Sucks to be you, Uno!"

Arion glared at Jazmyn, followed by a smile. He played his card.

"I win!" Jazmyn yelled.

"What is that the third time in a row, Your not cheating are you. Maybe using some mind trick?" Arion said then pick up a glass of water and took a gulp.

"No, never. You just can't handle it, husband of mine." Jazmyn snickered.

Her phone buzzed, and she saw it was Izzie.

"Hey, Izz."

"What ya doing?" Izzie said.

"Just whipping the ass off of Arion," Jazmyn winked at Arion.

"Oh, sounds kinky, I'm not interrupting anything saucy am I?" Izzie laughed.

"Izzie!, no in a card game. What do you need?"

"Just wanted to know if you two guys want to go on a double date with my boy, Mike and I?"

"When?"

"Maybe tomorrow night?"

Jazmyn shook her head, "Can't. Mom and dad invited us

over for dinner. We're free Saturday."

"Something illin' you?" Izzie said.

"No, it's been five years ago I defeated Diomedes." Jazmyn said.

"More the reason to party, See ya Sat. Byeea."

"Ok, bye."

Jazmyn sat and thought,

Since that day things have sure changed. Theia and Abraham still have the twins and have adopted a few more witches to train them. Miryssia ended up going overseas to battle demons, with help of all of them at times.

Jazmyn got up and took Arion by the hand and lead them up the stairs and out of the tree where they live.

In the distance, she heard a familiar wolf howl and smiled.

"Do you think Allison is enjoying spending time with the pack.?" Arion asked.

"Yes, I do." Jazmyn said, then laid a kiss on his lips.

"What was that for?" Arion's eyes widen.

Jazmyn laughed, "Its..It is because I love…"

With no warning, a hole appeared in front of them, causing a gale-force wind.

Jazmyn covered her eyes from dust and when the wind stopped, there was a tall blond woman standing in front of them.

"Don't be alarmed. I am not here to hurt any of you," the woman said.

"Who are you?" Jazmyn asked.

The woman brushed her leather jacket off and dusted off her boots then approached Jazmyn, "My name is Morgan Windfield and I need your help."

Made in the USA
Columbia, SC
25 June 2021